'I laughed, I cried, I sat quietly and thought about

NHLI?P

We hope you enjoy this book. Please return or
renew it by the due date.

You can renew it at www.norfolk.gov.uk/libraries or
by using our free library app.

Otherwise you can phone 0344 800 8020 -
please have your library card and PIN ready.

You can sign up for email reminders too.

v

g'

h   l,

oo

D1419937

starts with a death and darkı

of hope and embracing

JUSTIN MYERS, THE G

Isaac
and the
egg

BOBBY PALMER

REVIEW

The right of Bobby Palmer to be identified as the Author of the Work has been asserted by him in accordance with the Copyright, Designs and Patents Act 1988.

First published in 2022 by Headline Review
An imprint of HEADLINE PUBLISHING GROUP

First published in paperback in 2023 by
Headline Review

1

Cataloguing in Publication Data is available from the British Library

ISBN 978 1 4722 8551 5

Designed and typeset in Adobe Caslon by Patrick Insole

Printed and bound in Great Britain by Clays Ltd, Elcograf S.p.A.

Headline's policy is to use papers that are natural, renewable and recyclable products and made from wood grown in well-managed forests and other controlled sources. The logging and manufacturing processes are expected to conform to the environmental regulations of the country of origin.

HEADLINE PUBLISHING GROUP
An Hachette UK Company
Carmelite House
50 Victoria Embankment
London EC4Y 0DZ

www.headline.co.uk
www.hachette.co.uk

For Nina

' "I have done that," said Toad,
and he crossed out:

~~Wake up~~ '

ARNOLD LOBEL

PART ONE
EGG

ONE

Isaac Addy stands on a bridge, unsure whether to jump or not. His hands clasp the freezing stone of the parapet. His breath blots out the view. The early morning frost on the pavement crunches beneath his feet as he shifts from leg to leg. If he's been trying to work up the courage to bring those frozen legs up, over the edge, into the void below, then he hasn't been having much luck. Leaning forward, Isaac can see the surface of the rabid river, foaming white over the weir. He blinks at it. He isn't crying, despite the fact he's cried a river of his own over the last few weeks. Perhaps the wind has knocked it out of him. Perhaps the tears have turned to ice before they've reached his cheeks. It's not like Isaac is incapable of feeling. He just feels nothing about the water, nor the sheer drop between himself and it. His mind is on other things. His soul is somewhere else entirely. The river roars up at him, but Isaac Addy is too far away to answer.

He breathes in, a shocked and rasping breath, as if he's suddenly arrived from another place. Icy air fills his lungs. He looks along the bridge, in one direction, then the other. He's numb from the cold, but he's so numb to being numb that he barely shivers as he tries to work out how he got here. Isaac squints. He knows this place, and he knows he didn't walk here. He can't have. He's in the middle of nowhere. He's been drinking, which is a bad sign, because he's clearly been driving. He knows he's been drinking because his tongue is carpeted with the taste of hours-old alcohol, and he knows he's been driving because he can see his car at the end of the bridge, headlights still on, driver's door still open. It idles in the ditch like roadkill, the sky above it bruised. The distant *ding ding ding* of the warning signal is just about audible over the noise of the river. Isaac doesn't remember leaving the door open. He doesn't remember the drive itself, nor does he remember dawn breaking somewhere between the car over there and this spot, here, on the bridge. He doesn't remember how he got here, where he came from. He doesn't remember much of anything any more.

Isaac looks back down at the water, which greets him with a whiplash of wind. Now he feels the cold. It wraps itself around his throat, creeps down the collar of his dirty shirt and constricts his ribs. It squeezes the breath out of him, until all he can do is shudder and grip the parapet tighter. Though there's no snow, Isaac feels as if he's caught in a blizzard. He imagines his nose and ears turning blue. Isaac doesn't know where his coat is, and the suit he's wearing is

4

far from suitable protection for the bracing river wind. But his hands won't budge, even when he tries to move them to rub his shivering arms. Isaac watches the river, transfixed, as it rolls over shining rocks and broken branches, wondering if it rolls over dead dogs, too.

THE DOG SUICIDE BRIDGE

He can picture the headline, in a local paper. Can't he? Though Isaac doesn't remember much of anything any more, he remembers this: a news story, forced from a few loose anecdotes stitched to a local urban legend. Apparently, dogs that crossed this bridge had a strange tendency to jump off it. Some said it was haunted by the spirit of a malevolent mastiff. Others, actual experts, blamed the scent of wildlife in the nearby undergrowth. Pine martens, they suspected. The dogs don't know that they've made a fatal mistake until it's too late. Imagine jumping to your death in pursuit of a meal. Isaac wishes he had that kind of conviction.

Who's he kidding? Isaac was never going to jump. Even the imp of the perverse, that little voice in his head which *should* be telling him to take the plunge, is warning him off it. *Don't jump!* it's saying, in a mocking little tone. *You have so much to live for!* Isaac knows the imp is being facetious, but he also knows he's going to follow its orders. He closes his eyes, rocks back and forth on his heels, pushes his torso out over the edge of the parapet as if willing himself to fall accidentally. Gravity could do all the work, if his hands would just

5

let go. He opens his eyes again, the sheer magnitude of the drop opening up with them. Isaac's stomach lurches. Self-preservation, perhaps. The booze, more likely. He coughs, splutters and vomits into the abyss. Now the contents of his stomach are in freefall, carried off into obscurity by the wind. Isaac blinks back tears, and a different kind of bile rises in his throat. The water below seems to boil, black as tar, and his empty stomach boils with it. A vein in his forehead threatens to burst. He grips the parapet so hard that it cuts into his fingers. Then, finally, he screams.

It's a painful sound, one which would cause the birds around to take flight if there were any birds to hear it. His cry echoes off the stones of the bridge, off the trees of the forest lining either side of the water, off the surface of the river itself. Even the weir stops bubbling, as if it's paused to listen. The forest holds its breath. Time seems to stand still. Then, out of nowhere, something screams back.

Imagine Isaac, hanging over the parapet of an old stone bridge, spittle swaying in the wind, cocking his head like an inquisitive canine and staring at the trees on the bank of the river where he'd abandoned his car. Imagine an impenetrable forest, its muddy slope covered in roots which slither into the water like eels. Imagine a sound, not the *ding ding ding* from the idling car nor the roar of the water, but a scream – a blood-curdling, skin-crawling, stomach-churning scream which takes Isaac's anguish and blows it out of the water. It's not a human scream. It doesn't sound like a pine marten, either, whatever a pine marten is. No animal on earth screams like *this*. Imagine a scream that isn't human, isn't animal, and isn't anything in between. Imagine the murky river of possibilities *that* plunges you into. Anyone in their right mind would straighten up, get back in their car and drive off into the dawn as fast as they could. But Isaac is far from in his right mind, and he felt something in the cry. Something hopeless. Something helpless. Before he's even wiped his mouth, Isaac knows he's going to follow the scream.

He wipes his mouth. He straightens up. Then, after a slight tumble backwards into the road, Isaac staggers away from the edge. He heads towards his car, still idly *ding ding ding*-ing, his shoes scuffing on the frigid tarmac. At the end of the bridge he turns again, away from his car and towards the forest. Mulched flowers and discarded plastic wrappers squelch beneath his feet. He catches his breath against the first tree he reaches, then peers into the shadows beyond. All good kids' stories start with a journey into the woods, but Isaac's isn't a story for children. He's too old to be raised by wolves, too large to tumble down a rabbit hole, too jaded to be tempted into a gingerbread house. His happy ending has been and gone. Isaac hesitates, glancing back at his car. As if on cue, he hears the scream again. There's pain in it, and it's painfully familiar. Without so much as a second glance, Isaac launches himself into the undergrowth.

Moss slimes down the back of Isaac's suit as he descends the bank. He crawls through wet leaves and beats away low-hanging branches. Thorns and twigs puncture his forearms and hands. Twisted roots try their best to trip him up. They succeed a number of times, enough to ensure that the legs of his black suit trousers are soaking and that his once-smart shoes squelch like sodden kitchen sponges. He thinks not of hypothermia or frostbite, but only of the scream, a scream which already seems impossible in a forest where even the roar of the nearby river is muffled by a wall of trees. He hesitates once more. Perhaps the forest is playing tricks on him. Isaac spins on his axis, as if he's being watched from behind the branches by a thousand eyes. He's sobering up, still spinning, peering backwards in the direction of his car, peering forwards in the direction of something else. He's disoriented. He can't even remember from which direction he came. He thinks of screaming himself, of crying out for help. Then the brightening dawn brings divine intervention. The darkness of the woods rises in a moment like a curtain, a miraculous burst of early sunlight breaking through a gap in the branches and illuminating the entire forest floor. That's when Isaac sees it.

It is an egg. The egg sits resplendent in the middle of a clearing, bathed in a heavenly light which seems to defy the darkness of the night that came before it. But then, everything about the scene in front of Isaac defies logic. The clearing itself seems manufactured, perfectly circular and perfectly undisturbed, illuminated by light streaming through a perfect hole in the canopy above. The egg takes centre stage, beneath an awning of dripping leaves and branches, atop a flattened thicket which could almost be mistaken for a gigantic nest. The egg itself is white. Eerily so, like a pearl at the centre of the biggest oyster on earth. Or, no, whiter than that. It's as white as nothing at all. An oval of blankness cut out of a pristine sheet of paper with children's scissors, or an oval cut from that same pristine paper and pasted on to the clearing with a stick of children's glue. It's only the dew drops quivering on the white egg's surface which convince Isaac that it's actually there, and that it's actually a three-dimensional object. Isaac rubs his eyes. The egg is still there. The egg is still three-dimensional. And the egg is still magnificent, made even more so by the dullness of the muddy browns and the muted greens around it, by the beads of condensation which sparkle on its white surface like diamonds. In the shaft of light streaming through the gap in the canopy above, it glitters like a Fabergé under a spotlight in a display case. Although larger. Much larger. This egg must be two feet tall.

For the first time in weeks, Isaac feels an emotion that isn't despair. He blinks his red eyes a few times and rubs them. Hello, curiosity, old friend. With a slack mouth, Isaac peers through the branches on all sides of the clearing, looking for any clue as to the egg's origins. He looks down at the earth for enormous footprints. He looks up at the sky for the shadow of some even more enormous beast. He thinks of *Jurassic Park*, of the ripple made by the approaching T-Rex on the surface of a glass of water. But the clearing is dead silent, deathly still. Isaac's eyes trace a path back to the egg. He can't help it. There's something magnetic, something all-encompassing, about it, as if its sheer bleached-white weirdness is sucking all of the colour out of the surrounding flora. There's not a spot of dirt on it. And the size! You couldn't crack an egg like this with a spoon, Isaac thinks to himself. You'd need a shovel, a sledgehammer. Isaac swallows, becoming suddenly aware of his surroundings. He notices a sour taste at the back of his throat. Of all the questions posed by the egg's existence he hasn't yet answered the most pertinent one. Where did the scream come from?

Isaac glances around the clearing again. He shifts nervously from one leg to another, causing some twigs to crack beneath his feet in the process. The sound scares him into a foetal crouch. He screws his eyes shut, grabs hold of his knees. But nothing attacks. Isaac opens one eye, then the other, then creeps into hiding behind the nearest tree. He continues to scan the shadows for something large, something looming: a mother enormous enough to lay an egg like this. But every time his eyes wander, they're drawn back to the egg. Isaac saw an ostrich egg once, at a farmers' market in town – this must be four, perhaps six, maybe eight times as big. It's the size of a dinosaur egg. Yet he's seen a dinosaur egg, too, at the Natural History Museum. That was tea-stain beige, not Tipp-Ex white. Isaac thinks about what might be lurking inside, waiting to hatch. He recalls the scream, its source still unknown. Already his memory is making the sound aggressive, not anguished. In another life, Isaac would have already been fleeing to his car. In this one, death-by-pterodactyl would seem mercifully quick.

Isaac looks back over his shoulder. His eyes return to the egg. He wishes it were bigger, big enough to topple over and flatten him beneath its smooth, white shell. What an easy way to go. If Isaac couldn't work up the courage to fall from a bridge, perhaps gravity could work its magic the other way around. If an egg falls in the woods, will it kill Isaac Addy? If Isaac Addy dies in the woods, will his misery die with him? Already, the bridge seems long ago and far away. All Isaac can see now is the egg. And, when he looks at it, all he can feel in place of the desire to die is its polar opposite: life, and the urge to preserve it. Some prehistoric mothering instinct seems to have awakened within him. He knows the cry was a cry of hopelessness, of loss. In his heart, Isaac knows the egg has been abandoned. Like him. He already knows he's going to take the egg home.

Anyone else in Isaac's sodden shoes would feel the same. What is he supposed to do? Leave it, to be gouged by foxes and pecked at by owls? A rotting meal for dead dogs and pine martens? Isaac isn't even aware that he's moved, but it seems that his legs – so reluctant to carry him before – have pulled him out from behind the tree and deposited him in the middle of the clearing. Now he finds himself standing over the egg, swaying unsteadily, squinting between the trees for the telltale sign of an accusing maternal talon. Now, Isaac's clearing his throat. Take the egg, his subconscious urges him. So, after one last glance over his shoulder, Isaac bends down and picks up the egg. It's lighter than he'd expected. Softer, too. Its exterior isn't hard and cold, like the shell of any normal egg. It's soft and wet, like a ball of freshly proved dough. A boiled egg. It does, indeed, feel shelled. And while the egg has that age-old odour of wet dog, this dog smells far from dead. Despite the dewy exterior, it radiates an inner heat that could only come from something living. This heat ignites something in Isaac, a latent muscle memory. It feels, to his touch, less like an egg found on a forest floor and more like a hot-water bottle in a fluffy cover. What makes him think of this? Isaac is twenty-nine years old, and hasn't had need of a fluffy hot-water bottle for at least twenty of those years. Why the intrusion? It's her, of course. It's always her. While Isaac runs hot, it's she who runs – it *was* she who *ran* – cold. She had a hot-water bottle, in a fluffy cover. It lay between them in bed.

An awful sensation grips Isaac, one he's starting to recognise. It feels as if the forest floor is giving way beneath his feet, as if every tree around him has suddenly been wrenched from the ground, as if everything on the whole earth has been flattened except for Isaac, and he's been left with nothing but a wide expanse of nothingness which rips through him with the force of a thousand winter winds off a thousand icy rivers. Imagine all of this, contained within one body. It starts with a tremor in his gut, as if his stomach has reached the highest point of the upper atmosphere and has nowhere to go but down. Then, with a lurch, down it goes. His heart drops with it. Everything inside him is dropping, his very core collapsing beneath him, and he's struggling to breathe. Gravity is certainly working against Isaac now. In the middle of the clearing, he's too far away from the tree against which he'd steadied himself before. Isaac gasps as if he's drowning, choking as if all of the air has been sucked out of the clearing. He drops to his knees. He does not drop the egg. If anything, he's clutching it harder than before.

What am I doing? Isaac asks himself, his breath catching in his throat and his blood clotting in his veins. He kneels in a ruined suit in a sodden clearing in a strange wood, cradling an enormous white egg he found on the forest floor, trying his hardest to breathe again. What am I going to do?

For a moment there, Isaac was lost. He could barely breathe, barely see, barely find his way back through the undergrowth. Then a distant *ding ding ding* and the morning light through the trees drew him back to the road, to his car, to real life.

To a passer-by it would look absurd: an exhausted-looking man, hobbling out of a forest at the crack of dawn, struggling to carry a strangely light yet surprisingly cumbersome egg. He holds it as one would hold a bag of shopping while one roots around for one's front-door keys. That is, awkwardly, cradled between one elbow and the crook of his neck, hiccupping as he fumbles for the passenger door handle. There are no passers-by to pass judgement. Isaac opens the door, carefully moves the old Walkers shortbread tin to the backseat and deposits the egg in its place. In the driver's seat, he grips the steering wheel and studies himself in the rear-view mirror. His skin has been turning grey of late. His hair is greying, too. The only remaining colour is in his tired eyes, and that colour is red. His shirt is tie-dyed with mud and moss, and his best suit is ruined. Add his tie to the list of things he's lost. He's gained one thing, though: an enormous egg, about two feet tall, with a slick white shell and a distinctly musty odour. Isaac buckles the egg's seatbelt. He doesn't know what's inside, and he doesn't want to spend the morning clearing up pints of yolk from the footwell of his Ford Fiesta. He looks at the egg, looks back into his own bloodshot eyes in the rear-view mirror, looks at the yawning white sky over the slick tarmac. He turns up the heating, vaguely recalling the warming lamps they used on chicken eggs back in school. He remembers egg-and-spoon races, too, the sheer adrenaline of getting an egg to the finish line without allowing it to break. Isaac shakes his head, puts his car into first gear and drives away.

The bridge is on the outside of town, about fifteen minutes from Isaac's house. It's reached by country lanes, all thankfully deserted. The lack of passers-by gives Isaac ample time to ask himself, and the egg, and the biscuit tin on the backseat, all the questions preying on his quickly sobering mind.

What's inside?

Will it be dangerous?

Will it hatch anytime soon?

Should I have left it in the forest?

Should I take it back to where it was?

Would going back just make things worse?

Is it a crime to find an egg and take it home?

If so, what's the likelihood of being caught?

Do I really need to go to prison over this?

If so, what's the custodial sentence?

Should I dispose of the egg?

Should I *cook* the egg?

Boiled or fried?

Isaac's head is scrambled, so he has no answers. Neither does the biscuit tin. Nor does the egg, which is an egg, so cannot speak. Still, Isaac fires off questions, unsure if he's speaking out loud. He beats the steering wheel with nervous palms, casting the occasional angsty glance in his rear and side mirrors lest he sees approaching blue lights and hears the wail of a siren. For all he knows, the egg is contraband. It could be filled with drugs, or weapons, or worse. *Nee naw, nee naw.* He'd swear under his breath. The policeman might tap on his window and Isaac would be forced to roll it down. The policeman might say, 'Early start, sir?' Isaac would be sweating, and the policeman might frown and point to the passenger seat with his pen and say, 'Making an omelette?' And Isaac would laugh just a little too loud, betraying that he's smuggling . . . something. He's way over the limit. He'd fail a breathalyser, and what then? Isaac looks across at the egg in the passenger seat. He wants to ask another question. He wants to know if he's going insane. But before he can, he realises that he's driven himself home.

Isaac gets out of the car, which he's parked on the pavement. Unimportant, right now. The pale winter sun is rapidly rising, and the neighbours' curtains will soon be rising with it. They'll put his shabby parking and his even shabbier appearance down to *everything that's been going on*, but the egg? They'd have questions about the egg, and Isaac's already established that he doesn't have any answers. The egg is something he wants to keep to himself. Don't take this away, too, he thinks. After ensuring those curtains lining the street are all

16

still closed, Isaac unbuckles his uncommunicative passenger and carries it up the path to his front door, half attempting to hide it beneath his sodden suit jacket. At least he doesn't have to worry about keys this time, seeing as he never locked the front door in the first place. Pushing against it, Isaac meets the resistance of an avalanche of unopened letters, bills and leaflets. Anyone would think the house was abandoned. In a way, Isaac vacated it weeks ago. He's not been *living* here, just existing. Yet the house has a life of its own, as evidenced by the post around his ankles, the dead and drooping flowers on the console table, and the rancid smell of gone-off food wafting in through the gap in the kitchen door. A tap drips somewhere in the house. A fly buzzes somewhere else. For a moment, a silent Isaac sways drunkenly on his feet with the egg in his arms, and listens. It's as if he's waiting for someone to welcome him home. No one does. His throat tightens. His eyes glisten. The hallway is Baltic, and a shiver runs down his spine. The egg in Isaac's arms seems to feel it, too, its inner heat dwindling rapidly. He thinks once again of the hot-water bottle, the fluffy cover. She used to stuff it down the front of her pyjama bottoms to keep warm. It wasn't a great look. He had a picture on his phone. *Don't you dare put that photo anywhere.* They cried laughing. Cold feet, cold hands. They'd graze him in bed, like ice cubes smuggled under the duvet. She'd hook her bare foot under his bare leg to warm it up, or her bare hand under his bare back. He'd swear, wriggle away.

'How are you always so cold?' he'd ask.

It's relative. How are you always so warm?

Isaac's house is as cold as the river he wishes he'd thrown himself into. The post swamps his legs like a snow-drift, and his breath in the hallway comes out in clouds. He sniffs and looks down at the egg. His eyes widen. He swears. He drops the egg, which lands in a bed of credit card statements and takeaway menus. Isaac is already back outside, sprinting down the path to his car, two doors of which he'd left open. He finds the biscuit tin in the back-seat and grabs it, pressing the cold metal to his forehead and closing his eyes. Then he closes his car doors and returns to the house. Back in the snowdrift, he considers his options. He looks down at the egg, nestled in the letters by his feet. Its whiteness has dimmed, like a light going out. What to do? She'd have known. She'd have had all the answers. He searches their back catalogue of conversations for some-thing which might help. She'd told him a story, once, about an orphaned lamb on the farm where she grew up. If any of the lambs were ever left without a mother, it would be her job to bottle-feed them. But there was one which couldn't get warm. They'd tried wrapping the lamb in blankets, in towels, in the duvet from her bed. Nothing had worked. Then, a stroke of genius – someone had thought of the Aga. At the risk of ending up with a roast lamb for lunch, they'd popped the trembling little thing inside the warming oven. It had worked. The lamb was saved. And Isaac, who hadn't even *seen* a real-life farm until he was at the tail end of his teens, had laughed and shook his head and told her she'd grown up in a Beatrix Potter story. No one has an Aga. No one bottle-feeds lambs. She'd shrugged and told him there was a whole world he was missing out on, if he'd only step outside and see it.

Isaac bolts the front door behind him. He heads to the living room and places the biscuit tin carefully on the mantelpiece. Then he retrieves the egg from its resting place in the pile of post. The house is small and pokey, the kitchen devoid of an Aga, not that the egg would even fit inside. There's a rudimentary fireplace under that same mantelpiece, though, so it's there that Isaac takes the egg. Sunlight is starting to work its way in through the slatted blinds, but Isaac keeps his eyes low and the lights off. He works with slow, effortful movements. He builds a basic fire in the grate, using an old newspaper, a few logs and some forgotten scraps of kindling. He lights it, then snuffs the match out quickly so as not to illuminate anything in the room that he does not want to see. He grabs cushions and blankets from all corners, and on the floor in front of the fireplace he crafts a makeshift nest. He places the egg inside the nest, stokes the fire behind it. The flames begin to catch. Isaac sits back on his knees, watching the egg. Here, on the living-room floor in front of the fire, its white shell is at its brightest. But there's something else, too. Away from the cold, wet clearing, in front of the crackling flames, the exterior of the egg is finally starting to dry. And, as it dries, it blooms. Parts of it which previously lay flat are sticking up and popping out in all directions. Isaac's mouth pops open with them. His breath falling low, the hair on his arms standing up, Isaac begins to realise that the egg's exterior was never a shell at all. It was a coat. What was previously slicked down by the morning dew is now fluffing up, like the wool on that orphaned lamb in that warming oven. Isaac can't quite believe what he's seeing. The egg is covered in shaggy white fur.

'What are you?' Isaac whispers.

But the egg is still enough of an egg not to answer. Isaac watches, entranced, for he doesn't know how long. The fire burns, the egg is silent, and Isaac stares. Then, when his knees are aching and the flames start receding, Isaac's eyes begin to droop. Perhaps it's the warmth of the fire. Perhaps it's because he hasn't slept since the previous morning. With a yawn, Isaac retreats to the sofa on the other side of the room. After a few further minutes of watching the egg from there, he covers his lap with a spare blanket. He never saw the point of having so many blankets – he hot, she cold – but now he's thankful for their abundance. Soon he's fighting to keep his eyes open, then he's horizontal and snoring, slipping into the first proper sleep he's had since January began. As Isaac drifts off, he's only dimly aware of the children on their way to school outside, of the morning light spilling in through the venetian blinds, of the occasional crunch of the shifting fire. He's fast asleep by the time the egg begins to move.

It starts with a slither, as one element of the egg's shaggy coat comes away and slides around its side like an intricately fashioned lock. Then another piece gives way, slithering in the opposite direction. The whole outside of the egg is moving now, loops of its furry shell sliding round and round itself like a tornado in a cartoon dust bowl. Almost as soon as this peculiar display begins, it's over. White coils pile on either side of the egg. And while what's left in between them is still egg-shaped, it's not really an egg at all.

A log breaks in the fireplace, emitting a crack and a hiss. As if in answer, the egg opens its eyes.

TWO

'Are you sitting down?'

And, just like that, everything fell apart. It's a question which always precedes bad news. And if that question is asked over the phone by your mother-in-law, you might already have an inkling what the bad news is going to be. Her daughter had spoiled the fun years before, anyway, over coffee in bed. They'd been having a conversation about their parents' quirks. Isaac's father was constitutionally incapable of texting without using capital letters. His mother was singularly scared of dogs, but had a name for every single cat on the estate. His father-in-law couldn't do a task big or small without humming, even though the tunes he'd hum weren't strictly songs but rather a cacophony of mismatched notes. And his mother-in-law? She could never dive straight into bad news, no matter the gravity of the situation. Whether the family dog had an ear infection or a classmate you hadn't seen in seventeen years was getting a divorce, she'd always have to ask if you were sitting down first.

'Are you sitting down?'

Everything after that call has since congealed in Isaac's mind, but his memory of the moments before it is crystal clear. The speaker had been on at full volume, a playlist called 'Italian Cooking Songs' which Isaac used to cheer him on when experimenting in the kitchen. He'd been standing at the counter, attempting to sing along in nonsense language as he pinched together minced lamb and onion and coriander and wrapped it around wooden skewers. He was making kofta kebabs. Outside it was dark and below freezing, but the saucepan boiling on the stove was making the windows perspire. Isaac had made a mental note to draw the blinds, once he'd washed the raw meat from his hands. He never got that far. Barely had he shaped the third kebab when the music had stopped playing, replaced with a ringtone, the same melody as his morning alarm. Perhaps that's why he was on edge before he'd even picked up the phone. Or perhaps it was his messy hands, covered with diced onion and raw lamb, which he scalded under the hot tap as his phone continued to ring. By the time Isaac had dried them on a tea towel and darted over to the kitchen table, his phone had stopped ringing. He loosened up slightly. Then, almost as soon as it had stopped, it started again. Isaac looked down at the screen.

Esther Moray

Seeing that name caused the first stab of panic, because why would Esther be calling him? Why not her daughter?

'Hi, Esther. Everything OK?'

'Are you sitting down?'

No 'Hello, Isaac.' No 'How are you, Isaac?' No 'How was your weekend?' Just those four words.

Isaac wasn't sitting down. He was cooking kofta kebabs. He *could* sit down, if he needed to. Should he? He should. It's at this point that things begin to get foggy, as if answering the phone had been a ruse – a trigger for setting off the sort of knock-out gas they'd use in old spy movies. As soon as Esther started talking, the invisible fumes started seeping in through the gaps in the windows, under the doors, out of the oven and the fridge. Isaac remembers reaching for a chair with an unsteady hand, remembers lowering himself on to it with wobbling legs. He'd gripped the table for support, as if the room itself were lurching and he were about to be thrown from his seat. His mouth was dry. His chest, neck and head were filled with the sound of his own thudding heartbeat.

'I'm sitting down.'

He didn't recognise his own voice. He didn't recognise Esther's, either.

'Something awful's happened,' she said. And she didn't even need to tell him. Isaac already knew that Mary was dead.

Isaac Addy lies on the sofa, somewhere between sleeping and waking, unsure whether his wife is dead or not. There's nothing quite like it, emerging from a calming dream and into a waking nightmare. He keeps his eyes closed for as long as possible. He hopes that reality is the bad dream, that he can imagine an alternative life into being. In the world Isaac creates behind his eyelids, that imp he heard on the bridge tells him that Mary is upstairs. *It was just a fight*, the imp says. *Put on some coffee and apologise, and everything will go back to normal.* Isaac wishes it were an argument which had consigned him to the sofa. He prays for the worst fight they've ever had. They screamed at each other, sometimes. He wishes they could scream at each other now. *Grow up.* That was one of her favourites. *Why can't you act like an adult, for once?* He thinks of how he'd do anything to make her laugh, pulling her away from a work call to attend to 'a leek in the bath', only to be met with an exasperated eye-roll when she saw the leek in question. He thinks of the arguments about how he never ironed their clothes or cleaned the hob or learned how to use the smart meter – how, when confronted, he'd laugh or stick his tongue out or brush off any criticism with an 'Alright, Mum'. Taking things seriously had never been Isaac's strong suit. How that had changed. Groggily, Isaac starts to come back to the real world. He starts to remember what's happened. As he does so, he starts to slip off the edge of the sofa. His memory sends him to the carpet with a *thump*.

Eyes still closed, face against the floor, besuited body tangled up in a blanket, Isaac feels his chest tightening. Pressing his forehead into the carpet, he shudders as it dawns on him why he's not sleeping upstairs, in their bed, with her. The very thought of it is enough to make him sob. He fell asleep on the sofa, and Mary's dead. Now he's on the floor, and Mary's dead. His head hurts, and Mary's dead. Once he's remembered the big, bad thing, he allows himself to remember the smaller-yet-still-bad things, as well. Like his hangover. His head is beginning to throb with each tearful gulp, his skin taut and his throat tight with dehydration. His mouth tastes like the inside of a Hoover bag, a dusty tongue between teeth as dry as the carpet beneath him. If his memory serves – and it often doesn't – he's been told several times in the last few weeks to stop drinking. He's hurting himself. He's hurting others. His body is scraped, his ego not so much bruised as blown away. Yet no one hurts as much as he does, and nothing hurts as much as her not being here. Face down on this carpet, or the linoleum of a hospital ward, or the concrete floor of a police cell, the pain would be exactly the same.

The police. Isaac vaguely remembers worrying about them earlier. He remembers building a fire, too. Though it's long since dwindled, he can still hear its sputtering embers. And though the room has regained its chilliness, there's something about being trapped in a suit between a carpet and a blanket that makes Isaac feels like he's being roasted on a spit. Why did he light the fire? He can't help but think of a furnace, of the crematorium. There she is again. Mary's dead, and how can Isaac think of anything else? He wrenches a hand out from under the blanket, but only to bite down hard on one dirt-caked knuckle. Crying and shivering on his living-room floor, waiting to be put out of his misery, Isaac must look like a deer caught in a trap. He definitely sounds like one. With his eyes closed and his face scraping the rug, he makes the same noise he now makes every time he wakes up. Every time he remembers. It's a horrible, strangled sound, not unlike the one he made on the bridge. It starts as another sob, pathetic and small, then grows in a crescendo to a full-on wail, ghastly and ghoulish and goosebump-inducing. It's the scream of a man who's lost everything, a man who is truly alone. Which is why it's all the more surprising that something screams back.

Isaac opens his eyes. He removes his knuckle from his mouth, blinks tearfully at the floor. Something just screamed. Something loud. Something close. Now he's stopped howling, Isaac is suddenly aware of a presence next to him, the musty warmth of breath and the damp heat of a small body. Isaac, still trapped in his blanket, thinks very carefully about his next move. He pushes himself up off the floor by his forehead, as if rising into a headstand. From upside down he can see his dirty shirt, nicked all over with the snags of thorns and branches. His torn and trodden suit trousers, mud and moss all over their knees. He remembers. The forest. The clearing. Lighting a fire, building a nest. Putting something in it. The . . . no, surely not. Next to his right ear, there's the sound of curious snuffling. Isaac would shudder, but he's frozen still. Slowly, he manages to dislodge his scraped hands from beneath the blanket, placing them on the carpet beneath his chest as if he were about to do a press-up. Then he steels himself, takes a sharp breath, and pushes himself off the ground. He spins to confront the intruder. He kicks the blanket away. He lands in a seated position against the sofa, pinned back and wide-eyed, directly facing the source of the scream.

Its eyes are black

It is the egg. But it is not *an* egg. Out of its nest, between Isaac's outstretched legs, the egg has become something else entirely. It blinks up at Isaac with eyes that definitely weren't there before, and Isaac blinks back with his own, sleep-addled and tear-filled. What does Isaac see? The first thing that comes to mind is *E.T.*, the moment when the child first encounters the alarming little creature in the forest. But Isaac isn't in a forest, not any more. He's on the living-room floor, staring at two pudgy yellow feet pressing down into the carpet and two enormous black eyes blinking up into his. Isaac thinks of *E.T.*, not because he thinks he's looking at an alien, and not even because he found said alien in the forest near his house. He thinks of *E.T.* because of the scream. Isaac and Mary used to fill their favourite weekends watching feelgood films together. It had become something of a tradition. *Dirty Dancing* on Valentine's

Day, *Ghostbusters* at Halloween, all half glimpsed over a jigsaw and a steaming mug of tea. Mary hadn't watched a lot of the classics as a kid – she'd been more of a book-worm than a cinephile – but Isaac had, and had taken it upon himself to educate her. They started with *Babe*, an understandable lead-in for a farm girl like herself, and then ran down a list ranging from the critically acclaimed to the ironically enjoyed, from *Ferris Bueller* to *Flashdance*. For Isaac, *E.T.* was a childhood favourite. He remembers glee-fully acting out certain scenes, already way too old for that sort of thing. Him wrapped in a blanket playing the alien, his begrudging, bike-straddling sister filling in for Elliott. *Isaac phone home.* He remembers watching the film itself on VHS, over and over. Laughing when Elliott first finds E.T. in the forest and screams. Laughing even more when E.T. screams back, the human child just as repulsive to the alien as the alien is to the child. Now Isaac finds himself face to face with an ugly, bug-eyed alien creature of his own, and he's screaming, too.

Isaac screams. The egg screams back. The egg screams, and Isaac screams in return. This goes on for a minute, Isaac wide-eyed and loudly screaming, the creature wider-eyed and screaming even louder. Isaac screams himself hoarse, his bloodshot eyes straining and his dry mouth getting ever drier. It's nothing like when he and Mary used to scream at each other. Those screams were fuelled by emotion. Here, Isaac is only screaming because it feels like it's the proper thing to do. And the egg, which screams when Isaac screams and stops when Isaac stops, seems only to be screaming because Isaac is doing so.

Its fur is <u>white</u>

Isaac stops screaming. The egg stops screaming, too. It stares up at Isaac. Isaac stares at it, too. So, the scream in the forest didn't come from the egg's mother – it came from the egg. So, the egg isn't an egg at all. While Isaac had half expected the furry white casing to break open and unleash some sort of horrible creature, the casing appears to be a horrible creature in itself. It still *looks* like an egg. Just poached, this time. A bright yellow yolk sits in the middle of the previously blank white oval. Or, no, not a yolk. It's a face, an overeasy-looking face with rough skin the exact same colour and consistency as the rind of a lemon.

Isaac's eyes settle on the furry piles on either side of the creature. Piles of arms. Just two limbs, but each of them probably five times the length of the egg itself. They must be what allowed the creature to cover its face in the first place. Now unfurled, they drop down from either side of its body and pile up on the carpet like discarded laundry. No elbows to speak of. No bones in the arms at all. Isaac could have mistaken them for white feather boas, did they not each end in a set of three fingers, sausage-shaped and custard yellow. Apart from those fingers, and the face, and the stubby yellow toes poking out under its belly, the egg is a blaze of white fur. A white beard beneath its mouth, a white firework display above its eyes. And then those eyes, enormous and black, around which the rubbery yellow skin is stretched tight. Beneath these owl eyes, the yellow skin puckers into a pinched little pug snout, two pinprick nostrils and a downturned mouth. Though the egg's mouth is grimacing, its eyes betray nothing but curiosity.

Its face is <u>yellow</u>

Then the creature is gone. Not into thin air, but into the hallway, wobbling away without urgency like a wind-up toy. It skirts round the living-room door and disappears, its continued presence marked only by the slither of its long, limp arms trailing after it. A few moments pass, then its yellow fingers disappear around the edge of the door. Isaac is left alone. He stares at the blank space the egg left behind, the empty middle distance between himself and the remains of the fire, with the biscuit tin above. His breath rattles ever so slightly between loosely parted lips. Isaac knows this can't be happening. He knows this *doesn't* happen. He knows that, in the real world, monstrous little egg creatures don't just unfurl themselves on your living-room carpet and trundle off for a look around. Yet, for Isaac, the real world has already been turned on its head. And *his* head – still thick, still throbbing – is simultaneously unable to process what's happening, and totally willing to accept that this is just the sort of absurd thing that happens to a man whose life has already fallen apart.

Isaac slumps back into the sofa and rubs his face. He's heard of fugue states and cognitive lapses, but he never expected to experience one first hand. *He's gone mad*, they'd have tutted and said, back in the day. *The grief drove him mad*. They wouldn't be wrong. He's estranged from his own sanity, like an egg from its mother in a lonely forest clearing. He's so far from his normal self that he's not sure he'll ever be able to find his way back. He's not sure he wants to. He thinks of the alternative, of accepting the very real thing that's happened in his very real world, and he can't help but whimper. Isaac bites his knuckle again, stifling that same old sound. It's quieter this time, more inward. After a moment, he straightens up. He wipes his eyes. He sniffs. He looks down at himself, sitting tear-soaked and dew-soaked on the once-pristine carpet in a ruined shirt and a pair of mud-caked trousers. Then he looks at the door into the hallway, from behind which a new noise can be heard. *Glom glom glom*. Isaac swallows, rubs his sunken cheeks. If he's going mad, perhaps madness will at least offer some kind of distraction. If madness gives him something to focus on, Isaac will embrace madness with open arms.

Glom glom glom. There it is again. A low and wet and grumbling sound coming from the hallway. The unmistakable sound of eating. Once upon a time he would have been terrified if he heard a sound like this, but nowadays fear is as alien a concept as smiling or laughing or looking on the bright side. So, feeling only mild bewilderment, Isaac swallows and finds his way to his feet. He walks as if injured, constantly having to prop himself up. First against the coffee table, then against the back of the sofa, eventually against the door itself. By the time he reaches the hallway, the *thwap thwap thwap* of tiny duck-like feet indicate that the creature has had ample time to flee. Isaac can see the kitchen door creaking closed. In the afternoon light streaming in through the frosted window of the front door, he can also see the mess the creature has left in its wake. It's made a feast of the post pile. Some envelopes are shredded while others have been chomped in half, still soggy with saliva. Isaac averts his eyes, as much to avoid the destruction as to avoid seeing what has been destroyed. The envelopes bearing Mary's name, the cards containing deepest sympathies and heartfelt condolences, even the nagging letters from HMRC that a living, breathing Mary would have pressed him not to ignore. Isaac's eyes swell, but a new noise distracts him. There's a resounding metallic *clang* from behind the kitchen door. Then a pause. Then, again, *glom glom glom*. Isaac takes a tentative step, dislodging an unstable mound of envelopes which skid across the floor. He keeps his eyes up, trained on the kitchen door. Then he sets off, stiffly, using the wall for balance. After the four strides it takes to reach the kitchen, he catches his breath against the doorframe. With a final, beleaguered intake of breath, he pushes open the door.

Has he even been in here since that night? His memory is a blur, but the room seems untouched. The blinds remain open, making a sun-starved Isaac wince and raise his hands in defence. Then, as his eyes adjust, it's as if a photo from his past is developing in front of them. A negative. *Are you sitting down?* He'd thought he'd just imagined it, the chair clattering to the floor behind him like a dramatic moment in a weepy movie. But here it is, upturned on his kitchen floor. The table above it is still half set, two plates, a knife each but no forks. The fridge is still pinned with relics of his former life. A roll of expired pizza coupons Mary refused to bin. An unexciting magnet from one of his sister's legal conferences. And a shopping list in Mary's handwriting. *Washing tabs, peanut butter, bananas, milk.* The crippling normality of it all makes Isaac's breath come short. Or perhaps that's the smell. Even next to his stale shirt and his even staler breath, the stench unleashed by the now-open kitchen door is stomach-churning. A pot of something mouldy sits semi-cooked on the hob, but even that seems appetising next to what's on the floor. A baking tray lies upended, its contents catapulted over the tiles. A splattered array of uncooked kofta kebabs, in varying degrees of preparation, all in the same state of noxious decay. It smells like – well, it smells like three-week-old raw meat, left to become a rancid meal for maggots in an uncleaned, unoccupied kitchen. The creature, which is eating the mouldy meat, doesn't seem to mind.

Isaac gags. His eyes are watering. He pinches his nose to shut out the smell. The egg watches him do so, but doesn't stop eating. Its arms are in action, swooping down into piles on the floor then curving back up like the prehensile tails of two hyperactive monkeys, the fat yellow fingers at each end busily forcing fistfuls of rotten meat into its constantly chewing mouth. The movements would be graceful if they weren't so gross. *Glom glom glom.* Isaac watches, horrified, occasionally rubbing his eyes to try to make the creature disappear. It doesn't. Either Isaac is seeing things, which is bad, or there's a bona fide monster in his kitchen, which is worse. He slaps himself, pinches himself, even tries to push the vision out of his head with the flats of his palms. Every time, the egg remains. It watches him, intrigued, all the while shoving handfuls of decaying raw meat into its mouth like popcorn in front of a movie screen. Today's entertainment: Isaac Addy.

Glom glom glom. What is the creature thinking, as it chews and watches Isaac with those inquisitive, grapefruit-sized orbs? If it's never seen a human, it must be *E.T.* levels of repulsed: this human nose, those human ears, the fur which grows only in tufts above his small eyes and in spikes above his creased forehead. Perhaps Isaac looks naked to the egg, like a plucked chicken. Perhaps the egg doesn't know what a 'chicken' is. It gives nothing away. Whatever the creature is thinking, that squashed-up little face – if it *is* a face – remains expressionless, its stare unbroken.

'Wh–What . . .' Isaac stammers, but stops. 'How . . .' Isaac stops, but starts again. 'What are you?'

Its name is ____

The egg stops chewing the putrid meat, considering the question for a moment. It answers with a startlingly loud belch. Then it sets off again, wobbling from side to side, its feet slapping against the kitchen tiles as it goes. *Thwap thwap thwap.* The creature disappears, this time through the door into the living room, dragging its arms along the tiles behind it like ropes across a gymnasium floor. Isaac stares after it, at the living-room door, behind which the *glom glom glom* has started again. He looks at the fridge, at the shopping list, and feels suddenly pained. He looks at the tap, at the unwashed glasses in the sink, and feels impossibly thirsty. He's about to get a drink, have a cry, curl up on the festering kitchen floor, when something stops him. A creak, from the direction of the living room. He turns. The egg is back. Or, half of the egg. Its tufted head is poking round the edge of the living-room door, its huge eyes staring up at him. Isaac blinks at the egg, and the egg blinks back. It takes Isaac a moment to realise what's happening. The egg is expecting him to follow, to give chase. The egg thinks they're playing a game.

'I . . .' Isaac begins, unsure where he's even going.

It doesn't matter. Acknowledgement was enough. The egg has disappeared again. And, right on cue, the *glom glom glom* has resumed. Isaac sighs, shakes his head, but trudges towards the living room, anyway. He pushes open the door. Same room, same scene. Sullied blankets on the floor, cold ashes in the grate. But in front of those ashes, pushing its meaty yellow toes into the same broken nest of cushions and rags, the creature now stands. Its arms are gathered on the carpet, its hands cramming one of the Christmas cards from the mantelpiece into its mouth. Its eyes dart to Isaac, whose appearance only makes it chew faster. It's as if it's worried Isaac will take the card away from it. When Isaac does nothing, the egg burps again, turns back to the fireplace, and surveys the other cards on the mantelpiece as if selecting from a cheeseboard. Its arms rise puppet-like up above its head. Its pudgy yellow fingers wiggle. It makes a sound like *ooooooo*, somehow both squeakily high-pitched and grumblingly low. Then several things happen at once. The egg makes its selection, and its hovering hands grab at one of the Christmas cards on display. In its excitement it dislodges the biscuit tin in the centre of the mantelpiece, which shifts on its axis and begins to teeter on the edge like a spun coin. And Isaac, whose face has now switched from wretched weariness to awful realisation, lunges forward.

'No!' he shouts.

He moves faster than he's moved in weeks, crossing the living room in three strides and knee-sliding over the rug into the tangle of cushions in front of the fireplace. In his sudden movement, he sends the creature sprawling, rolling over and bouncing off the opposite sofa like a punted rugby ball. Isaac makes it. The biscuit tin, catapulted off the edge of the mantelpiece, lands safely in his outstretched hands. The frightened egg picks itself back up, squeals and flees towards the hallway. Isaac doesn't notice. He's doubled over on the carpet, eyes closed, heart hammering, struggling to breathe.

It feels like he's in a blizzard again, with the windows and the slatted blinds blown out, an icy wind roaring in and robbing him of his ability to speak or think. He tries to cry out, but he can't. He tries to breathe, but he can't do that, either. No, not a blizzard. The opposite. He's burning up. He's kneeling in front of the fireplace, sweating, but he may as well be kneeling in the fire with flames roaring around him. He's in hell, but he knows hell doesn't exist. He looks up to heaven, but he knows there's no such thing, either. If there was, he'd be able to feel her there. And he can't. He can't feel her. Not there, not here, not anywhere.

What use is praying, when you don't have faith? Isaac thinks about trying to talk to her, to God, to anyone who might be listening. Anything to get a message to her, to get some sort of indication that he might one day see her again. He knows it's hopeless. Didn't the Bible condemn lapsed Christians? She'd not exactly had the chance to repent. Both of them were a constant disappointment to their families, she born to staunch Scottish Presbyterians and he dragged along to dreary Mass every weekend of his long childhood. And for what? He'd still grown up agnostic. Mary was an out-and-proud atheist, subjected to a Christian funeral because she hadn't left behind any concrete instructions beyond where she wanted to be scattered. Even that much detail was impressive, at thirty. She'd have baulked at the solemn service with prayers and hymns, and she'd have laughed if she saw Isaac here now, at the altar of their living-room mantelpiece, searching for salvation.

Everyone said Isaac was the confident one, but he'd never held a candle to her conviction. Mary lived with the quiet confidence of someone who didn't need to prove anything to any higher power than herself. It infuriated her parents, her brothers, sometimes her husband. But wasn't Isaac's way infinitely more infuriating? This never-say-never dithering, this wishy-washy inability to believe in either anything, or nothing at all. To admit that Mary had returned to dust and only dust. To her, religion was ridiculous. *An excuse to get away with all manner of sins.* Yet to Isaac, nothing could be more ridiculous than the prospect of a life without her in it. Isaac sobs. Because God isn't listening, he turns his eyes downwards and speaks to the biscuit tin instead.

'What am I going to do?' Isaac asks. 'Please, tell me what to do.'

In response, a squeak. Not from the biscuit tin, nor from heaven above. It came from the doorway. The frightened egg has poked its head back into the room and is watching silently from the shadows. It looks like a told-off toddler. Isaac sniffs and wipes his eyes, clutching the biscuit tin a little closer to his chest. The egg had been abandoned. He'd brought it home. What on earth can Isaac do now? He isn't a carer. He couldn't even keep a cactus alive, and he wouldn't babysit for the neighbours without Mary coming, too. She was the one who was good with kids. She was a children's author, for Christ's sake. Isaac remembers watching her through the doorway as she did a reading at a library, every one of her audience mesmerised, sitting hypnotically still.

She was a veritable Pied Piper, while he's always seized up around children, shied away from responsibility. He's little more than a man-child himself. He breaks things, spills things, messes things up when he's left to his own devices. Last time Mary went away, he shrunk all of their bedsheets in the tumble dryer. *Why can't you act like an adult, for once?* Now he's home alone with a monstrous little toddler, and Mary isn't there to guide him. Isaac stares at the egg, two foot tall and statue-still, its white fur shining in the shadows. Its huge eyes gleam like polished marbles, blinking with expectation. Isaac wonders whether the egg expects him to be its mother. He shakes his head. His own mother had always told him only fools deal in what-ifs. But watching the expectant egg as it watches him from the doorway, Isaac can't help but think: What if?

'Hello,' Isaac says.

The creature blinks back. Then it screams. And while Isaac can't help but flinch in response, there's nothing scary, nor scared, about the noise.

Sure, the egg is screaming. But it's only screaming, *'Hello.'*

THREE

Isaac Addy might be a robot. Here on his sofa, in low-power mode, it's as if he's been abducted and replaced by an unfeeling machine. Perhaps the thing on the other sofa has something to do with it. While Isaac used to think his life was a rom-com, then a tragedy, now he knows it's a creature feature. Still, one glance at the innocent pair of eyes on the other side of the dirty coffee table is enough to assure Isaac that the creature of this particular feature isn't here with ill intent. It's just . . . here. Isaac feels no need to question why. He simply vegetates on the sofa in a perpetual state of 1 per cent charged. Behind the ever-closed blinds, the sun rises and sets, rises and sets. Isaac doesn't know if it's weekday or weekend, morning or afternoon. Robots don't have body clocks, and the internal computer which counts the hours for Isaac is malfunctioning along with everything else.

Proof that Isaac is a robot: his face, a taut grey mask

with red eyes and a rictus mouth, a cross between the Tin Man and the Iron Giant. Further proof: he's stopped crying. Whereas last week he was a sobbing, weeping mess, Isaac woke up this morning and found himself entirely devoid of emotion. It's like the tears seeped into his switchboard and fried all of its circuits. Before, Isaac would cry every time he saw Mary's shoes lined up by the front door, or Mary's perfume sitting by the sink in the upstairs bathroom. He'd even cried at a knife mark in the tub of butter in the fridge, a fossilised imprint she'd left behind. She was the one who was careless with crumbs. Like the Tin Man, Isaac has an aching hole in his chest, a cavity which has been scooped out like that butter, the hole filled instead with bile and baking soda and battery acid. Unlike the Tin Man, a replacement heart is off the cards. Yesterday, the egg found Isaac crying into that same butter, collapsed on the floor by the fridge. Self-loathing and embarrassment fried those circuits. Now Isaac has resolved to bottle up his emotions, and, in doing so, he's powering down. So, yes, Isaac Addy has been replaced with a robot. But he's only done that to himself.

Isaac has taken to sitting very still. If he sits still enough, subsisting on a diet of stale bread and featureless films, he can almost pretend he doesn't feel anything at all. It's like he doesn't even exist. And if it weren't for the perpetual scribble of bright white fur in his peripheral vision and the pug-like sound of flat-faced breathing, Isaac could even pretend the egg didn't exist, either. As if intuiting this train of thought, the egg is becoming increasingly enthusiastic about making its existence known. Even when Isaac goes to the bathroom, the curious little creature won't be far behind. It'll announce its presence with that familiar *thwap thwap thwap*, getting gradually louder as it makes its way from the adjoining room until it's suddenly there in the doorway, breathing heavily. Then it will scream. It hasn't stopped screaming to say '*Hello*' since that first meeting in the kitchen, something Isaac can't help but reinforce. Even when he hears the approaching *thwap thwap thwap*, Isaac never fails to jump out of his skin when the creature appears in a doorway and screams its little heart out. Isaac will always fumble whatever he's holding, whether it's a toothbrush or a towel or a cold tin of beans. And, yes, he'll always scream back, which is taken by the egg as a simple return of its greeting. Isaac's been trying to suppress his screams along with his crying, but without much luck. While the Iron Giant wouldn't allow himself to be frightened by something only two feet tall, Isaac clearly isn't made of such stern stuff.

Today, Isaac and the egg are watching *The Wizard of Oz*. While Munchkins lark about on screen, Isaac tries to ascertain when he last showered. His head hurts, and he winces at the slivers of light coming through the cracks in the slatted blinds. The sunlight burns. He picks a cold baked bean off a lapel of his dressing gown and eats it, then blows his nose on a used tissue, which he chucks on to the coffee table. In a past life, that table was reserved for whatever half-finished jigsaw puzzle he and Mary had on the go. Now it's reserved for dirty crockery and crumpled Kleenex. There's even a small spill-off pile of plates accumulating at the other end of his sofa, presumably because the coffee table had run out of space. He doesn't remember putting them there. At least the egg's sofa is clean. While he shared some of his breakfast with the egg this morning, the egg's chin – unlike his – is remarkably free of dried baked bean juice. Isaac looks back at the dirty plates on his sofa and feels ashamed. He smothers this shame in a metaphorical blanket, his customary response to all of his emotions. The egg stares at the TV, transfixed. Isaac sniffs, throws an actual blanket over the dirty plates, and turns his attention back to the TV.

While Isaac might feel an affinity with the Tin Man, it's the flying monkeys which have caught the egg's eye. As they run hooting through the forest, the egg makes shapes with its puckered little mouth as if it's trying to hoot along with them. Isaac looks at the egg. He cocks his head to one side, imagining a mechanical whirring sound accompanying the movement. He looks back at the monkeys on the TV screen, then the egg. Monkey, egg. Egg, monkey. There's something undeniably simian about the egg. Could it be an exotic animal, escaped from some eccentric collector's private menagerie? After all, the egg is far more primate than zygote. Its haircut is that of a marmoset, the squarish top and the unruly, monk-like tufts on either side. It has the snow-white fur of an albino gorilla, the saucer-like eyes of a tarsier, the eardrum-shattering greeting of a howler. Isaac knows Mary would berate him for conflating his apes and his monkeys. He also knows that the egg is none of these things. It's too tiny, too rotund. Too unnervingly yellow, too blindingly white. It looks like an abominable snowman, albeit one painted on to the shell of a hard-boiled egg by a child at a village fete. Isaac can imagine its arms as wiggly white pipe cleaners, stuck wonkily into each side of the egg.

Gibbons are the underdogs of the primate world. Don't you think?

Isaac cocks his head further to the side. Just like the egg's, a gibbon's arms are comically long in relation to its body. And the way a gibbon sits – sloped shoulders, raised knees, crossed hands – gives it a silhouette a little like an egg. But Isaac knows his gibbons, and he knows the egg is not one. Gibbons spend their entire lives in the treetops. The egg spends its entire life on the sofa. Gibbons move at thirty-five miles per hour, the fastest of any tree-dwelling mammal. The egg is nowhere near as fast – it has no legs to speak of, and just getting down from the sofa seems to require a monumental effort. And gibbons are social animals. They mate for life. They live in family units. They sing together, complex harmonies that resound through the dense forest canopy for miles around. When the egg screams, Isaac is the only one who screams back.

Isaac watches the egg, wondering if it knows that it's alone. Is it missing anyone? Is anyone missing it? Isaac thinks about being alone, and his pity for the egg turns to self-pity. Self-pity soon becomes self-loathing, for making it all about himself. Then panic. Then despair. He shouldn't have thought of gibbons. He can feel his circuits tripping again, and the sound of screeching monkeys is soon replaced by a pressurised throbbing in his eardrums, the witch's cauldron-like bubbling of bile in his throat. It's like the far-off beating of a drum, a drum whose every thud sounds the words MARY'S DEAD MARY'S DEAD MARY'S DEAD MARY'S DEAD MARY'S DEAD MARY'S DEAD MARY'S DEAD MARY'S DEAD.

The seismic rumble grows harder to ignore, both inside his diaphragm and under the ground beneath the sofa on which he sits. He sways. He swallows. He balls up his fists and presses them against his temples. Then, as the drumbeat reaches a crescendo, Isaac the Robot malfunctions. He whines, tears escaping from his closed eyes. One mechanical arm reaches up, swings like a lever and breaks the closest thing within his reach.

CRACK

Isaac's eyes shoot open. The panic subsides. The movie returns to its normal volume, the room to its everyday stillness. Isaac gulps. He knows he broke something, and he's worried that it might have been the egg. Had it come to sit next to him? If so, Isaac hadn't heard it. With a wince, he raises his hand. No yolk. Just a graze. He looks to his right, to the other cushion. No shell. Just a broken plate poking out from beneath a blanket. He turns to the other sofa, where he can already feel a pair of black eyes boring into him. No egg. Just an egg-like, gibbon-like creature staring back at him. Only now does Isaac realise that tears are streaming down his cheeks, his sobs coming half stifled and near-silent. So much for not crying. He wonders if the creature knows what it means, to cry. Despite its perpetual grimace, the egg rarely shows emotion. Isaac has seen no sign of tear ducts. Yet the sight of the egg now – so small and wintry white in the expanse of such a large sofa – is enough to make Isaac feel lonely on its behalf. He wonders why it's here, presumably so far away from home. If it's on a fact-finding mission, it's chosen the wrong host. Its research has a sample of just one, and a deeply flawed one at that. Isaac isn't typical of a human being. His tears don't line up with the tears the egg sees on the screen. On TV, people cry at train-station goodbyes, at babies being born or at unconscious loved ones in hospital beds. Here in real life, people cry at lined-up shoes, tubs of butter, and forests filled with flying monkeys.

●

Isaac wakes himself up on a park bench. Would a robot do that? The fact that Isaac often finds himself in places with no idea how he got there seems too chaotic for something pre-programmed and precisely assembled. It happened on the bridge, and now it's happening all the time. Sometimes he'll find himself in his empty bath, or in the long grass at the end of his garden, or swaying on his feet outside the locked door at the top of the house. At others he'll find himself in public. He found himself, last week, in the sterile white corridor of a local hospital. Three days ago, he found himself outside his hairdresser's, shivering in pyjama bottoms and a dressing gown. Tommy, his barber, knocked on the window. Isaac stared through the glass with the glazed eyes of a man lost both within and without. Today he's materialised in the local park, half dressed and half asleep, rooted so firmly to a bench that he's become a landing pad for pigeons. He wakes himself with that usual blood-curdling scream, as if he's being butchered, as if he's an abattoir cow at the business end of a stun-gun. He always screams like this, always gasps, always pants, but always eventually returns to sanity. You've wandered off, he tells himself, as if he's elderly before his time. He feels ashamed, embarrassed, abnormal. Isaac sits on the park bench, screams, and the pigeons who've been keeping him company scatter in fear. Now he stands up and staggers back home, alone once again.

Isaac arrives at the house, covered in cuts, bumps and bruises. He's been tripping up more often, falling over like a child trying to run before it can walk. He can't remember where most of the injuries came from. He feels like he's lost something else alongside Mary, something integral to his body, some part of his inner-ear function which controlled his ability to balance. Everything is off-kilter now. He wants to tell Mary this, this weird fact, this strange symptom of her leaving that she'll never know. Sometimes, he finds himself composing texts to her. After he deletes these ghost messages, he scrolls back to random samples of past conversations just to feel as if he can hear her again.

Isaac I have a confession

                                        Oh God
                                        Tell me

I've ordered an electric blanket

                                            . . .
                                        A what

An electric blanket
I used to have one but it broke

                        Please say you're joking

It's the dream
Don't knock it till you've tried it

                        It sounds like a fire hazard

It does start to burn sometimes sure
But you roll with it

                Have you ordered a zimmer frame too

You laugh
But you'll be cold sleeping on the sofa xxx

Isaac can't accept that Mary won't text him back. He still feels his phone vibrate and convinces himself it's her, as if she's scrolled past something so funny she couldn't help but share it from the other side. He still sees her in his peripheral vision, still glimpses her through doorways or in the backdrop of his reflection in the hallway mirror. He finds himself knocking on the bathroom door in the middle of the night, half asleep, calling her name. But she's never there. His only housemate is a two-foot-tall egg-shaped creature, which silently watches Isaac as his mind unravels.

Ever since Isaac cried during *The Wizard of Oz*, the egg has taken to staring at him quite intently. It's like a long-forgotten teddy bear with a nanny cam behind its eyes, those enormous, unblinking orbs that miss nothing. Isaac's disappearing acts may be a mystery to Isaac himself, but the egg must be drawing its own conclusions. After all, it sees Isaac leave the house for hours, sometimes days, on end. It sees him pack a toothbrush into a hastily filled duffel bag, then drive off into the night. It sees him sneak back in through the front door the next day, looking sheepish and smelling of someone else's soap. It sees the ever-present guilt in his eyes, a guilt which has defined Isaac since the night he lost Mary. Perhaps that's why he always follows his clandestine trips out with a night spent cradling the biscuit tin he keeps on the mantelpiece, or crying in his bedroom when he assumes the egg has gone to sleep. Perhaps that's why he refuses to talk to anyone but the egg, even when the shadows of other people pass behind the blinds or rap their knuckles on the front door. Perhaps Isaac only speaks to the egg because he knows the egg can't speak back. The egg can't ask him questions which he doesn't want to answer.

What would Isaac's mates say, if they could see him now? What questions would Mary's friends ask, if he was confronted by them face to face? Isaac can't think of anything worse than explaining himself to the couples they used to see for drunken dinner parties or coffee in the park. He had friends of his own once, sure, from college or uni, or the one or two desk jobs he did in his early twenties. But Isaac is a man on the cliff-edge of thirty, and he's just as bad at keeping in touch with old friends as old friends are with him. They have their own lives now. Isaac had his own life, too. And while he'd readily blame Mary's death for his enforced isolation, becoming a widower was only the last little push needed to seal him off completely from the rest of the world. *Here if you need me*, those friends say, over text. But Isaac doesn't know what he needs. *Want to go for a drink?* they ask. But Isaac isn't drinking any more. His little sister has been keeping a close eye on that. Guys meet at the pub and talk about their jobs, their wives, their Sunday league football teams. Isaac and his mates talk about superhero films, stupid injuries they accrued as teenagers and 'Who would win in a fight, a bear-sized duck or a hundred duck-sized bears?' Contemplating throwing yourself off a bridge or finding yourself screaming in anguish in public parks isn't exactly cheery conversation to be had over pints and peanuts.

Isaac settles back into the sofa. He turns on the TV,

switches over to *Dirty Dancing*. He avoids his phone, face down on the coffee table, and the egg, facing him from its seat on the other sofa. Isaac hasn't seen his mum and dad for over a month, despite the fact that they've been calling constantly. He's just about blocked Mary's mother, too – their once-fraught relationship made even more so by the biscuit tin on the mantelpiece. The one person who actually sees him is his sister, Joy, albeit only via snatched glances through the crack in the latched front door when Isaac reaches out to grab the shopping bags she leaves outside. Joy has always acted older than Isaac. Or, no, Isaac has always acted younger than Joy – she'd abandoned fancy dress long before him. As an adult, Isaac could hardly look after himself before his life got a death sentence, and now he doesn't even have the energy to drag himself to the Sainsbury's Local down the road. Lawyers like Joy barely even get lunch breaks, yet she still finds the time to deliver his groceries once a week. More guilt, more shame. Mary would smack Isaac if she found out he was making Joy do all of his shopping. But Mary isn't here, and Isaac feels nothing. He's a robot, and to thank Joy for her efforts would be to risk an overspill of human emotion. Besides, there's a strange little egg-shaped creature on his sofa, and Isaac doesn't want Joy discovering it. Isaac has formed an attachment to the egg, and he can't risk anyone taking it away.

As Jennifer Grey dismounts the stage and launches herself into Patrick Swayze's arms, Isaac attempts to dissociate from his corporeal form. He's still avoiding the egg's gaze, worried that if he gives it the time of day it'll want to try the lift that he and Mary would attempt when drunk, always ending up in a heap on the floor. Isaac puts the egg in the corner, metaphorically, but is less successful at ignoring his phone. It's ringing. He can't help but flip it over and check the name on the screen.

Esther Moray

Who did he expect? She's been calling twice a day since that night on the bridge. Isaac's eyes dart nervously to the biscuit tin. He swallows, one eye twitching. No one makes him more antsy than his stern-talking and aggressively Scottish mother-in-law. It's not like she was ever less than civil, but their conversation would always shrivel and die in any room without Mary in it. Isaac had always felt like Esther blamed him: for stealing Mary away from Scotland, for ensuring Mary would never move back, for the sixteen-hour round trip that constituted the privilege of going to her own daughter's wedding. At the wedding itself, the meeting of their families was about as much fun as the Battle of Stirling Bridge. Clan Addy versus Clan Moray. Joking had always been Isaac's first line of defence, hence his wedding speech, sweaty-palmed and self-conscious. That awful *Braveheart* impression. *You can take my wife, but you can never take my freedom.* Isaac still cringes to think of it. At least Mary had laughed. Esther's face had been like a battleaxe. Yet Mary told Isaac that it was all in his head, that his favourite hobby was convincing himself that people found him disagreeable. *Nobody dislikes you but yourself,* she'd say, only half joking. Isaac was inclined to agree. He'd always thought his biggest fear was people not liking him. Turns out, it was only his second biggest.

Isaac lets the phone ring out, its vibrations on the coffee table replaced by the tuning-up of the saxophonist next door. A saxophonist who'd practised every single day since Isaac and Mary bought the place, yet whose face they'd still never seen, and whose skills still hadn't improved. Over three years since they moved in, the same daily repertoire. 'Baker Street' into 'Careless Whisper', the *Pink Panther* theme, a blasphemously bad Chet Baker medley and, finally, for the big finish, 'What the World Needs Now is Love'. Every tune always a millisecond too fast or too slow, the fifth note always fluffed and the sixth always flat. Mary called it *quirky.* She used to say she quite enjoyed it, liked to pretend that it was the corny movie soundtrack of their life. This only makes hearing it now so much worse. For Isaac, the very existence of neighbours is a cruel reminder of a world outside these four walls. And while Anna and Adam on the other side have been nothing but lovely, the care packages they've been leaving on his front doorstep are somehow more grating than the saxophonist. *What a lovely family,* Mary and Isaac used to say, about the pair of them and their perfect twin toddlers. *We'll probably make friends with them, when we've got kids of our own.* Now they're one of the very friend-couples Isaac has been doing his best to avoid.

Isaac feels a surge of anger. He stares at the wall, at the rough point beyond which he imagines the saxophonist is standing. Then he hurls the television remote. It narrowly misses the biscuit tin, and Isaac's heart skips a beat. When he turns to the opposite sofa, as if to say 'Phew', he's surprised to find that the egg has disappeared. Isaac panics, briefly, then sees it standing on the nearside of the coffee table. Its arms are spooled on the carpet, its eyes trained on the kitchen door. It doesn't look happy.

'The smell?' Isaac says.

The door is firmly closed, but that hasn't stopped the worsening stink of old, rancid meat creeping in through the gap beneath it. Only now that the creature has addressed it does its full force hit Isaac. He wonders how he's been blocking it out, how he's been eating food in there without immediately expelling it back into the kitchen sink. The egg nods in agreement, wrinkling its nose. The expression is surprisingly human.

'OK,' Isaac sighs. 'I'll get rid of the smell.'

He rises slowly, pulling himself towards the kitchen door as if he's put down roots in the sofa. He turns the handle with weak fingers. Isaac was expecting it to be bad, but the noxious wave of stink that hits him is almost enough to send him sprawling to his knees. He coughs and splutters as he grips the doorframe. The egg, which was bobbing after him, bumps into the back of his legs and is now upturned, beetle-like, on its back. As Isaac retches, the egg rights itself again and pushes him forwards into the room. He shields himself from the bright windows and the wall of flies and rotten-meat fumes. Meanwhile, the egg plods around the kitchen, plucking bluebottles out of the air, two at a time, and stuffing them into its mouth.

Isaac re-engages his robot sensibilities. He flings open the cupboard under the sink, arms himself with a scouring pad and a bottle of bleach, and gets to work scrubbing. He wipes his brow, pauses to retch again, then scrubs some more. He prises the remainder of the meat from the floor with his Marigold-clad fingers, banishing each grey piece to the depths of a black bin bag, which he ties, for safety's sake, in a quadruple knot. He thrusts the bin bag at the egg and nods towards the front door, then bungs the baking tray in the sink and turns on the hot tap. By the time Isaac turns back, the last shreds of black bin bag have already disappeared into the creature's chewing mouth. Isaac shakes his head as he retrieves the mop from the cupboard under the stairs, then, sighing all the while, sets about cleaning the floor. The creature reverts to watching Isaac, the flat saxophone on the other side of the wall providing a soundtrack to his exploits. The egg watches Isaac bleach the countertops to 'Careless Whisper'. It watches Isaac load the dishwasher to the *Pink Panther* theme. And finally, as Chet Baker begins to play, it watches Isaac pick up the upturned chair from the floor, place it back by the kitchen table and slump into it. Isaac rubs his tired eyes. The egg climbs into its own seat opposite him. Isaac looks at the creature and yawns. After some consideration, the egg yawns back. Isaac can tell it's mimicking him.

'Where are you from?' Isaac says.

He doesn't actually expect an answer. It certainly doesn't occur to him that it's the first time since that first day that he's asked the egg anything about itself. The creature scrunches up its little yellow mouth, making that same old monkey-like hooting face. Its thick, rubbery lips come together, and in its concentration a bubble of spittle pops out. Isaac's own lips part a little, his eyes opening a little more. He realises what's happening. The egg is forming its first word.

'*Wawooo*,' the egg says.

Its voice is laboured and throaty, like that of a cartoon frog. Isaac blinks dumbly, his own voice wavering.

'Wawooo?'

'*Wawooo.*'

'You're from . . .' Isaac trips over his words. 'Wa—Wawooo?'

'*Wawooo.*'

Isaac blinks, thinks for a moment. The egg waits.

'Where is "Wawooo"?'

The egg blinks at him, breathing with its characteristic wet rumble, its waking snore. Either it doesn't understand the question, or it's lost interest in the conversation. It just stares, only half of its tiny face visible over the edge of the kitchen table. In the light of the newly cleaned kitchen, the egg seems less cartoonish, more tangible. Its white fur floats atop its head like candyfloss, its skin mottled and pock-marked like a well-aged cheese. Isaac had assumed the egg was a toddler because of its diminutive size and its clumsy demeanour. But it now occurs to him that the egg could easily be older than Isaac himself. Like Yoda. It watches Isaac with eyes that seem suddenly wise, eyes larger than the two dried-up grapefruit sitting in the fruit bowl between them. Eyes like black holes.

The egg has noticed the grapefruit as well. Those elastic arms are now hovering over the table and its fingers, like an exploratory brigade of tiny yellow soldiers, are marching their way towards the fruit bowl. The fruit was bought by Joy, always keen to impose her own healthy regimen on her couch-potato brother. Her recommended breakfast is half a grapefruit, a matcha tea and a turmeric-and-ginger shot. Isaac's favourite used to be Coco Shreddies, because they turn the milk chocolatey, but his new go-to is a perilously black coffee and cold baked beans, eaten straight from the tin. Either way, he's always hated grapefruit.

'Still hungry?' Isaac says, pushing the fruit bowl towards the creature. 'Be my guest.'

The egg's fingers slither into the bowl and grab hold of the fruit. It picks them up and holds them in front of its similarly grapefruit-sized eyes, enthralled. From where Isaac's sitting, it looks like it's wearing goggles.

'It's food,' Isaac says, miming the action of putting food in his mouth. 'You eat it.'

'*Wawooo*,' the egg says, uninterested.

Before Isaac can ask why grapefruit is also *wawooo*, his phone starts ringing again. He hadn't realised he'd brought it with him. Here it sits, face down on the tabletop, vibrating harshly against the wood. Isaac stares at the phone. The egg stares at the grapefruit, putting one back in the bowl, turning the other over in its tiny palms. Isaac fidgets, glances at the egg, at the grapefruit, at the phone. He flips it over, reads the screen. Then he's off. He bolts from the kitchen to answer the call, closing the door behind him. The creature stares at the grapefruit as a terse conversation begins in the hallway. Through the wood of the door and the din of the saxophone, only a fraction of the words are audible.

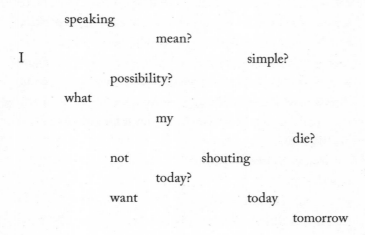

In the hallway, Isaac hangs up the phone. He considers smashing it to smithereens on the wooden floor. He slides it into his dressing-gown pocket and presses his forehead against the cold hallway mirror instead. Isaac straightens up, resolves not to lose his temper. He crosses the hallway with gritted teeth, opens the kitchen door with white knuckles.

Judging by the state of the kitchen, the egg also doesn't like grapefruit. For instead of eating the fruit, the creature appears to have lifted it over its head and, with all the force its arms could muster, smashed it repeatedly against the surface of the table. Then, with the grapefruit already flattened on the tabletop, the egg has set to work pummelling the fruit into the wood with its tiny yellow fists. The grapefruit clearly wasn't as dried-up as it had seemed, judging by the limp, wet shreds of skin on the table, and the kitchen whose floor and walls and cabinets are now painted with juice and pith. Isaac surveys the kitchen. He breathes slowly out of his nose, doing everything in his power not to start shouting. His mouth is tight. His fists are clenched. He steps carefully over chunks of grapefruit flesh and puddles of grapefruit juice, until he's standing directly over the egg. The egg, or the egg's just-about-visible eyes over the edge of the table, stare up at him defiantly.

'*Wawooo.*'

'You don't like grapefruit?'

'*Wawooo.*'

'You could have just said.'

Isaac walks slowly over to a kitchen cabinet, his mood betrayed by his shaking hands and the force with which he opens the cupboard. The resulting bang even stops the saxophonist, albeit only momentarily. While the door shudders as it rebounds, Isaac reaches into the cupboard, pushing aside assorted jars and tins until he finds something the creature might like. He settles on a half-eaten, half-stale pack of biscuits.

'Here,' he says, returning to the table and slamming the biscuits down. 'Hobnobs. Everybody likes Hobnobs.'

The creature blinks up at Isaac. Then, as if to test Isaac's theory, it puts the packet into its mouth. Isaac stops the egg before it can bite down, prising apart its wet gums and opening the packet on the egg's behalf. He hands the egg a biscuit. The egg holds it up to the light, as it did the grapefruit. The Hobnob hovers there for a second, held in a yellow hand at the end of a snaking arm which sways ever so slightly, like a puppet on a string. Just before the egg moves, Isaac realises what's about to happen.

'Don't—'

'*Wawooo!*'

The creature does. It slams the biscuit down on the table like a poker player with a winning hand. Then, with its free fist, it pulverises the biscuit into the already-grapefruit-soaked tabletop. Its fists slam downwards, sending clouds of rolled oats over the front of Isaac's dressing gown. Then, not satisfied, the creature takes another biscuit and does the same. Then another. Then another. Isaac watches all the while, a stormy expression brewing on his face.

'Are you done?' Isaac says eventually. He's still not shouting, but one eye is twitching violently. Combined with the angry vein standing out on his temple, it makes him look particularly deranged.

'*D'oh*,' says the egg.

'D'oh?' Isaac repeats. No need to guess what that one means. 'Fine. No Hobnobs.'

Isaac returns to the counter by the oven. He slams open the bread bin, pushes aside his go-to loaf of stiff white bread, finds a stale croissant lurking at the back. He grabs it, stomps back to the table, hands it to the creature.

'Eat that.'

The egg sniffs the croissant. It considers it with suspicion, from a number of angles. Then it begins to eat. Instead of devouring the whole thing in one bite, it nibbles from one pointed end to the other, working away at the flaky pastry with a seemingly toothless mouth. Once again, Isaac watches. And even though his just-cleaned kitchen is already a mess, something about the way the creature is eating – expelling an avalanche of pastry crumbs out of the corners of its mouth, down its furry belly and all over the chair and tiles below – is making him even more annoyed. Lacking a bib, Isaac grabs a plate from the plate rack and sets it down so hard in front of the egg that it almost breaks. The creature stops eating and blinks up at Isaac. Isaac points at the plate, the muscles in his neck straining as he tries to keep his voice measured.

'Eat off this,' he commands, miming eating once again. He makes a cross with his hands. 'No crumbs.'

The creature blinks at the plate. It blinks up at Isaac. Isaac's eyes are wide, red and, if possible, even more bulging than those of the bug-eyed creature in front of them. The egg looks back down at the plate. For one blissful moment, it even looks as if it's going to use it. Then it sets its croissant down on the table, and picks up the plate instead.

'No,' Isaac says, already sensing the inevitable.

Blink. Blink.

The plate rises higher, until it's hovering above the egg's head.

'Don't even think about it.'

The plate rises higher still, until it's higher even than Isaac's own head. Isaac stares at the creature, adopting his tersest schoolteacher tone.

'If you even—'

His voice is drowned out by the crash of the plate shattering into a hundred pieces on the kitchen tiles between them. Chunks of porcelain explode in all directions, rebounding off the chair legs and Isaac's shins, and the cupboards and the counters and the door of the fridge. Isaac stares, incredulous, at the point in mid-air where the plate had previously been. The egg hasn't once taken its eyes off Isaac.

'*Wawooo.*' It purses its mouth, a non-verbal full stop implied.

Isaac – who is about to explode, too – is barely able to control himself. He kicks a piece of the mottled porcelain, as if using his foot as a probe to check that what he's seeing is real. The plate is broken beyond repair, which would usually be manageable but is, in this circumstance, beyond the pale. It was Mary's plate. They're all Mary's plates. She picked them all out at an independent shop on the high street, the plates themselves from an even smaller design house she loved in Copenhagen. What will Isaac do now? Buy more plates? It was Mary who chose the plates. Even if he bought the same plate, it wouldn't be the *same* plate. And if he bought different plates, what then? He'd have to smash the rest. And what about the matching bowls? The side plates? Christ, the serving dish? She'd matched the whole set. Now he'll have to get rid of it all. He'll have to start again. How is he supposed to start again? It hits him, all at once, as if the plate had been smashed over his head and not on the kitchen tiles. How is he supposed to throw away the mugs only she liked to drink from? How is he supposed to keep making only one cup of coffee, every morning, in a kitchen where he only ever made two? Isaac's heart hammers in his chest, his mouth dries up, his jaw clenches and he finds himself scarcely able to breathe. They always said they'd adopt a dog. Now they won't. They always said they'd buy a farm. Now they can't. They always said 'always', and now the only 'always' in Isaac's life is the fact that Mary will always be gone, and Isaac will always have to live without her. How is he supposed to keep on living, knowing that his reason for living is gone for good?

Silence descends on the kitchen, like the void at the centre of a tornado. Then the saxophonist behind the wall dives into the first few notes of the Burt Bacharach big finisher, and Isaac screams.

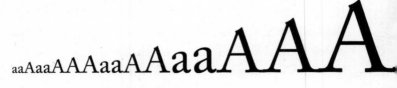

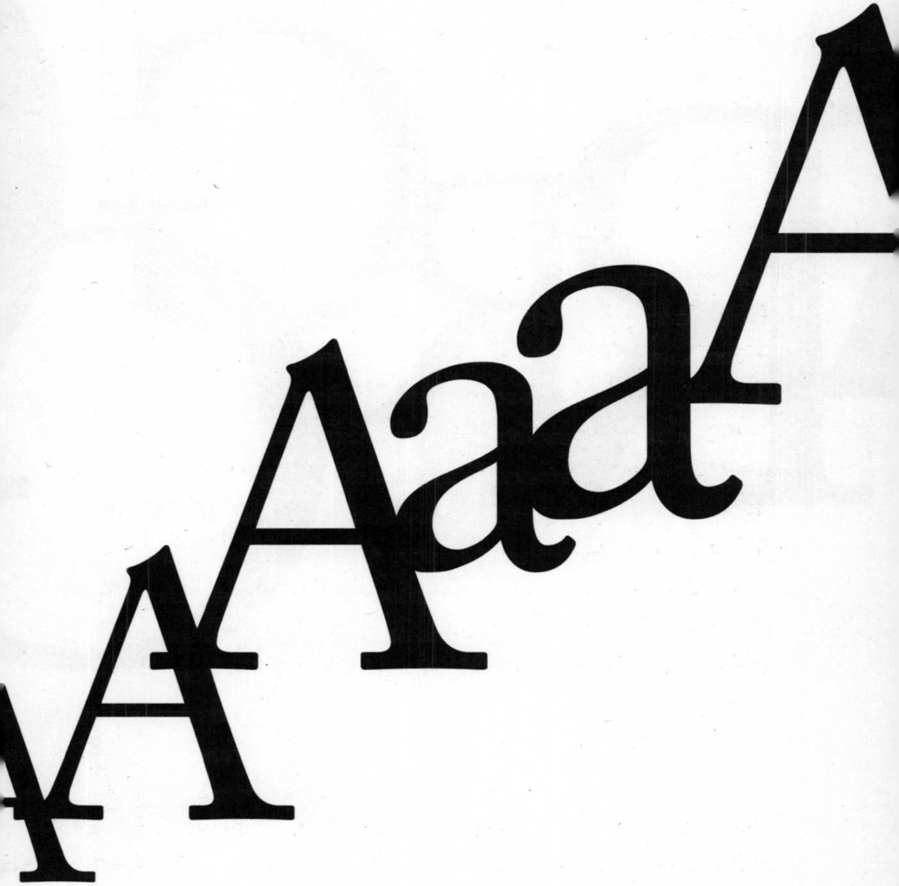

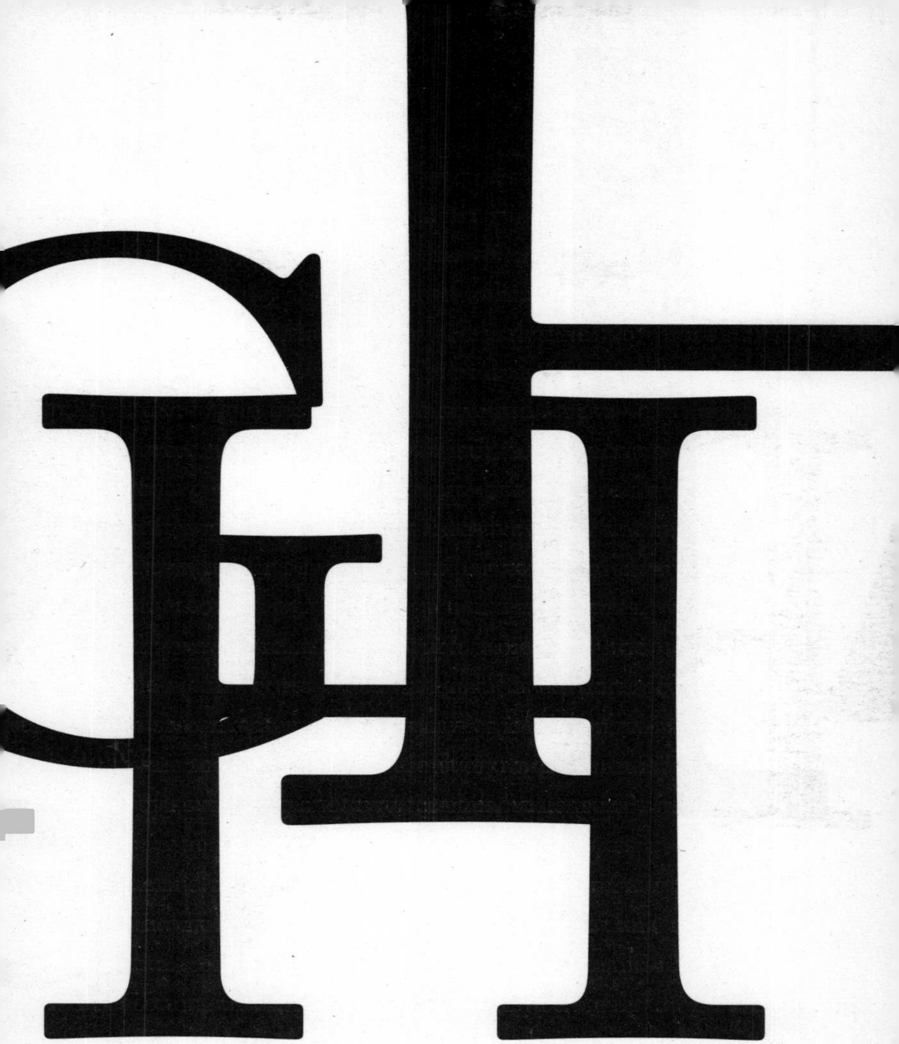

The saxophone stops. More porcelain smashes. Isaac looks accusingly at the egg, but the egg is staring at Isaac's hand. With every muscle in his body still tensed, Isaac realises what's just happened. He's pulled a plate from the plate rack. He's raised it over his head. And with this hand, the shaking hand he now holds in front of his face, he's brought it down on the kitchen tiles with a crash even more thunderous than the one before. He'd blame the imp of the perverse, but it's the egg who started it. Isaac looks at the egg. The egg looks at Isaac. Then Isaac lets go, and all hell breaks loose with him.

Isaac reaches for the same plate rack. He screams again. This time, the creature screams with him. The egg leaps gibbon-like from the table to the counter by the hob, settling on a wooden spoon which it begins to bang against the base of a metal saucepan. Isaac, meanwhile, grabs the furthest plate on the rack and wrenches it forwards with all his strength. This liberates every other plate in the rack, sending them crashing like a mighty waterfall to the tiles below. As the plates cascade, Isaac sets to work flinging side plates one by one, like frisbees. They shatter against the door of the fridge. The egg, meanwhile, has flung open the door of the cupboard in which Isaac found the Hobnobs, then used its monkey-tail arms to wrench the cupboard door clean off its hinges. It hurls the wooden door to the floor, then hurls a barrage of dried herbs and condiments after it. Damson jam, see kitchen tiles. Peanut butter, say hello to the far wall. Mustard powder, meet the floor. The latter explodes on the tiles in a cloud of yellow smoke, which fills the kitchen and makes them both sneeze. As paprika explodes by his left foot like a red flare, and as cumin blooms up in a tawny billow to his right, Isaac crosses to the kitchen table and flips it on its axis like a Viking berserker at a pagan feast. Over the sound of his screaming and the egg's pot-banging cacophony, one can barely even hear it fall.

The rest is a blur. Isaac smears pesto across his cheeks like a commando. The creature dances upon the wine rack as it uses the base of a rolling pin to shatter each bottle beneath it. Red wine washes over the tiles in an awful wave as Isaac pulls open the fridge door and licks his lips. Then, through a multicoloured cloud of powder, an impromptu game of baseball begins. Isaac lines up the shot, then pitches a jar of mayonnaise towards the creature. Isaac made the egg watch *Field of Dreams* last week, so it knows exactly what to do. It swings the rolling pin, connects with the jar, and is rewarded with a head-to-toe coating of goo. If the resulting *oooooooo* is anything to go by, it sees this as a success. Isaac bowls a bottle of ketchup, and the creature hits a home run. The game continues with pickled onions, preserved lemons and the contents of a particularly old bag of potatoes, each one exploding on impact like a water bomb. It's only when the pitching of a soft old lime causes a juice explosion which imperils the eyes of both players that Isaac loses control of the game.

He turns. The egg watches him turn. He screams. The egg screams in unison. But when Isaac hits the wall, the egg doesn't join in. With no food left to pulverise, no bottles left to smash, Isaac takes his rage out on himself. His right fist connects with the plaster and causes a startling *thwack*. A rosebud of red appears on the crumpled surface, but Isaac feels nothing. He hits the wall again. *Thwack*. And again. *Thwack*. Isaac punches the same spot over and over, a spider's web of chipped paint and dripping blood spreading ever wider and wider as he punches and screams and punches some more. *Thwack*. *Thwack*. *Thwack*. Still he punches and still he feels nothing, his crushed knuckles swelling and the wall caving in beneath his ruined fingers. *Thwack*. *Thwack*. *Thwack*. Only when he feels like either the wall or his wrist will give way does Isaac stop. He feels sick. He staggers backwards. And, with a broken hand already starting to swell, he slumps to a floor coated in Marmite and Merlot.

The room is quiet once again. The sound of wanton destruction has clearly alarmed the saxophonist into silence. Isaac sits with his back against the bottom of the fridge, coated from head to toe, his wrist shaking, his fingers fattening with swollen blisters and clotted blood. He surveys the walls, so covered in splattered sauces and streaked condiments that the whole room looks like a Jackson Pollock painting. Then he surveys the egg, wading towards him through a shin-deep pool of vinegar and wine, like a priest at a river baptism. There is no judgement in the egg's eyes. And remarkably, considering all the claret and blueberry and tomato ketchup, its fur remains unstained. Rather than trailing through the sticky liquid, the egg's saggy belly seems to hover above it. Isaac thinks of Jesus, a two-foot Jesus egg with pipe-cleaner arms, and would laugh if he weren't in so much pain. At least he's not thinking about the phone call, which is as much as can be asked for right now.

'We'll need to clean the kitchen again,' Isaac mutters.

The egg stops walking and stands next to him, its limp arms floating like pool noodles on an ocean of passata and Pinot Noir. Isaac feels like he should apologise, or say thank you. On both counts, he doesn't know what for. Instead, he resolves to awkwardly ruffle the egg's hair, reaching out with his ruined hand and placing it shakily on top of the creature's head. With some effort, he tousles the egg's white fur with his tingling fingers. That's when something strange happens.

The egg doesn't make a sound. It merely closes its eyes, the first time Isaac has seen it do so, huge yellow lids drooping on to a bulbous and now-eyeless yolk. For a moment, Isaac thinks it's fallen asleep. Then there's a jolt, and the wet floor falls away beneath both of them. The edges of Isaac's vision are fringed with black. The kitchen spins into nothingness, the whole of his consciousness seemingly sucked through an airlock into some otherworldly vacuum. And though Isaac can still feel the cold metal of the fridge against his back and the soft fur of the egg's crown between his bruised fingers, his eyes are somewhere else entirely. He's floating in a void. An enormous metal structure looms over him, yawning in the dark. It must be fifty feet tall, this thing, lights blinking all across its upper ridge, spotlights flaring and fanning out beneath it. At the front is what looks like a glass pyramid, the vague suggestion of movement behind the glass. Above and behind that is the great body of the beast itself, an enormous cube of shifting obsidian and iron which twinkles all over with lights. An arcing sound like whale song fills Isaac's ears as the vast mechanism threatens to swallow him up. But his startled hand has already let go of the egg's head, and he's been vortexed back into the kitchen, slumped on the floor between a fridge cleaned out of contents and a being from out of this world. He gasps, gathers himself, and stares at the creature, which is slowly opening its enormous black eyes once again.

'What was that?' Isaac says, his skin prickling under the sleeves of his dressing gown.

The egg simply blinks. Isaac blinks back, his back-from-the-void head now filling with guilt about everything he hasn't learned, about a visitor he knows nothing about.

'Where did you come from?' Isaac asks, his voice barely a whisper.

'*Wawooo*,' says the egg.

FOUR

When Isaac pictures Mary now, he can't help but see her in a crowd.

It's a memory. But why this one? Mary hated crowds. If she needed company, she'd choose books. Or animals. Or Isaac. Yet this is an image of her that Isaac can't shake. Picture their third, maybe their fourth, date. Isaac is ascending the stairs of Brixton tube station. Now he's on the wide pavement outside, but it's half-past six and so is everyone else. Impatient pub-seekers and hurried headers-home push past him. Someone is preaching on a megaphone, someone else is playing a one-man violin concerto for cash. The two sounds wrestle with each other for attention over the laughter of a crowd which knows it's nearly the weekend, and the moan of the buses and taxis which know it's still rush hour on a Thursday. Someone is burning incense at a stall, a strong, sweet smell which overpowers the Routemaster exhaust fumes and the cigarette smoke. Someone in a branded red jacket thrusts a copy of *Time Out* into his hands. He protests. He doesn't need a magazine. He's got a date to get to. He's off to meet Mary.

And there she is. Looking up from the magazine, he sees her. It's like divine intervention, the way she appears so suddenly and so serenely, visible over the rushing masses as if a spotlight is trained on her from the heavens above. Really, it's her height which makes her stick out – at just over six foot, she's a whole head taller than any of Isaac's ex-girlfriends. Not that she's his girlfriend. Not yet. There she is, about fifty yards away, cold greenish eyes and warm reddish hair springing out of a crowd of grey faces like a flower between the cracks in a pavement. She's looking for him, and Isaac lets her look. He stands on the busy concourse, barely noticing that he's being jostled, barely caring that it's starting to rain. He holds the magazine over his head as he watches her, and he smiles. He doesn't want to forget this moment. He paints her in his mind like a Botticelli Venus. Her broad forehead, her sharp chin, her eyes which seem to shine out across the crowd as they search for him. Her lips, which will turn up at the corners when they find him. Perhaps Isaac always pictures this moment because it's the moment that he knew, really knew, that there'd never be anyone else. And there never *will* be anyone else, not now. There'll never be another Mary. And Mary will never be anything other than this, a painting of Mary, a painting of a painting, etched on the backs of Isaac's eyelids every time he closes his eyes. He sometimes wonders if the image will fade. Or, worse, he wonders if the image will falter – if his memory of Mary will shift with every day, week and year until the Mary he sees in his head is nothing like what Mary was at all. How will he know? All she is now is a product of his imagination. Mary, tall and pale and auburn-haired against a grey sky, peering out of a sea of grey umbrellas and grey faces, not knowing she's being watched.

Mary wasn't like Isaac. She was never at ease in busy places. She loved London, but she'd always rather be back home. Sitting on the bridge over the river near the farm where she grew up, breathing in the great wide-open air. Which is funny, because whenever Isaac spent time in the country, he'd always yearned for the bustle of the big city. They disagreed on a lot, but this was the big one: the constant bickering over how rural their life together should be. While Isaac wouldn't consider himself an out-and-out urbanite, staying south of Hadrian's Wall was just about where he drew the line. Their current house had been a compromise, a green-enough county town with good-enough trains to get Isaac straight back into the city if he was ever feeling homesick. The farm? That would come later.

Mary would never inherit her family's farm, which had been passed down from generation to generation. The honour was going to her twin brothers, Duncan and Dennis, whom she called Tweedle-Dun and Tweedle-Den on account of their inseparability and the fact they were both built like Highland cattle. They never really *got* these nicknames, just as they never *got* their sister, though they smiled accommodatingly nonetheless. Neither had abandoned lambing for the bright lights of London, so despite being younger they were natural successors to the Moray plot. But even down here, in the city, Mary wore her Scottishness as a badge of pride. She couldn't exactly hide it: rust-brown hair which, in the sun, could just about pass for ginger – and sheet-white skin which, in the sun, would burn unless smothered in Factor 50. Yet Isaac, who was a Londoner through and through and thus approached everything with the obligatory cynicism, used to enjoy annoying her about it. You moved down here when you were eighteen and you never go back, he'd say. Your brothers are Scottish, but you? You're not even northern now, let alone north-of-the-border.

You're an eejit.

'Eejit? That's Irish.' This was one of his favourites.

Scots say it, too.

'You're not Scottish any more, though.'

More Scottish than you, eejit.

Mary was outdoorsy, but she was far from a born farmer. Too much heavy lifting for someone so bookish. And Isaac? He'd barely picked up a spade, let alone driven a tractor or milked a goat. Their own farm was more of a concept, a picture-perfect idea of how they'd eventually settle down. Sure, he'd have to learn to shear the sheep, but Mary said she'd collect the eggs from the hens and top up the troughs with chicken feed. 'OK, when we're old,' Isaac had said at first, then 'OK, when we're rich,' then 'OK, when we're forty.' Mary wasn't the Renaissance painting Isaac made her out to be. Her headstrong could be pig-headed; her idealistic teetered on the verge of unrealistic. Yet while the farm was a far-off dream, she always genuinely believed in it – less a failing of practicality, more an impatience for good times to come. And while Isaac's being a people-pleaser normally equalled being a pushover, with every busy year that passed he became more enamoured of Mary's idea of a rustic, bare-brick farmhouse with only his wife, their kids, five cows and forty chickens for company. Oh, and a dog. Border Collies had been an ever-present fixture on the farm on which Mary grew up. She'd known a succession of three or four in her thirty years of life. Kirsty, Clodagh, Bonnie and Clyde. Only Clyde remained, which was more than could be said for Mary. They were going to adopt a dog for themselves, maybe next year. There was always next year. Now Isaac lies in a lonely bed in a lonely town away from London, thinking about how he'd buy a thousand cows if doing so would bring Mary back.

Hello, stalker. Did you think you'd lost me?

That's what she'd said, in real life, on the pavement outside Brixton station. And he did think he'd lost her. She'd noticed him, her lips turning up at the corners, growing into that goofy smile he'd grow to know and love. But the commuter crowd were like cattle, bucking and ploughing and herding him in directions he hadn't wanted to go. A raised newspaper here, a flower stall there, a tall man in a trench coat and a short woman with a large umbrella, and suddenly Mary was nowhere to be seen. Isaac's heart had stopped in his chest. *Where is she? Where has she gone?* It was as if she'd been abducted by aliens, first there in a gap in a crowd, then vanished completely, even though the gap remained. Perhaps that's what the heavenly spotlight had been – a tractor beam from a spaceship, taking Mary away from him, forever. *But what would they want with Mary? And wh—*

Hello, stalker. A tug on his arm, and Isaac's heart rate slowed. His face must have given something away, because Mary flashed a knowing grin. In his memory, her greenish-grey eyes sparkle. *Did you think you'd lost me?*

Isaac had never lost anyone. He'd lost no end of wallets, phones and keys. He'd lost his favourite denim jacket on a work trip to Frankfurt, a handful of low-stakes poker games, more socks than he could count, and even, to Mary's bafflement, the odd shoe. But he'd never lost *someone*. His sister, her husband, his colleagues, his friends, even all the best teachers from his school, all still fit as fiddles. His parents, though pushing seventy, had never been healthier. He had two ancient grandmothers, and two grandfathers who'd died before he'd ever had a chance to know them. He'd never had a pet, so had never had to reckon with the loss of one. Isaac Addy was lucky not to have lost anyone, to have had a life devoid of bereavement. But now he looks at it another way. Now he wonders if all those deaths that never happened had been tallied up, filed away by a higher power who clearly had Isaac's card marked. Isaac wonders if each loss he never endured was like a little wave meeting another little wave. Wave upon wave upon wave which, when combined, had rolled together into the tsunami which had washed his whole life away. For Isaac, losing Mary might as well have been losing everyone. And though he'd never say this to anyone, he'd rather lose everyone else if it meant not losing her.

In real life, Mary found him. But in Isaac's dreams, she never does. And if he has those same dreams every night, that means that every night he loses her, again and again. There she is, Mary, as if singled out by a heavenly beam of light. Isaac stands at the doors of Brixton tube station, but it doesn't feel like the Brixton he knows. Something's missing. He calls Mary's name, but she can't see him. She isn't wearing her glasses. It's starting to rain, too, and Mary is forced to shield her eyes. She looks distressed. He needs to reach her, to tell her it's all going to be alright. Isaac is shielding his eyes now, too, but the commuter crowds are like cattle. Bucking. Ploughing. Herding him where he doesn't want to go. Isaac shouts louder and louder and reaches for Mary over the fray, but it's no use. A raised newspaper here, a flower stall there, a tall man in a trench coat and a short woman with a large umbrella, and suddenly Mary is nowhere to be seen. Isaac's heart stops beating, and it doesn't start again. He screams her name, but no one answers. He beats his fists against grey coats and grey umbrellas, attempting to part the sea of grey faces like a latter-day Moses. He reaches the space where she'd previously been, but the gap in the crowd remains a gap. No hand tugs on Isaac's arm. The rain starts to come down in sheets, a torrent so heavy that Isaac feels like he might drown. He screams her name, but Mary is nowhere to be seen. This time, he knows he's lost her for good.

dING DONG

Isaac's eyes snap open. At first, with one foot still on the Brixton pavement, he doesn't know where he is. Then, as he feels the pillow under his head and the duvet over his body, he leaves the bad dream behind and settles back into his waking nightmare. Isaac emerges into consciousness laboriously, like a bear coming out of hibernation. His head is so thick and foggy that he assumes he must be hungover, but at least part of him knows he wasn't drinking last night. Still, his head hurts – and, Christ, his hand. He can't place *why* his hand is hurting, why everything from his wrist down throbs. He tries to cradle his hand, but it only makes things worse. He makes his customary waking sound – half whimper, half wail – then the doorbell rings again, and a barely conscious Isaac actually decides to crawl downstairs and answer.

'Yes?' Isaac grunts as he opens the front door.

He can't remember when Joy last delivered his shopping, but he isn't ready to allow her in. He keeps the door on the latch, but even through the gap the morning sun blinds him. It's only hearing the reply that tells him he's not talking to his sister.

'Oh, hi,' says Anna, Isaac's next-door neighbour.

He can just about see the concern written on her face, the way she self-consciously rubs one arm with her hand. Isaac retreats a step, into the shadows.

'There's been a lot of, erm . . . screaming. And smashing. A couple of the other people on the street are concerned. I just wanted to check in, see if you're doing OK, or if we can—'

She stops speaking. Even in the darkness of the hallway, she can see what he's done to his hand. And, to be fair to her, she's managed not to gasp. She does lose her footing, though, and her hands shoot up to cover her mouth. It's only her reaction that makes Isaac observe his own injury in the harsh light of day. She's not overreacting. Isaac's right hand, so deliriously painful that it feels detached from his body, is a sight to behold. Every single finger is bent and bruised, every single knuckle is flaking and caked in dried blood, and the whole thing – the fingers, the hand, the wrist – has turned purplish-red and swollen up to twice its normal size. It looks like he's growing a lobster claw.

'Oh my—'

Anna doesn't get to finish her sentence, on account of Isaac slamming the door in her face. He double-checks the latch, then hides the hand back under his dressing gown in an attempt to pretend it isn't there. He turns and trudges back up the stairs. In the bathroom, he necks two co-codamol. Back in the bedroom, he closes the door and climbs under the sheets, wrapping a pillow around his head to drown out the deafening noise of the world outside his house.

dING DONG

He thinks he can hear Adam, Anna's husband, calling through the letterbox. He blocks it out. The painkillers help. In fact, he even manages to drift back off to sleep. He must have, because when he opens his eyes again, the doorbell has stopped ringing and Adam has stopped shouting. There's no sound whatsoever. But there's a smell, wafting in through the doorway. A smell of burning. The room is still dark, the curtains closed and the door pulled to, but the smell is unmistakable. Someone is burning breakfast. At first, Isaac assumes it must be Mary, making a hash of some hash browns, using her anti-Midas touch of turning anything she tries to cook to ash. Then reality rears its ugly head, and he realises it can't be. This is why he'd been avoiding the bedroom, until now. It's like the hibernating bear has reached the entrance of its cave, only to see that winter has barely even begun. Taking a deep breath, Isaac looks to the side of the bed where Mary used to sleep. He's not surprised to find she isn't there.

It's not like there's a Mary-shaped indent in the mattress. The bed has forgotten her long before anyone else. But there's a coldness to the side on which she used to sleep, and the room is filled with all the other indents she left behind. A Booker-longlisted novel she'd now never finish reading, page marked, on her bedside table. A childhood teddy bear she'd always feared losing, now outliving her in the crook between their pillows. A pyjama top, crumpled on the floor by the bed, never to be worn or washed or ironed again. She was a head taller than all her classmates by thirteen, called Pippi Longstocking on account of her knobbly knees and ginger pigtails. The pyjama tops she slept in as an adult were all just T-shirts she'd accrued in her early teens, ones she was too embarrassed to still wear out but too sentimental to bin. True to form, each was emblazoned with some variation of 'I Love', each with a varying degree of irony: *I Love My Bed*, *I Love New York*, *I Love Goats*. The last was bought more recently, from the farm on the outskirts of town, on the weekend they'd first viewed their first home. Isaac picks up the T-shirt and presses his face into it. Then he looks at the thing on the floor next to it, the hot-water bottle in the fluffy cover. His brow furrows. He sniffs the air. Suddenly, Isaac realises who's burning breakfast.

Scenes from the night before crash into Isaac like a brick through the bedroom window. His stomach somersaults as he remembers the phone call, the grapefruit, the saxophone. Then it shrivels as he recalls eviscerating his entire kitchen, with the help of the egg he found in the woods. At least he remembers what happened to his hand. Not for the first time, Isaac wonders if he's losing his marbles. He wishes he was. He knows full well it was real, and he knows full well the mess he'll find on the floor and the walls and, most likely, the ceiling when he gets out of bed and heads downstairs. He flipped the kitchen table, didn't he? The egg played baseball with the contents of the fridge, and Isaac punched a pretty sizeable hole in the wall. What else? Isaac vaguely recalls being helped up the stairs, being encouraged to change his wine-soaked trackies for a pair of clean pyjama bottoms, being put to bed and tucked in by a pair of long and winding arms. It might have been a dream. The last thing he really remembers is being slumped against the fridge, overcome by an overwhelming tiredness. He touched the creature's head and . . . yes, that's it. He saw something. Isaac leafs through his mental movie-encyclopaedia. Can't Spock feel someone's pain with four fingers on their face? Can't E.T. heal things with his glowing fingertips? It makes sense that, in real life, touching an otherworldly egg on the forehead would be a gateway to its thoughts. Judging by how much his hand is starting to hurt, Isaac would rather it have been the E.T. thing.

Isaac tries to picture what he saw. A vast structure in the abyss, fronted by a glass pyramid with shadowy shapes behind. A huge thing, made of metal, floating in the ether. It would make sense for the creature to have crash-landed in the forest. But did it crash-land alone? Perhaps that enormous structure is right now floating, *Independence Day*-style, above them, as big as the town itself. Perhaps it's already light years away. Perhaps it's been destroyed, wiped out, and the egg really is as stranded as it seems. Even as he's thinking it, Isaac shakes his head and banishes the idea. He knows he's lost his mind, but now he's just getting carried away. Still, Isaac wonders why he hasn't yet seriously considered the egg, where it really came from, why it's really here. He finds himself filled with a burning desire to get to the bottom of it . . . just as soon as he's found out what the egg is burning. Isaac sniffs the air, detecting baked beans. This makes sense, as most of the other food in the house was demolished last night. He and Mary kept their tins in the cupboard under the stairs, in shrink-wrapped crates bought in bulk from Costco. So, the creature has found the beans. So, the creature is trying to cook the beans, having seen Isaac do so several times before. Judging by the scorched smell and the smoke and the fact that the fire alarm has just gone off, the creature is not succeeding. With a grimace, Isaac endeavours to swing his stiff legs out from under the duvet and investigate the problem. But he doesn't have to. The problem has come to him.

The bedroom door opens with a creak. A dense cloud of smoke rolls in. The egg appears as if shrouded in dry ice. Isaac coughs and splutters, beating away the smoke, trying to get a clear picture of the tiny silhouette in the darkened doorframe. The fire alarm continues its piercing *beep beep beep*. The creature is staring up at Isaac with large, wet, expectant eyes, totally unbothered by the smoke. It's holding something, and it seems to want to give that something to Isaac. Isaac can't quite believe what he's seeing, but it would appear that the creature has brought him breakfast in bed. Or, an approximation. If Isaac were making beans on toast for the egg, he'd probably have toasted the bread, heated the beans, then topped the former with the latter on a plate. A pinch of salt, a twist of black pepper, perhaps a fistful of grated cheese. But the egg has not done as Isaac would have done, mainly because the egg has presumably never cooked anything until this morning. The very little it knows about human food has been gleaned from watching a tearful, clumsy Isaac, hence the meal at hand. To the egg's credit, it's remembered parts of the process. It clearly knows the toaster is involved. It obviously knew where to find the beans. And it's definitely got the topping part right. The problem is, the creature has assembled the beans and the toast within the toaster itself, then toasted the whole lot, together, a number of times. And because there are no plates left in the house after their impromptu game of crockery frisbee, the creature has proceeded to unplug the toaster and drag the whole fiasco upstairs, like a child with a toy dog on a lead. It looks like a toy itself. A Furby. Or maybe Gizmo. Here stands the egg, in the doorway of Isaac's bedroom, picking up and showing off an unplugged toaster stuffed with charred-black bread and coated thickly with browned, sputtering bean juice. Beans abseil stickily over the creature's fat yellow fingers, down the toaster's outsides and on to the cream bedroom carpet. Isaac stares at these beans, then at the creature. The fire alarm is deafening, but at least the egg has apparently stopped screaming, '*Hello.*'

'Good morning,' Isaac ventures.

The creature blinks back, blankly. Then it sets off towards him, waddling across the bedroom and around the side of the bed, cradling the ruined toaster in its arms like it's presenting him with a present on Christmas morning. The toaster cord and plug trail along the carpet behind it. The egg comes to a stop next to Isaac, between the fitted wardrobes and the bed itself. Then, with the same expectant look as before, it unravels its arms and brings the toaster up to Isaac's eye level. Now that the toaster is hovering in Isaac's eyeline, he can better see the extent of the damage. The toast is pitch-black and still aflame in places, while the beans are crackling and popping like pieces of popcorn. The toaster itself seems to have been brought to such a heat that its silver exterior has started to go bronze. The whole contraption is chugging out fumes like a steam engine, powering nothing in its unplugged state but the grating noise of the fire alarm overhead. Isaac now realises that the egg is trying to hand him the scalding toaster. Isaac looks from the toaster to the asbestos fingers of the little monster holding it. Then he holds up his hands, one normal-sized and one definitely not. He shakes his head.

'I can't,' he says. 'Too hot.'

The egg nods sagely. Then it drops the toaster in Isaac's lap. Isaac squeals, feeling the heat through the duvet, shunting the toaster up into the air with a thrust of his hips then stuffing a pillow beneath it before it can land. His thighs may well be scalded by the hot metal, but he's more worried that the pillowcase is about to burst into flames. Isaac winces, fanning the toaster. Nothing has been set alight. He peels open one eye, then another. The toaster seems to be cooling down, though its bean-coating is now soaking into a pillow. The pillow isn't Mary's, so he doesn't panic. The fire alarm has stopped, and the smoke seems to finally be dispersing. Isaac breathes a sigh of relief, then looks back down at the egg. He was intending to tell it off, but one look at those puppy-dog eyes makes him falter. The egg nods at the toaster. Then, with the one arm that has slid back off the bed, it mimes eating. The movement is a perfect mirror of Isaac's own, in the kitchen, the night before. Isaac can't help but feel a little impressed.

'*Wab wob*,' the egg says.

'Thank you,' Isaac says. 'It looks delicious, but—'

'*Wab wob*.'

'I'm not really very hung—'

'*Wab wob*.'

Isaac can already tell that the creature isn't going to take no for an answer.

'I don't wan—'

'*Wab wob*.'

'I can't—'

'*Wab wob*.'

'I—'

Isaac isn't stopped this time by '*Wab wob*' but by the fact that the creature has grabbed hold of one of the bean-soaked slices of black bread and, utilising the length of its arm, jammed it into Isaac's face. The brittle toast splinters against his cheek, smearing warm bean juice across his lips and nostrils. If only to stop the misery, Isaac opens his mouth and accepts the offering. It's somehow both uncomfortably moist and incredibly dry at the same time, and it takes Isaac a while to chew and swallow. It catches in his throat, but he forces it down. Mission accomplished, he wipes his face with his good hand, then rubs his stomach.

'Good,' he says, though it wasn't. 'Very good.'

'*Wab wob.*'

'Even better than it looks.'

'*Wab wob.*'

Isaac can see that he's expected to take another bite. Feeling guilty, he does. It's a dainty one, mainly because the toast is so charred that he fears chipping his teeth. Carefully, he begins to chew again.

'Mmm-hmm,' he says, with a shudder that disagrees.

The creature looks pleased. Its work here is done. With one final '*Wab wob*' and a face that seems to say '*You're welcome*' it turns on its heels – if it has them – and toddles off. Not towards the door, but around the bed and towards the window. The egg is actually opening the curtains. Isaac thinks back to the scene in the kitchen the night before, wondering whether he'd missed the part where he'd paid the egg to be his butler. Maybe it's been watching *The Remains of the Day* while Isaac's been in bed. Before Isaac can interrogate the thought further, he's interrupted by a more pressing matter.

dING DONG

Isaac casts a weary look towards the bedroom door. How many hours has it been since he spoke to Anna? Is Adam trying to force his way in again? Isaac looks down at the egg, which is looking up at him. Its huge eyes are curious, its rubbery yellow brow furrowed. It hasn't let go of the curtains, its long white arms hanging down from them like tasselled tie-backs.

'Wait here,' Isaac says.

He frees himself from the duvet and shuffles out of the bedroom. As soon as he's on the landing, he can tell that the egg hasn't waited. In fact, he can feel it, nipping at the tail of his dressing gown. Isaac shakes his head, steels his nerves, then lets himself into Mary's office at the end of the landing. In the room, he keeps his eyes firmly fixed on the carpet. Away from the framed pictures, away from the bookshelf, away from the computer screen. He hasn't broken down yet today, and he wants to avoid doing so before he's figured out who's at the door. He leans over the desk, the fingers of his bad hand grazing the yellow notebook upon it. Its author such an open book, but the contents of her notebooks always so secret. Isaac winces and pulls his hand back as if he's been stung. Then, with his good hand, he pokes a finger around the edge of the blinds so that he can see outside. The cherry blossom tree across the street has started to bloom. He hadn't realised. Fat green buds cover the branches, split open by brightly coloured petals. Even brighter is the sky, an unimpeded blue above a street where several of the passers-by have undone their scarves and shed their winter gloves. A tired-looking father on the other side of the road pushes an empty pram, his crying toddler balanced in one arm. Further down the street, a far-too-big car tries to parallel park in a far-too-small space. Closer, below it all, below Isaac and the egg

94

and the window that separates them from the outside world, stands the ringer of the doorbell. It's Anna again, flanked this time by a man and a woman in hi-vis jackets. Paramedics. No, more like police. Community support officers? Whoever they are, they look official. They look concerned. And they're looking right at him.

'Shit!' shouts Isaac.

'*Blip!*' shouts the egg.

Isaac dips back behind the blinds. He flattens himself against the bookcase. They must have heard the fire alarm. Anna would have told them he looked like a man not opposed to self-immolation. Isaac looks down at the egg, now flattening itself against the bookcase next to him. The egg doesn't seem as concerned as Isaac, mainly because it can't reach the window so it doesn't know what it is they're supposed to be shouting '*Blip!*' about. It blinks up at him, looking for some sort of answer. Isaac looks down and – in a hushed voice – gives it one.

'Police,' he says.

This is a mistake. The egg's seen both *Bad Boys* and *Bad Boys II*. It knows that, in the movies, it's always a bad sign when the police show up at your door. It pictures SWAT vests and helmets. It pictures angry men with assault rifles raised. It pictures one of those miniature battering rams ready to batter down the front door, smoke grenades and flash-bangs and being pinned down and put in tiny handcuffs and sent down for crimes the egg surely hasn't committed. Quite understandably, the egg freaks out.

'*Blip!*' it shouts again.

The egg grabs the ripcord which controls the blinds. Before Isaac can intervene, they shoot upwards like an opening parachute, and the room is filled with blinding light. Isaac shields himself and yelps, as if he really will burst into flames. Then, as his eyes adjust, he's faced once again by Anna and her PCSO companions staring up at him and gesturing for him to come downstairs. Isaac does the first thing that springs to mind: he ducks. He drops out of sight of the window, uncharacteristically fast, hitting the floor with a thud that knocks all the wind out of his chest. This abrupt movement is enough to send the egg into a state of high panic. It squeals, spins on the spot a few times, then manages to get caught in a fold-up chair which clatters to the floor just inches from Isaac's head. The egg seems to think the pair of them are now fugitives in a stand-off with the law, so it bounces anxiously around the room, wailing all the while. When it finally finds the doorway, it launches itself out on to the landing. Isaac watches as the egg flees down the landing, although, since Isaac is once again lying with his cheek pressed against the carpet, it looks more like the egg is fleeing horizontally across a wall. Its usually limp, noodle arms flail upwards and squiggle cartoonishly, like one of those inflatable tube men one sometimes sees at funfairs.

'Can you come down, Mr Addy?' Isaac can hear from outside.

In his dressing-gown pocket, his phone is now vibrating. Lying underneath the desk, he swears under his breath.

On the landing, a shrieking egg darts between the bathroom and the bedroom and the bathroom again, arms still flailing, the volume of its scream rising and falling as it scurries in and out of view. Peeling his Velcro-like beard from the carpeted floor and spitting out a clump of what must be either Mary's hair or the egg's fur, Isaac tries to stand up. He forgets about his right hand, presses it against the floor and squeals in agony, knees drawn up into the foetal position. Then, sighing heavily, he climbs carefully to his knees and shuffles out of the office. He closes the door and sits up against it, trying to block out the sound of the intruders outside on the path behind him and the screaming egg darting about in front of him. *Think, Isaac*, he thinks. *How are you going to get out of this one?* He now understands, too late, why Mary hated crowds. Wasn't this house supposed to be their refuge? He feels as if the enemies are at the gates, and he's lost his only ally. He wishes Mary were here to scoop him up and tell him everything is going to be alright. He wishes Mary were here to stroke his hair. Isaac slams the back of his head against the door, looks up at the ceiling, bites his lip. His breath is quickening. His chest is tightening. His eyes are flooding with hot tears. He feels like someone's grabbed him by the throat. It's not fair, he thinks. None of this is fair. Why did she have to leave me? And why can't everyone else just leave me alone?

dING DONG

The sound of the doorbell isn't any different this time, but the voice which accompanies it is.

'Isaac,' the voice calls, from the path. 'Please can you come down? I just want to talk.'

Isaac sniffs. He straightens up. He takes a few breaths. Then he staggers to his feet and wipes his eyes. The egg seems to have tired itself out. Isaac can just about see it cowering in the bath, huge black eyes poking out through a gap in the shower curtain. He makes a gesture for it to stay quiet, to stay hidden, then he turns and takes a few more breaths and descends the stairs. In the hallway, he kicks his way through the post and undoes the latch. Then – a few more deep breaths – he opens the door to the outside world.

'Isaac,' says Joy, her voice weak.

Isaac looks down at the ground.

'I'm sorry,' he says.

He doesn't know if he's saying it to her, or the police, or Anna, or himself. It doesn't matter. Isaac has surrendered. And, for the first time in a long time, Isaac is letting someone give him a hug.

FIVE

Isaac Addy has agreed to therapy. In his mind, it was either that or get sectioned. He pictured being restrained by the police, bundled into the back of a van and carted off to some secure facility in the woods. He doesn't fancy that. He doesn't even know what 'sectioning' really is. Joy told him he was talking nonsense. Why can't he understand that they're all just trying to help? Now Isaac's trying, too. He's accepting that help, even if it means leaving the house on a regular basis and speaking to another human being for more than ten seconds at a time. Joy thinks it's because Isaac wants to get better. Really, he just wanted to get her, and Anna, and the PCSOs, off his doorstep. If the police were to do a sweep of the place, they'd have found the mess all over the kitchen. They'd have noticed the blood all over the wall. They might have kicked down the locked door at the top of the house. And they'd definitely have found the egg, cowering behind the shower curtain in the upstairs bathroom. Isaac won't freely admit it, but he's starting to feel responsible for the egg. He wouldn't want to get the egg sectioned, too.

It's a couple of weeks since the incident in the kitchen, and Isaac is sitting in a cool, white room, heavenly shafts of light streaming in through tall windows. He arrives here as he tends to arrive from anywhere: like a film character waking in the rubble of an explosion. There's a ringing in his ears, a hazy white mist obscuring his sight, which slowly lifts to reveal high ceilings, clean walls, an office in a leafy suburb not too far from his house. Suddenly, he's sitting down. Opposite him, behind the therapist's desk, is a large bay window with a window seat and a couple of cushions. He blinks at it. He assumes the seat is for sitting pensively, reading and reflecting. He blinks again, and the light gives way to an Edenic garden beyond. A bird bath. A pond. A nice big willow tree with plenty of shade. Isaac doesn't know if the garden is shared or private. He doesn't know if it's the garden of a doctor's surgery, or the garden of his therapist's house. Though he won't admit it to the woman behind the desk, Isaac can't remember getting here. All he knows is that he's sitting in a chair by a desk in a therapist's office, and that his rucksack is on the armchair by the door. This rucksack is strategically placed in his line of sight, and out of the therapist's. Ah, yes. He remembers. The egg is in the rucksack.

What? Isaac couldn't exactly leave it at home. He's seen

how it makes beans on toast. He knows it's a walking fire hazard. Isaac wonders what the egg would do if left to its own devices. He imagines it sliding like Tom Cruise across the hallway floor in sunglasses and Y-fronts. He imagines it building Macauley Culkin's elaborate booby traps for next time the police come calling. He imagines it opening the locked door at the top of the house.

'What are you thinking about, Isaac?' the therapist says. 'You're miles away.'

Her voice sounds slightly distorted, as if she's speaking through a cardboard tube. Isaac attempts to tune into what she's saying. He blocks out the ringing in his ears, clenches his jaw in order to avoid saying something he doesn't want to say. I'm thinking about how I didn't want to come here alone.

'Nothing much,' he says.

Dr Abbass is a grief counsellor. She's middle-aged and highly regarded, with a soft accent and a hard stare. She gained her degree in Nazareth and her doctorate in Tel Aviv, and now she's one of the best therapists in the NHS. All of this is information regurgitated to Isaac by Joy, who'd presumably spent a lot of time studying her website. Joy has always been good at these sorts of things. She's a lawyer, don't you know, his parents would say. She's been the one sorting out the insurance, dealing with the solicitors, changing all their 'joint accounts' to just 'accounts'. Isaac had nodded politely on the other end of the phone when she'd suggested Dr Abbass, not letting on that even hearing the word 'grief' had been enough to make him feel like he was going to collapse. Joy said she worried that Isaac wouldn't take the therapy seriously. He said that he would. Now Dr Abbass is looking at Isaac as if he isn't taking the therapy seriously, because she knows that he isn't. There's a thousand people Isaac would rather speak to about the empty hole in his chest than a trained medical professional. Like his barber. Like the egg. Like Mary. He wishes, beyond anything, that he would just be allowed to speak to Mary. Isaac blinks at Dr Abbass. What am I thinking about? I'm thinking that bringing the rucksack was a bad idea. I'm thinking that it's too early to allow the egg into the outside world. I'm thinking that I can see two sets of stubby yellow fingers poking out from the space between the zips.

'Nothing much,' Isaac says. His voice is flat, a monotone.

'What happened to your arm?'

Dr Abbass gestures at his right forearm with a pen. Isaac bows his head towards it. He blinks once, twice, feels his full consciousness finally arriving in the room. He flexes his bruised fingers underneath the thick plaster. They barely move. Isaac looks surprised not only to find that his broken hand is in a cast, but to discover that he even has an arm, or a body, at all. For a moment there, he felt like nothing more than a floating head. Isaac stares at the arm for a while, then his body. Clean T-shirt, freshly laundered tracksuit bottoms, although still stained in places with red-wine reminders of that messy night in the kitchen. He turns his gaze to the rucksack on the armchair by the door. Then he looks back at his arm. He wishes they could have put a cast over his entire body. A carapace. A cocoon. Dr Abbass frowns, writes something in her notebook. Did he say that out loud? Isaac stares at the pen, watches it dance over the page. Then he stares, once again, at the rucksack. It's partially open, now. Isaac can see two black eyes watching him from inside.

'I hit a wall,' Isaac says.

'A metaphorical wall?'

'No,' Isaac says. 'A physical one. I punched a wall.'

'Why did you punch a wall?'

'Because my wife is dead.'

Dr Abbass sighs and leans back in her chair. She clicks her pen shut. Then she smiles. A warm, genuine smile which takes Isaac off guard.

'Do you think you *need* therapy?' she says.

The rucksack wobbles. The rucksack topples. It lands on its side on the chair, and those two sets of yellow fingers wiggle their way out. Isaac wiggles his own painful fingers, jiggles the knee on which the cast rests, but tries not to draw too much attention to the cause of his concern. In the corner of his eye, he sees one of the creature's spaghetti arms flop out of the fully open rucksack, then the other. They hit the floor and begin to unroll. Now, the egg is hopping out of the rucksack and off the chair. Now, two pigeons are battering each other on top of the stone bird bath outside, either fighting or flirting. Now, Dr Abbass is looking at Isaac, waiting for an answer. Isaac tries to find one.

'I don't think I can be helped.'

'Why is that?'

'Because—'

'Because your wife is dead?'

Isaac winces.

'I think I *can* help you,' Dr Abbass continues, her fingers making a bridge on her lap. 'But you have to be open to being helped.'

One of the pigeons has flown off. The other one has been left alone. And the egg is . . . the egg is gone. Panic fastens its fingers around Isaac's throat. He looks at the empty rucksack, at the door which has been left ajar. He swallows thickly. He shakes his head.

'I guess we'll agree to disagree,' Isaac says.

'Would you say this is out of your comfort zone?'

'Oh, no,' Isaac says, closing his eyes. 'There's nowhere I'd rather be.'

Dr Abbass doesn't laugh. 'Do you do that often?' she says.

'Do what?'

'Turn things into jokes.'

Joking *had* always been Isaac's first line of defence. But now he's been rumbled, he can't find the ammunition with which to fire off another retort. Isaac's eyes are still closed. He swallows, looking for an answer. *Act like an adult*, a voice says. *For once.*

'I don't like serious subjects,' Isaac says. 'I like to keep everyone happy.'

'But you're not happy.'

Isaac opens his eyes. 'I'm—' he begins, but he's distracted again.

The egg is outside. How did it get out there so fast? Isaac's eyes widen as he watches it toddle into his line of sight, heading down the garden, swinging from side to side like a buoy on a choppy sea, its arms dragging along the grass after it. Isaac can't see where the arms end. Perhaps they haven't left the building yet.

'I'm—'

The egg has caught sight of the pigeon. And the pigeon has caught sight of the egg. The egg stops, looks up, stares at the bird as it sits on the mossy rim of the bird bath. It stares down at the egg with tiny, beady black eyes. And though Isaac can only see the fluffy white oval which signifies the back of the egg, he knows that it'll be staring up at the pigeon with enormous, curious black eyes of its own.

'I'm—'

Outside, a tussle begins. The pigeon has descended from the bird bath and is flapping its wings at the egg. The egg, in response, is flailing its arms at the pigeon. Isaac watches, nervously picking at the edge of his cast with the fingers of his free hand. Dr Abbass watches Isaac, moves her shoulders a little, threatens to turn. He coughs, and she doesn't. She frowns at him instead.

'Why are you here, if you think you can't be helped?'

'My sister made me come,' Isaac says, in a petulant tone. He's trying to avoid looking out of the window, at the pigeon and the egg.

Dr Abbass arches an eyebrow. Then she finally turns, looking over the back of her chair and out of the window. Thankfully, the fight is over. All that's left is a few dirty feathers blowing across the grass. The egg now seems to be hiding behind the willow tree. You'd need to squint to see the telltale heaps of its white arms on either side. For a while, both Isaac and Dr Abbass stare out of the window, sitting in their respective chairs on either side of the walnut desk. Isaac wipes his brow with his good hand. Dr Abbass turns, stands, walks around the desk, and sits in the chair right next to Isaac. She smiles again. The effect is unnerving.

'I don't feel like you're telling me the whole truth,' she says.

And she's right. He isn't. It occurs to Isaac that if he was like the upended rucksack on the chair, his own zips would be permanently closed and padlocked for good measure. He isn't telling Dr Abbass about the times he wakes himself up in the middle of the night, screaming Mary's name. He isn't telling her that he smells her perfume or hears her voice just around the corner of every doorway, and how this frightens him more than it comforts him. He isn't telling her that he still calls Mary's phone just to hear her voicemail, that her sing-song voice still says *we both know I'll forget to call you back*, that Isaac still sobs and sobs after the tone. He isn't telling her about the panic attacks, the fainting fits, those first three weeks where he found himself waking up on the funeral directors' carpet or the doctor's linoleum floor. He isn't telling her about the screaming, the materialising out of nowhere, the times he's found himself half dressed and terrified and in tears, in supermarkets and car parks and sterile waiting rooms. He isn't telling her where he goes, where he stays, how guilty he feels when he finally returns and finds the egg waiting for him, blinking judgementally from the hallway floor. And, oh, yes. He isn't telling her about the egg. He isn't telling anyone about the egg.

'Where were you yesterday?'

'What was yesterday?'

The egg is out from behind its tree. The pigeon is nowhere to be seen. In fact, some of its dirty feathers are poking out from the corners of the egg's mouth. The egg itself has become distracted, having noticed Isaac through the window. Is it? No, surely it can't be. But it is. The egg is waving at him. Perhaps it wants him to come outside and play.

'Yesterday was supposed to be our first session,' Dr Abbass says. 'You didn't turn up.'

Isaac keeps his eyes in the room, away from the egg. He distracts himself from the distraction by counting the chairs. One for him, one for Dr Abbass, one by the door for the egg, and one for Mary, behind the desk. He shakes the thought away. He tries to train his thoughts on what Dr Abbass just said. Yesterday?

'I thought today was our first session,' he says.

'It is now,' she says. 'Joy called me to rearrange.' A pause. 'Do you think it's possible you might be suffering from blackouts?'

'Blackouts?'

'Yes. Short-term memory loss.'

'Like in *Memento*?'

Isaac is well versed in the theoretical concept of short-term memory loss. He knows it as something that happens to people in films. Something unrealistic. Something absurd. Isaac dispels the idea, instead making a mental note to watch *Memento* with the egg when they finally make it home. He looks back out of the window. The egg has disappeared again. Panic rises once more.

'Sure, like in *Memento*,' Dr Abbass says.

'Oh. Then, no.'

Isaac doesn't seem to fully believe himself. There's a flutter in his chest, a strange tickle in the back of his throat. He's worrying about what's happened to the egg, sure. But that's not quite it.

'When people go through something traumatic, they can dissociate,' Dr Abbass says. 'The brain switches off from what's happening. They get mind blanks. It's a coping mechanism.'

'Like the jokes,' Isaac says.

'Exactly, like the jokes.'

Isaac bites his tongue, annoyed at himself for engaging. Yet while he wouldn't say that he's suffering from memory loss or mind blanks, he can't deny that he's lost huge swathes of his memory, and that his mind is filled to the brim with blanks. As it happens, he doesn't remember yesterday. Or three days of the week before. Or most of the week before that. If pushed, the last thing he'd be able to remember with any actual clarity is the night that *it* happened. He remembers being curled up in an uncomfortable wooden chair, staring at the tubes and wires, listening to the morbid bleeping of the machines. He remembers being shown her body, how pale she'd looked, even for Mary. He remembers melting into a puddle on the floor. Isaac shudders. Perhaps he does need help. Perhaps he should be taking therapy a bit more seriously. Mary had always been more on it with the mental health stuff. He remembers London, that low point when insomnia and writer's block came calling. Some days she couldn't even bring herself to leave the house. She sought out therapy for anxiety. And Isaac? He'd said, 'Don't you think you're just a bit shy?' A trickle of guilt slides down the walls of Isaac's stomach. *What else?* says that little imp in Isaac's head. He remembers Scotland, more recently. At his lowest point, still refusing to let her in. Isaac had laughed when Mary had told him he might benefit from therapy, too. *Why can't you act like an adult, for once?* Half an hour in the barber's chair with Tommy every few weeks was more than enough time to spill his deepest secrets. When he'd been ashamed of his struggles to make friends in a new town, or near-crushed by the weight of deadlines pressing down on his chest like an anvil, it was Tommy to whom he'd turned. He'd never wanted to worry Mary. But in not wanting to worry her, he'd shut her out. He'd been defensive, dismissive. She'd been hurt. Isaac's lip trembles. He wishes he'd taken it more seriously. He wishes he'd taken *her* more seriously. He wishes they'd had more time.

'Sometimes it's helpful to try to open up,' Dr Abbass says. 'To *really* try to open up.'

'Open up how?'

'Trying to remember things would be a good start.'

The hairs on the back of Isaac's neck stand up. 'I don't want to,' he says, instinctively. His voice is small, childish again.

Dr Abbass leans back in her chair, folds her fingers. 'What don't you want to remember?'

Isaac swallows thickly. He feels like there's a trapped and dying pigeon inside his chest cavity, trying to beat its way out. He clenches his fist beneath his cast. The effect is excruciating. His eyes water, but not from the pain.

'I don't want to remember anything,' he says, his voice breaking. 'I don't want to remember why I feel like this.'

Isaac has started to cry. The tears come thick and fast as he speaks, his voice pathetic and nasal and far away. He scrunches up his face and he scrunches up his fists, shaking his head as if to will the outside world away. Heavy tears roll down his cheeks and snot streams out of his nose. He finds himself unable to continue. Instead, he breaks down in sobs. Dr Abbass watches him, lets him cry. The sounds he's making are embarrassing, great racking *hyuck hyuck hyuck*s. He convulses. He kicks the ground. He cries some more. And then, when he's all out of tears, he sits with his head down and his eyes closed and his arms, one in a plaster cast, one not, wrapped around his knees. Dr Abbass gives him a moment.

'Then let's remember something else,' she says. 'Something better.'

Isaac looks up at her. There's a tissue in his hand, now, which means she must have handed it to him. He uses it to blow his nose. His cheeks are puffy, his eyes bloodshot. In the corner of his tear-fogged vision, he thinks he sees the egg climbing back into the rucksack.

'Better?' he says.

'Exactly,' Dr Abbass says. She smiles encouragingly. 'Why don't you tell me how you and Mary met?'

Until his life skidded off the edge of a cliff like a cartoon coyote, Isaac was an illustrator. His pictures of robots and aliens had become very popular with the under-twelves – which in turn made him very popular with those who commissioned his work. That's where the gibbons came in. Mary used to say it was gibbons that brought them together. Isaac would always follow up with '. . . and it will be gibbons that tear us apart', a joke he characteristically repeated to death because it made Mary snort with laughter the first time he said it. Isaac had been roped in by his agent to have a meeting with an up-and-coming Scottish author about a book she wanted to write, a book about monkeys or something. 'I can't draw monkeys,' he'd protested, but his agent had pushed him head first into the meeting room, anyway. That's when Isaac laid eyes on Mary Moray.

Who was Isaac before Mary? A jobbing illustrator, a people-pleaser, a man whose perpetual fear of missing out meant he hit the pub far too many weeknights and missed far too many morning meetings as a result. Blame Isaac's illustrating success on a persistent failure to let himself fail, which itself could be blamed on a conversation he had with his parents when he told them what he was going to do with his life.

'I'm going to be an illustrator.'

'But what will you do for money?'

'Well, I'm going to be an illustrator.'

'Hear this? He's going to be an illustrator.'

'Yes, I'm going to be an illustrator.'

'What will he do for money?'

Isaac's mother always said that only fools deal in what-ifs, and 'What if Isaac can make it as an illustrator?' was one of the biggest what-ifs of all. But after a fine art degree, countless overnighters and a partnership with a publisher who saw his potential, Isaac had, just about, made it. His parents had stopped hounding him by then – Joy was studying law, so they'd got the lawyer they'd always wanted. But he struggled. With expectations, big or small. With making a living from a not exactly lucrative career. And with the deadlines, though he didn't exactly help himself by dating every weeknight and spending every Friday and Saturday afternoon holding court in any Peckham pub that would have him.

In that first meeting with Mary, Isaac did what he always did: overcompensated by being overconfident. And while

Mary would later claim she could see straight through his class-clown schtick, he still remembers how she stole glances at him, how she laughed just a little too loudly at his jokes. Though the age of Mary's readers was lower than Isaac's usual target market, he said yes within the first five minutes. *That's Not a Dog*, Mary's book was called. It followed the adventures of a hapless father who kept getting his hands on the wrong kind of pet for his dog-coveting son. 'That's not a dog!' the child would laugh, every time the father brought home a quokka, or an echidna, or a naked mole-rat. Mary wanted the book to teach kids about animals they'd never usually encounter.

Gibbons are the underdogs of the primate world. Don't you think?

Who was Mary before Isaac? An aspiring author, an antisocial reader, a wide-eyed new arrival in the city with a point to prove to a family of disapproving farmers. Mary had always known she wanted to write books, and had always known she wanted to write those books for children. She had no interest in the snooty, the stuffy, the serious. To her, 'literary' was just a synonym for 'lacking imagination'. And though the rolling hills of her childhood looked like something from someone else's fairy story, she knew she needed to be somewhere else if she was ever going to do something with all these ideas of her own.

I'm going to move to London.

'What's London got that we haven't?'

Opportunities. London's the place to be.

'Hear this? She's going to move to London.'

Yes, I'm going to move to London.

'What's London got that we haven't?'

Though Mary was the eldest, her parents couldn't exactly deny that Dennis and Duncan's thick necks and tree-trunk forearms were better suited to farming. 'Away with the fairies,' her father used to say, when she'd sit on the bridge at the edge of the farm and write stories for readers who didn't yet exist. Down in London, when she was working as a journalist and then a jack-of-all-trades freelancer, her readers finally existed. And while the city could be overwhelming at times, she loved the urgency, that feeling of a shoal of individuals swimming towards a common goal. Plenty more fish, too, though Mary was more of a relationship-hopper than a one-night-stander. She'd not long ago ended things with the Goldsmiths grad who wore a gold hoop in his left ear, himself a rebound from the clean-shaven banker who'd read *Animal Farm* and rooted for the pigs.

The first time Isaac heard Mary laugh, he felt his centre of gravity shifting. So, naturally, he did everything he could to impress during that first meeting – little sketches of quokkas, of echidnas, of naked mole-rats. Mary's own research was more impressive, the last two years spent volunteering with kids on Vauxhall City Farm, an opportunity to be around the animals so abundant in her own rural upbringing. She'd even spent time with the keepers at London Zoo, asking endless questions like *Do platypuses really sweat milk?* (they do) and *Do skunks really spray stink in green clouds?* (they don't). Mary's audience would never notice these things, but that thought never crossed Mary's mind. Isaac would soon come to learn that children loved her because she treated them like equals. She took them seriously. Perhaps that's why she liked Isaac.

'I can't draw monkeys.'

That's fine, because gibbons are apes.

Isaac agreed to illustrate *That's Not a Dog*. Contracts were discussed, hands shaken. Long after their agents and publishers had departed, the pair of them sat in a cramped meeting room in a fourth-floor Soho office and bonded over gibbons. The gibbon was the star of the book. The beleaguered father would first bring home a gibbon, and the gibbon would act as the boy's confidant and guide during his adventure through the less illuminated corners of the animal kingdom.

Gibbons are golden
With great big black eyes
And they sleep in the trees
with those eyes on the skies

Isaac brought out watercolours and fineliners and, under Mary's direction, set to work designing the very gibbon that would eventually end up on the cover. Turns out, he wasn't so bad at drawing apes. When the sun outside the window had set over Soho, they'd packed their bags and put on their jackets and rode the lift together to the lobby. On the street outside, Mary had made as if to leave. Then she'd hesitated, turned back to Isaac and fielded a suggestion.

I'm going to a friend's book launch, up at Foyles. Nothing fancy. Do you want to come with me?

Yes, I do. I really do, he'd thought.

'Sure. Sounds fun,' he'd said.

The party was, indeed, nothing fancy. And though Isaac was good at parties, always comfortable working the room, tonight he only had eyes for Mary. While Mary chatted to author friends and the odd parent and proxy fan, Isaac kept one eye on her. He got caught in conversation with a big-eared comic-book writer who was working on something about time travel. He kept one eye on Mary. He was cornered by a wire-haired older fellow writing a too-long tome on talking foxes. He kept one eye on Mary. He found himself alone, by the drinks table, fondling a plastic cup of warm Prosecco. He kept both eyes on Mary. She spotted him, smiled and threaded her way over.

Shall we get out of here?

'I thought you'd never ask.'

Where next? They found themselves at a naff wine bar in Covent Garden. The drinks were three times as much as they would have been in the Wetherspoons down the road, but Isaac made a show of paying for both. At a dimly lit table in the back, they shaded in any missing details.

Why are you an illustrator? she asked.

'I didn't want to grow up and get a real job.'

For shame, she bellowed. *It is a real job!*

'My mum would disagree.'

Then I think our mums would get on. She took a sip. She smiled.

'Why do you write children's books?'

They're not children's books. A wagging finger. *They're just books, and children happen to like them.*

'Apologies. Why do you write books which children happen to like?'

Because children have so much imagination, she said. *Even when things are awful, they always manage to find the brighter side.*

Outside of work, Isaac and Mary didn't have much in common. But they couldn't have been more meant to be. What's that they say about opposites? Something clicked, and one drink turned into two, which turned into three in the morning, blind drunk and snogging on the platform at Oxford Circus. For a first kiss, it was sloppy and decidedly unromantic. Unprofessional? Definitely. Regretful? Not one bit. Within a month, they were 'official'. Within six, they had rented their first flat, a pokey hideaway on the edge of Tooting Common. When Mary had begun to struggle with the pace and expectations of city life, Isaac had saved her. When Isaac's work had dried up and the mortgage payments on their new house in the country had loomed large, Mary had saved him right back. They had a habit of saving each other. By the time their first book was published, they'd already bought that house. By the second, they were already married. And while he'd always be a city boy from Lambeth and she'd always be a country girl from Loch Lomond, in this perfect place away from it all they could be something else, together. 'Til death do them part.

Back home, Isaac kicks off his shoes and puts the door back on the latch. Then he takes off his rucksack, unzips it and unpacks the egg on to the bottom step of the stairs.

'You were very good today,' he says.

The egg is unfurling its arms, seemingly flexing a stiff back.

'Thanks for coming. I don't think I could have done it without you.'

The egg blinks up at him silently. Isaac can't tell if it understands.

'What do you want to do now?' Isaac says. He talks to the egg in a high-pitched voice, as one would talk to a cat or a dog or a young child. 'Film? Beans? Bed?'

At each option, the egg shakes its head. Then it turns and, with much difficulty, begins climbing the stairs. Each step takes it about thirty seconds to climb, and with each step it climbs it seems as if it might topple over and bounce back down like a Slinky. Isaac is impressed. And tired. He takes his eye off the egg and looks down the hallway, pointedly avoiding his reflection in the mirror on the wall. He looks towards the closed kitchen door, blockading the mess that Isaac knows he still hasn't cleared. He looks towards the open living room, the biscuit tin on the mantelpiece. Then he looks up the stairs, at the dark outline of the landing and the closed doors beyond. The egg has disappeared out of sight. Isaac frowns. He clenches his one good fist.

Thunk.

The sound comes from upstairs.

Thunk.

Isaac bounds up the stairs two at a time, practically skidding on to the landing. Yet as he arrives, he stops himself. He almost topples over as he does. The egg is not where he feared it would be. It's not on the second floor. It's not in his bedroom, either, nor back hiding behind the shower curtain. Isaac hesitates. Regular breathing resumes. He furrows his brow, cocks his head and wiggles the stiff fingers of his damaged hand like a cowboy primed to draw his gun. He breathes out quietly, waiting for the sound to come again.

Thunk.

It's coming from behind him. From Mary's office. Isaac frowns, turns and pushes open the door. The egg is in there, but it doesn't notice his arrival. It's too busy picking books out of the tall bookcase and flinging them on the floor.

Thunk.

The Isaac of a month ago would have been angry to find the egg in here. He'd have grabbed it by its fluffy white scruff and marched it outside and said, 'Not even I'm allowed in Mary's inner sanctum.' But he doesn't. He feels calmer today. He's not prepared to attribute his mellow mood to his session with Dr Abbass, so he decides it must be thanks to the sunset. Spring is here, and with it a pinkish, orangey hue which fills the office through the still-open blinds behind the desk. Isaac breathes out through his nose, shakes off his worries, thinking of nothing but the egg and the *thunk*s which signal each book hitting the floor.

'Why are you in here?' he says, eventually.

The egg looks up at him. Then it looks back down. It doesn't make a sound, just stares at the books on the floor like a baby orangutan peeking over its own pot belly. It's so silent in the room that Isaac swears he can hear the stiff old papers on the desk shift and crinkle, or see the framed pictures on the walls quiver ever so slightly as he passes. Isaac sighs and looks around the office. It's the first time he's allowed himself to do so in a while. The office was Mary's space, never his to look around. Isaac was always a hectic soul who didn't need a studio. He kept his materials scattered around the house, and did his best drawings on buses or in busy cafés or balanced on a book on his lap in front of the TV. But Mary? Mary preferred order, and she used to find it in here. The egg looks back up at Isaac, then shifts on its toes as it follows his gaze around the room. Together, they discover the office, as if for the first time. The three pristine frames on the wall, inside which are the three front covers of their three published books. *That's Not a Dog* on the left, *Undone-under-London* in the middle, *Fred Founds a Farm* on the right. They'd left room for one more, and had hoped they'd move to somewhere bigger by the time they were on book five. Isaac traces the space on the wall where book four would have gone. Then, as if in a trance, he takes a couple of steps forward and sits down in Mary's chair. The hydraulic base lets out an uneasy puff of air as he does so, as if it's aware he's an imposter. He doesn't notice. He's staring at the computer screen, which has come to life in his presence and presented him with a landscape screensaver of a bridge.

It's not the bridge in the forest near their house. It's another bridge. Her bridge. This is why Isaac has been putting off coming in here. In here, in Mary's office, *everything* is hers. He feels like he's encroaching. The notebooks on the desk are her private property, as are the stacks of diaries and the half-filled calendars and even the books on the shelves over his right shoulder. Even looking at the bridge on the screen feels like an intrusion. They literally called it 'Mary's bridge', *they* being Isaac and Mary and Mary's family, on the outskirts of whose farm the bridge still stands. It's a squat, sturdy specimen, cobbled together from huge chunks of mountain stone, turned white over time by the churning water below. Sit on the edge of this bridge, legs dangling over the parapet, and you could almost dip your toes into the ice-cold river. She used to try, summer after summer when the hills had turned purple with heather, lowering herself over the edge and stretching out her long legs. Splashing about in that water, or fending off rogue sheep from the nearby fields, or reading under the tree at the end of it despite the never-ending hail of conkers come autumn. She took him there straight away, the first time they visited her family in Scotland. Then she took him back, again and again, Isaac always feeling like an intruder every time he was allowed to sit on that parapet, to stretch his toes towards that water.

Everything's going to be OK, Isaac.

The clarity of the memory is startling, as if speaking to Dr Abbass has worked loose some shard of Isaac's mind that was stuck hard between the cracks. He can feel the wind off the water running beneath the bridge, the numbing onslaught of the ice-cold air on his nose and cheeks. But when Isaac remembers the surroundings, he remembers them without sound. No roar of rushing water, no breeze in the leaves on that tree. Just him and Mary, standing on a bridge, sharing a moment. How long ago was it? A year? Longer? The unbroken view of the rust-brown Highland hills had turned white with snow. That's all you could see for miles around: a dead, white, icy expanse. The atmosphere on the bridge was just as frosty. Why does he keep coming back to this?

'You wouldn't need to tell me everything's going to be OK if everything's going to be OK,' Isaac had replied.

He'd been having a hard time of late. When he and Mary worked together, they were golden. Her big ideas, her crystal-clear direction, the way she helped channel that chaotic creativity at the end of Isaac's pen, like sunlight through a magnifying glass. But their last book hadn't sold so well, they had no others in the pipeline, and money was already stretched with the honeymoon just gone and the mortgage payments still due each month. Mary was practical. She'd already found copywriting clients in chirpy health-food start-ups and soulless fintech apps. But Isaac? His eclectic style of drawing, his reluctance to follow a brief, meant he'd found himself the grinning face on the wrong side of a lot of slammed doors. Money was becoming an issue. And though Mary was too kind to admit it, the issue was all Isaac's fault.

It's in your head, Mary had said. *We'll manage with money, like we always do. So what's wrong?*

'I feel like I'm going to fuck it all up.'

Then we'll fuck it all up together.

She'd implored him to speak to her about his feelings. Better yet, a therapist. His response – he shudders to think of it, now – was to laugh in her face.

'Oh yeah, that'll help,' he'd said. 'A straitjacket and a padded cell are just what I need.'

Maybe it's not about what you need any more.

'Maybe I'd be better off alone, then.'

An excruciating silence. Isaac knew he'd gone too far, but he could barely bring himself to care. He'd failed in everything else. May as well let his marriage fail, too. Isaac shoved his hands into his coat pockets, pouted, looked down at the snowy ground. Mary stared out over the water, breathed out once. The air carried off her breath in a cloud of smoke.

Why can't you act like an adult, for once?

Her feet crunching on the snow as she walked away. It feels cruel, that Isaac's last memory of Mary's happy place would be a sad one. It feels crueller that he was to blame, and that he can't take that back. Cruellest of all is the fact that she'll never sit on the edge of that bridge again, that her toes will never touch that water. She'll never sit beneath that tree, never be hit by another conker. And she'll never see Isaac in therapy, see that she was right. Isaac will never get the chance to apologise. He'll never get a chance to introduce her to the egg. They'll never frame a fourth book cover and hang it on the wall above her desk, no matter how much space they'd left for more. Isaac shakes his head, massages the bridge of his nose. In the reflection of the screen, Isaac catches a glimpse of himself. An unruly tower of hair escapes upwards from his head, while an unsightly beard anchors him back down. The whiskers creep up his cheeks and down his neck like ivy on the exterior of a derelict old house. He's not sure which looks more haunted: his face, or this room. He's not sure which looks more wild: himself, or the grunting, egg-shaped creature on the carpet behind him.

As if reading Isaac's thoughts, the egg coughs. Or it makes a sound like a cough, presumably one copied from the TV. Isaac isn't even sure if the egg *can* cough, and this sound it's making seems more like it's ejecting a hairball. Still, Isaac can tell that the egg is trying to get his attention. He doesn't respond. He's looking down at the yellow notebook, stiff spine and bleached white pages. It sits inches away from his broken hand. It's the last one Mary wrote in.

The last one she *will* write in. He does his best to ignore it. The egg, on the other hand, is now doing its best to get hold of it. Isaac bats the egg's sneaking arm away, so the egg settles on a stapler instead. While the egg starts attempting to staple some printer paper to its forehead, Isaac stares at the yellow notebook and feels the slightest tremor in the fingers under his cast, an almost-imperceptible twitch running up his bruised arm and down his restless right leg. He swears under his breath. He swivels away from the notebook, takes the stapler off the egg, then unfolds the folding chair on the floor and places the egg upon it. The egg weighs about as much as a cuddly toy from a fairground, and here – plump as a cushion on its chair with arms trailing on the carpet below – it looks more like a seal pup than a monkey. Any human with half a heart would see that tubby belly, those puppy eyes, and call the creature cute. But Isaac's chest is empty, so he just calls it 'the egg'.

'Why are you throwing my books on the floor?' Isaac says. 'Don't you like them?'

The egg just blinks. Isaac sighs. He leans over, picks up the nearest book and reads the cover.

THAT'S NOT A DOG
Written by Mary Moray
Illustrated by Isaac Addy

Inside, on the back flap, Isaac knows he'll find two headshots. The author, grinning against a backdrop of the same bridge on the screen behind him. And the illustrator, smiling that all-teeth smile everyone remembered him for, a drink in one hand and his party guests in the palm of the other. If Isaac told the egg that the grinning crowd-pleaser in the picture and this pallid, sunken creature in the desk chair were the same person, it wouldn't believe him. Isaac might have abandoned the whole robot thing, but he's still a long way from being human. He's a long way from being anything at all. If grief does come in waves, then the tsunami of a few weeks ago has given way to a choppy battering of constant, relentless, low-level misery. Even the effects of the therapy session are already receding like the tide. Isaac wants to feel nothing, like a jellyfish. But he feels everything, like an ocean with no land in sight.

Thwap.

The egg's fat yellow hand slaps against the cover of the book and smears itself across the shiny page, its padded palm somehow sticky and oily at the same time. Isaac looks down at the hand, at the cover. Then he lifts the egg's furry wrist and drops it back to the floor, giving the creature a look that says, 'No touching.' The egg blinks back, nods down at the cover and then up at Isaac, with eyes that say, '*Read*.'

'You want me to read?'

'*D'ah*.'

Isaac raises an eyebrow. *D'ah*. That's a new one.

'OK,' Isaac says. 'I'll read.'

He opens the book at the first page, clears his throat, settles back in Mary's office chair. Then, as the sun sets behind them, Isaac starts reading.

'Gibbons are golden,' says Isaac.

'*Bibbubs ah bolbum*,' repeats the egg.

It speaks slowly and with considerable effort, enunciating every syllable of every mispronounced word. Isaac raises his other eyebrow. He stops for a moment. The egg stops, too. It blinks with expectation. Isaac shakes his head and continues.

'With great big black eyes.'

'*Bizz waybib bab whize.*'

'And they sleep in the trees.'

'*Abbay eebim ba wheeze.*'

'With those eyes on the skies.'

'*Biddoze whize odda schwize.*'

The next page comes more easily. By the page after that, Isaac and the egg have found a rhythm. The sun sets, but the pair of them hardly notice. It's only when the book is finished that they break off their impromptu English lesson to go downstairs and watch *Memento*. Mary would often say that Isaac was happy as long as he had a project, even if that project was just trying to untangle all of her necklaces, or trying to identify the neighbourhood squirrels from the kitchen window by the names he'd given each of them. All that chaos in Isaac's mind, channelled into something productive. Or at least something time-consuming. So, if the egg wants to learn English, Isaac will take Mary's advice.

Tomorrow morning, perhaps they'll start the alphabet. Next week, joined-up handwriting. Isaac would welcome the distraction. It'll take his mind off things, in the yawning gaps between therapy sessions and tearful breakdowns. Besides, if he teaches the egg to speak, maybe he'll have someone he can actually talk to. Maybe he'll find out where the egg is from. He thinks of the vision in the kitchen. He thinks of far-off planets, of worlds unknown. He thinks of an escape. Maybe, if he teaches the egg to speak, Isaac can tell it exactly where he's escaping to, what he's escaping from, when his memory freezes and his mind goes blank. Maybe, if Isaac and the egg can find a way to speak, Isaac can finally find a way to tell the truth.

Reality is fragile. All it takes is a gentle tap to break its shell. And while Isaac would have the egg believe that he's starting to heal, the egg knows full well that Isaac is lying. The egg doesn't get mind blanks. The egg's mind is sharp as a tack. And for all the mysteries Isaac has made the egg watch there's none quite as compelling as the mystery of what's going on with Isaac Addy. The egg has been watching. The egg notices that, for all his supposed forgetfulness, Isaac never forgets to charge his phone. The egg notices the phone calls themselves, which come from a woman whose name isn't *Esther*, isn't *Joy* and definitely isn't *Mary Moray*. The egg notices the late-night car trips, the one direction in which Isaac always drives when his mind supposedly goes blank, and the guilt written all over Isaac's face whenever he returns from a night spent God-knows-where. That's why, in the many hours that Isaac is out of the house, the egg is going to make like Shaggy and Velma and investigate the biggest mystery of all: the mystery of Isaac Addy, and the door at the top of his house which always remains locked. It's also why the egg has resolved to learn Isaac's language, so it can ask two pertinent questions; questions it's been pondering ever since its unexpected arrival in this strange, unnerving place.

'*Where do you disappear to, Isaac?*' the egg will ask, once it has the words with which to do so. '*And what exactly is it that you're hiding?*'

PART TWO
SHELL

SIX

Isaac Addy is getting better. He's growing, like his neighbours' garden, sprung into life with daffodils then bluebells in the month or so since that morning when Anna came knocking on Isaac's front door. He's healing, like his right hand, which has stopped hurting almost entirely, which is out of its thick cast and into a strict regimen of wrist and finger exercises given to Isaac by someone at some hospital, somewhere. And he's changing, like his house, transformed by an even stricter regimen of dusting, grouting and polishing in the latter weeks of the list which has taken over Isaac's life. If Isaac Addy is getting better, he has the list to thank. And he has Dr Abbass to thank for the list. She'd said making one might add some structure to his days, though she probably hadn't expected Isaac to throw himself into it with quite so much vigour. But Isaac, once an immobile robot, has a new theory. If he focuses on this list, everything else will melt away. If he keeps on moving forwards, he'll stop feeling like he's falling backwards. If he fixes everything around him, he just might be able to fix himself.

The crossing-off of the list began the morning after that first therapy session, back when the egg was still 'the egg', and was still screaming every time Isaac turned on the Hoover. The first task was cleaning up the mess in the kitchen, mopping red wine from the floor and knuckle blood from the crumpled hole in the wall. When the job was half done, Isaac rummaged for a Sharpie in the drawer beneath the living-room TV, ignoring Mary's old keyrings, Mary's old hairbands, thinking only of the task at hand, of the list. He tore a piece of paper from one of Mary's old notepads, thinking of anything but Mary. He pinned the paper in place of the old shopping list on the fridge door. He drummed the Sharpie against his chin. Let's press on, he thought. Let's not look back.

Then he wrote down thirteen tasks, and crossed off the first one. ~~Clean kitchen~~.

Next up was the fridge. Its contents were already sparse, but Isaac and the egg made sure to rid it of the last vestiges of shrivelled limes and mouldy garlic. In the following weeks, with a kitchen now needing filling, Isaac would start making tentative trips to the supermarket. He'd even make one trip further, to John Lewis, where he'd pick up a shiny new toaster and two new plates. While Isaac and Mary had made memories over banku and tilapia or bucatini all'amatriciana – he the accomplished home cook and she the hopeless-but-eager sous chef – his drive to experiment in the kitchen had gone out the window in recent months. Beans on toast carried no emotional baggage, so it was beans on toast every day for Isaac and the egg. Breakfasts in bed would quickly become a new tradition, the creature routinely turning up in the doorway of Isaac's bedroom at nine o'clock sharp with whatever it had decided today's breakfast should be. Some variation of baked beans, deconstructed like the world's worst gastronomist: cold beans in an old boot, beans off toast (and on a throw pillow), or baked beans and bread blended in the NutriBullet. The egg would always know to bring two portions: a larger one for Isaac, and a smaller one for itself. Then it'd hop up in bed and blink at Isaac, ensuring he finished every last disgusting bite. Mary liked her toast with poached eggs, but Isaac has noticed that the egg never cooks eggs. Perhaps it would deem it too close to cannibalism. Back in front of the fridge, after binning a rancid jar of green tomato chutney, Isaac realised that the egg never goes to the toilet. Or perhaps it does, in the back of a drawer or the bottom of a suitcase somewhere in the house which Isaac hadn't found yet.

Isaac shuddered at the thought. Then he crossed out ~~Clear fridge~~.

The pile of post by the front door had long needed sorting. And after their good work on the fridge, Isaac knew just the guys for the job. He'd started to think of the egg as his sidekick. The Luigi to his Mario, or the Robin to his Batman. Here, in the North Pole snowdrift of letters and bills, he was more like an elf to his Santa. They waded into the hallway, Egg's flat yellow feet slapping against the wooden floor like snowshoes on tundra. Beneath Isaac's feet, envelopes that betrayed the existence of a world outside his list: sympathy cards from the friends he still refuses to see; seats for a show at the Globe Theatre which will never be filled; a legal-looking letter which may have been a cease and desist from Esther Moray. Isaac glanced through the doorway at the biscuit tin on the mantelpiece, then disposed of the unopened post. He used the egg's mouth as a receptacle, rather than the shredder in Mary's office upstairs.

Glom glom glom. The egg paused occasionally to try to read a word, applying its now-daily literacy lessons with mixed results. 'Isaac Addy' became '*I'b a babby*'. 'Mary Moray' became '*Marv Morv*'. And the egg? It's probably around this time that it gained its own name. Isaac had already tried to ask it if it had one, but the *d'oh*s and *wawooo*s it answered with never seemed sufficient. So, Isaac's started calling it 'Egg'. Why not? Call an egg an egg, and all that. Besides, Egg seems to like it. Nowadays, anytime Isaac shouts 'Egg', he'll appear in the doorway with an obedient *thwap thwap thwap*, bearing a freshly cooked portion of beans on toast. There's that, too: Isaac has decided that Egg is a 'he'. It's mainly because of the mess, and the appetite, and because Isaac doesn't know that gender is as alien a concept on Egg's own plane of existence as Egg himself is on Isaac's. Isaac thinks he's been getting to know Egg. In actual fact, he's barely scratched the surface. He's too focused on other things. Like the list. Like his latest project. Like never looking back.

Isaac and Egg cleared all the letters from the floor. While Egg burped in satisfaction, Isaac crossed out ~~Sort post~~.

Mary's computer needed sorting, too. Isaac had promised Joy he'd send her some of the 'nicer' photos of him and Mary. The one where they're wearing silly hats, from the photobooth at Joy's wedding. The one where they're pulling silly faces, during the impromptu food fight at their own. Isaac had been putting off this particular task, so he took to using the five-minute gaps in between his and Egg's reading sessions to blitz the files on Mary's Mac, to drag and drop images into an email to Joy. Egg has clearly been benefiting from the uptick in learning time this entails, and has only grown more and more vocal as the weeks have run on. Isaac can barely shut him up, now. He pipes up most often from his sofa, in front of the TV. His voice never deviates from its habitual cross between mewling cat and mobile-phone-vibrating-on-a-wooden-worktop, and he always uses words from his own, strange vocabulary. There are the *oooooooo*s, an enraptured sound of appreciation, reserved for the most unimpressive and ugly of things. Slapstick mishaps, fart humour, and the dogs on *Crufts* which break off their routines to defecate in the arena. There are the *bleh*s, too, which are mainly directed at displays of human affection. Egg doesn't like romance. He seems allergic to hugging. When two characters on screen wrap their arms around each other, Egg *bleh*s, shudders and makes a retching sound like a cat ejecting a furball. Wherever Egg is from, he and his fellow eggs must be programmed to keep a wide berth. Perhaps that's why his arms are so long.

'*Wawooo.*'

What about *wawooo*? This is the one that still has Isaac stumped. It seems to come completely at random, directed at spinning volleyballs or porcelain egg cups, igloos in the Arctic tundra or termite mounds in the Australian outback. Every time Isaac thinks he notices a pattern, Egg will *wawooo* a Russian doll or a nest of anacondas, and Isaac will be back to square one. All he's able to ascertain is what *wawooo* probably doesn't mean. It doesn't mean 'ball', or even 'egg', nor does it mean 'ape' or 'monkey'.

'Does *wawooo* mean "gibbon"?'

'*D'oh.*'

'*D'oh*' means 'no'. Either the egg has a toddler-like ineptitude at pronouncing the letter *n*, or it's remembered '*d'oh*' from *The Simpsons* and thinks it means, well, 'no'. It makes more sense than its word for 'yes', which is '*d'ah*', something which had Isaac briefly convinced that the egg was a Russian spy.

'Are you from Russia?' Isaac asked.

'*D'oh,*' Egg answered.

'Are you from another planet?'

'*D'ah,*' he said, then reconsidered. '*D'oh.*'

'Where are you from?'

'*Wawooo.*'

'Were you trying to show me something, that night in the kitchen?' Isaac said. 'Was that a spaceship?'

'*Wawooo.*'

'Are you lost?'

'*D'ah.*'

'Do you need to get home?'

'*D'ah.*'

'Where *is* home?'

'*Wawooo.*'

Isaac wants Egg to speak English as much as Egg wants Isaac to speak Egg. If Isaac spoke Egg, Egg could ask *him* about home.

He could say, '*Why are you never at home?*'

He could say, '*Where do you go when you leave home for days on end?*'

Isaac and Egg don't speak the same language. They aim for some sort of mutual understanding. Isaac reads to Egg in Mary's office, these readings punctuated by the shredding of unwanted files and the filing of unfinished shreds of Mary's writing. The literacy lessons, like the list, distract Isaac from the darkness that hides just behind everything they're doing.

'How now, brown cow,' Isaac will say.

'*Bow wow, bow wow,*' Egg will reply.

That first time, as every time, Mary's yellow notebook remained unopened on the desk. Back in front of the fridge, Isaac crossed out ~~Sort Mary's computer~~.

That cast came off. Next door's bluebells bloomed. And Isaac, ever the worrier, started to worry that he and Egg are getting through the list too fast. He's worried about what comes after. That's why he'll drag out the next item, the general cleaning of the house, for as long as humanly possible. For his is a house with plenty to attend to. A narrow, terraced Victorian thing, with brittle old windows, bricked-in fire-places and high-ceilinged rooms. Every old-fashioned door has a lock and a key, and a brass doorknob ripe for polishing. Every room has a skirting board which needs a wipe, or retro lampshade which needs a dust, or an unreachable corner on the ceiling which Egg can use his pipe-cleaner arms to swipe cobwebs out of. He's been keeping any spiders and flies as treats for himself. The bookshelves want dusting, the windows require wiping, and the stray pine needles from the long-gone Christmas tree are in serious need of hoovering up. Isaac's become a veritable cleaning machine. He once read that there are more germs on a kitchen counter than on a toilet seat, but he could never quite work out whether this was supposed to reflect well on the toilet seat or badly on the kitchen counter.

'Which do you think it is, Egg?' he asked, one gloved arm wrist-deep in the toilet bowl.

Egg was too busy sucking the toilet brush to answer. Isaac scratched his chin with his gloved hand.

'Bit of both, I guess.'

Isaac sometimes watches Egg, while they clean, and wonders why he's still here. Not that he's complaining – he doesn't know what he'd do alone. But he still thinks, Why? What are you waiting for? He's asked Egg how he came to be in the forest, if he has family searching for him, whether there's anything he can do to help facilitate his safe return. Egg tends to just blink, shake his head and utter some variation of *wawooo*. So, for the time being, he's stopped asking. He's waiting for a sign, a garbled extradimensional call on his landline or that monolithic metal shape from the vision he had landing, uninvited, on top of his garden shed. Until such a thing happens, Isaac focuses on his list, and Egg seems happy to help. They live like hermits, in a house which is hermetically sealed. Within that fragile ecosystem, Isaac's getting better. He's moving forwards. He's . . . hiding something. Something big. Egg has noticed that Isaac never suggests cleaning the room at the top of the stairs.

Isaac doesn't think about that. And he never quite crosses out **Clean house**.

Up until recently, Isaac didn't know much about depression. He still doesn't think its definition applies to him, which would suggest he's not clued-up on denial, either. He zoned out when, in their last session, Dr Abbass tried to talk him through the 'stages of grief'. He does know about lists, though, and his list has at least given him a reason.

'A reason for what?' Dr Abbass might ask.

'A reason to forget about Mary,' Isaac might answer.

'*Just* Mary?' Dr Abbass might reply.

Isaac wouldn't have an answer for that. Mary was the one with all the answers. She was the one with all the ideas, too. Think of all her unwritten books, the one about the Yorkshire miners digging too deep and hitting live dinosaurs, the one about all of London's statues coming to life and battling each other, the one about the animals on Noah's Ark starting a mutiny and becoming marauding pirates. It was Mary's idea that Isaac should start making lists, a practical Mary move which worked just as well for an all-action man. She knew he liked a project. His unfinished ones ranged from a half-restored antique desk to a half-painted mural to an oil drum he tried to turn into a garden meat smoker and ended up taking down to the dump. He couldn't write to save his life, just as Mary couldn't draw to save a game of Pictionary. But lists? Lists helped him catch his thoughts, to bring some of Mary's order to his own disorder. They were the perfect intersection of action and ideas, like a Venn diagram of Isaac and Mary with 'lists' forming an egg shape in the middle. Or a coin. Yes, Isaac and Mary were two sides of the same coin. That's why losing Mary sent Isaac into a tailspin. If he stops moving, he'll flip. He'll be a paradox, a one-sided coin. All tails, permanently lurching, unable to land.

Isaac was never very good when it came to helping Mary with the *Times* crossword, just as Mary deferred to him for the more difficult bits of every jigsaw they ever assembled on that living-room coffee table. Choppy sea, stormy sky. They met in the middle on word searches. *Those* they could do together, although they laughed in secret shame because they were pretty sure word searches are supposed to be for kids. Is this the only thing we can agree on? This and *lists*? But Mary wrote for children. She was the first to admit that grown-up concepts are best understood through childish means.

```
K  J  X  D  M  A  B  D  J  J
D  E  N  I  A  L  P  E  H  N
T  G  X  J  U  H  V  P  G  T
Y  N  A  Q  Y  D  X  R  H  V
M  D  N  U  B  W  I  E  Y  R
U  B  G  A  H  J  V  S  F  O
I  I  E  H  S  W  M  S  Q  T
B  A  R  G  A  I  N  I  N  G
H  E  J  X  Y  R  S  O  A  G
A  C  C  E  P  T  A  N  C  E
```

It feels like this could last forever: Isaac and Egg, existing like monks in a secluded mountaintop monastery. As long as the windows stay closed, the living-room blinds stay drawn and the people listed in Isaac's phone stay in his phone and don't appear at his front door, things are just about manageable. Isaac's been keeping up with his texts, telling everybody he's 'Fine' or 'Keeping busy' or, of course, 'Moving forwards'. In reality, he's sitting still, albeit comfortably, ever propped up with pillows and tucked under the duvet with Egg next to him and a plate of beans on toast in each of their laps. Isaac had known how to throw up a smokescreen long before Mary died. He knows how to fake a smile, especially now he only has to fake one digitally. In person, the only person he sees is Dr Abbass, and he only sees her once a week. He's started leaving Egg behind when he does, on the condition that Egg will use the time to either further his education with something from the bookshelves, or dust the top of said bookshelves with those handy old arms. Isaac sees a lot of Egg, and a little of Dr Abbass. But *other* humans? That's what phones are for.

'Keeping the wolves from the door,' is how he describes it to Egg. Egg doesn't know what wolves are, but nods, anyway.

For about six weeks, this strategy really does seem to be working. It's only when Isaac's taking the dirty breakfast plates downstairs on one particular morning that he realises it isn't. The wolves are indeed at the door, and Isaac and Egg's version of domestic bliss is about to be shattered by a shadow behind the frosted glass. Isaac freezes. Through the open doorway between the kitchen and the living room, he sees the shape pass in front of the venetian blinds and grow larger, as if trying to peek in. Isaac puts the plates in the sink, his heart in his mouth. He pokes his head into the living room, but the shadow has gone. He returns to the kitchen. He pokes his head into the hallway. He shrieks. The shadow is back on the other side of the front door, staring straight in his direction through the frosted glass. It hesitates. A blurry hand moves towards the doorbell, but the noise doesn't come. Instead, a voice sounds from the other side of the door.

'I can see you, Isaac,' says Joy. 'Can you let me in?'

Isaac swallows. He looks at the dirty plates in the sink. He looks at the distorted outline of Joy in the window. He looks at the stairs, at the top of which he'll find the creature he's been so diligently hiding from other human beings. He swears under his breath. Then he rushes down the hallway, towards the front door, pivoting at the bottom of the stairs and starting up them. He shouts an excuse back to his sister.

'Door's locked!' he shouts.

It isn't. And even if it was, no one in their right mind would keep the keys upstairs. Still, he scurries up and away from the door, sprints across the landing and into the bedroom. Egg is still sitting in bed. Egg has been waiting for him to return. Egg stares up at Isaac, seemingly expecting an introduction to whoever is at the door.

'You have to hide,' Isaac hisses, keeping his voice low.

Egg blinks once, twice. Then, with arms which rise from

either side of the bed, Egg puts the duvet over his head.

'No,' Isaac says, rubbing his forehead. *'Hide.'*

Egg is currently little more than an egg shape under-neath a duvet, like the bump on the head of a *Looney Tunes* villain after a well-placed hit with a mallet. But even if Egg-under-a-duvet could be mistaken for a misplaced cushion or a balled-up pyjama top, his arms still give the game away – they've flopped out of either side of the duvet and across the carpet, as flat and lifeless as empty fire hoses. Beneath the duvet, Egg can't seem to hear Isaac.

'Egg,' he half shouts, through gritted teeth. 'Egg!'

Egg continues to sit in place, sandbag-stout and stock-still. Isaac marches forward and yanks the duvet, by the corner, straight off the bed. What's left is Egg, wide-eyed, sinking into the centre of the mattress and quaking a little.

'You have to hide,' Isaac says.

'Bibe?' Egg's voice is shaking. He thinks they're under attack again.

'Yes, hide,' Isaac says. Egg still doesn't move. 'Now!'

Egg seems to get the message. Or he just loses balance, rocking on his little yellow feet until he falls backwards on to the mattress. Isaac bites his lip as he watches Egg squirm on his back like an upended tortoise. Then, quite unexpect-edly, Egg does something amazing. First, he closes his eyes, and his face becomes a featureless yolk in the middle of an egg-white body once again. Then he rolls ever so slightly on to one side, then the other, as if he's trying to rock a boat. He rolls a little further, so he's face down, the top part of one arm beneath his face and the top part of the other behind his back. Then he rolls again, and again, until he's at the edge of the bed, wrapping his arms around himself with every turn. By the time Egg rolls off the bed and plops on to the floor with a squeak, his face, his yolk, has disappeared entirely. With a final *twang*, as if the hoses have been reeled in as far as they can go, Egg comes to a stop on the floor by Isaac's feet. He quivers a little more. As he does so, each yellow toe disappears into the fur at the base of his body. They do so one by one, with the rhythmic plopping of a leaking tap.

plop plop plop   *plop plop plop*

Just like that, Egg is once again a blank, white egg. It rolls across the floor slightly, bumping into Isaac's feet, then lies still. Isaac can't help but be impressed. He crouches down and picks the egg up, turns it over, palms it from one hand to another. It's as light as a rugby ball, and just as lifeless. Egg – or *the* egg – looks almost exactly the same as when Isaac found him in the forest, though a little less cold and a little less wet. And despite everything that's happened since then, it's hard for Isaac to believe that his only friend lurks beneath the colourless ovoid in his hands.

Noises in the hallway. Joy has already let herself in, and Isaac can hear her calling his name from downstairs. Panicking once again, Isaac looks for a hiding place in which to stash the egg. He settles on the wardrobe to his left, flinging open the doors and depositing the egg in a pile of swimming costumes, flip-flops and barely used goggles. Once it's in its impromptu nest, Isaac smooths down some of its more gravity-defying patches of fur. The egg is still shivering, and Isaac can't help but feel bad at having to leave it in the dark.

'Stay here,' he says, as softly as he can manage. 'Don't come out until I give you the all-clear.'

Then he closes the door, puts the duvet back on the bed, plumps the pillows and opens the curtains. Moments later, Isaac is strolling down the landing with as normal a face as he can manage. When he reaches the top of the stairs, he sees Joy waiting for him at the bottom.

'The door was unlocked,' she says.

Isaac swallows. He descends the stairs, avoiding eye contact. Joy, who seems as if she's trying her best to be angry at her big brother, can only manage a slight frown. Isaac hasn't seen her, in person, since the day he broke his hand. Now she looks him up and down, takes in the shrivelled right hand and the shamanic beard and everything else that points to him not doing quite as well as his texts would have had her believe. Her bottom lip starts to tremble. She bursts into tears, grabs Isaac and gives him a crushing hug. Isaac feels as if he might snap in her arms, or at least rebound off her sizeable stomach. How far along is she? How long has it been?

'You stink,' she says, but she doesn't let go.

It's probably deserved. Isaac doesn't know how many days it's been since he last showered, let alone since he asked about the baby. Before he can ask, or even answer, Joy has already pushed past him and headed towards the kitchen. It's as if she's worried Isaac will still bolt, pushing her back outside and bolting the door for good measure. He had been considering the strategy. Isaac glances back upstairs, then sniffs the armpits of his T-shirt. He wrinkles his nose. Then he looks up to see that Joy is watching him. Isaac leans with his back against the front door, his whole body tense, every muscle stiffened in an attempt to give a sufficiently normal outward appearance. Joy wipes her eyes with one well-manicured finger and waits for Isaac to say something.

'You're very big,' he says.

Bad start. Perhaps he is a robot, after all. Joy raises one eyebrow, looks down at her protruding stomach, then back up at him.

'Thanks,' she says. 'You're not. You look thin.'

Does he? Isaac looks down at the space where his paunch should be, and is surprised to find it isn't there. He would have thought the lack of vegetables was making him fat, but perhaps two portions of beans on toast per day counts as a calorie deficit for an adult human male who doesn't sleep. Eyes still lowered, he surveys his own outfit, and is even more surprised by what he sees. Joy is wearing a matching set of brightly coloured earrings, brightly coloured bangles and a brightly coloured necklace, with boots and a bag clearly chosen to match her impressively clean dress. Isaac is wearing old, moth-eaten socks inside slippers with holes at the toes. His tracksuit bottoms are once again dusted with crumbs and stiff with spilt sauce. As for his dressing gown, that hasn't been washed in . . . well, he doesn't know how long. Worst of all, Isaac now realises that he's wearing one of Mary's pyjama T-shirts. The one that says *I Love Goats* on the front. He doesn't remember putting it on. All he knows is that it would never have fitted him before.

'Have you been eating?' Joy says, worry written on her face. 'Mum insisted I bring you these.'

Joy holds up a carrier bag filled with Tupperwares, the Tupperwares themselves filled with all manner of soups and stews, bundled together with a couple of flimsy-looking elastic bands. It's his mother's way of telling him that she's thinking of him, but Isaac is only thinking of his T-shirt, of his own stench.

'Tell her thank you.' His voice is wooden.

'You can tell her yourself.'

'Tell her thank you,' Isaac says again, as if he hasn't heard her.

'You better eat them,' Joy says, as if she hasn't heard him, either. 'Or I'll tell her you said she's lost her touch.'

That was a joke. Isaac knows he should laugh, but he can no longer remember how. He coughs instead. In the awkward silence, Joy crosses the hallway and attempts to hand the bag to him. Isaac flinches, draws back, and waves his weak hand in the general direction of the kitchen. Joy sighs, shaking her head. She heads into the kitchen, puts down the bag, then pulls more items out of her capacious handbag: vibrantly coloured juice shots, rattling boxes of multivitamins, some sort of protein powder with an unnervingly algal hue. Isaac watches her through the doorway as she places them on the counter, keeping a safe distance as if he's worried the pills and potions will prove radioactive. Once Joy is finished, she faces him. There's another, even more awkward, silence. To save face, Isaac throws an empty statement across the void opening up between them.

'You've done your hair,' he says.

'You haven't,' she replies. 'You look awful, Isaac.'

Then she turns on her heels and disappears out of sight, leaving Isaac to consider just how awful he looks. He turns to the mirror on the hallway wall and inspects his face. His hair is, indeed, unruly. It looks Frankenstein-esque, defying gravity and shot through with prematurely grey hairs. Just looking at his beard makes him itch. Next to the mirror is a photo of himself and Mary, taken in the photobooth at Joy's wedding. In the photo, he's smiling. In the mirror, he's not. And it's not just that he isn't smiling right now, it's that his face seems entirely devoid of the ability to smile. His dimples have been absorbed into his barbed-wire beard, his laughter lines subsumed by hanging flesh which seems to be decaying before his very eyes. Isaac sticks an index finger into each corner of his mouth and tries to manipulate it into a smile. He bares his teeth, his gums exposed like a decomposing skull. He's surprised to see how awful he looks. But he's somewhat glad, too. It feels good to be told that he looks bad, like a self-flagellating monk paying penance. If Joy had told him he looked well, he might have worried he was getting better too quickly.

'Isaac!' Joy has been shouting his name over the sound of the kettle.

'What?' he says, entering the kitchen.

'Where are all your mugs?'

A hot flash of panic in Isaac's stomach as he remembers the egg in the cupboard upstairs. He casts a furtive glance towards the door into the hallway, then clears his throat.

'Spring cleaning.'

'Of mugs?' She looks at the plate rack. It's empty. The only two plates in the whole house are dirty with bean juice, idling in the sink.

'Plates, too,' he says, before she can ask.

Joy frowns at Isaac, leaning with her back against the kitchen counter. She flicks off the switch on the kettle, then crosses her arms. The saxophonist squeaks into action on the other side of the wall.

'How's your hand?'

Isaac had forgotten he'd ever broken it. Where the cast once was, the thin skin is sticky and yellowish. It looks like the hand of a dead man.

'It's fine.'

'And how are you?' Joy says, without missing a beat.

The question takes Isaac off guard. He doesn't have an answer. 'I'm fine.'

'Are you?'

'Basically, yeah.'

'You've been ignoring my calls.'

'I emailed you.'

'I saw.'

'I've been in therapy.'

'I know,' she says. 'Once a week. If that.'

'It's a start.'

'Not if you're spending the rest of the time on your own.'

'I'm not on my own,' Isaac says, before he can stop himself.

Joy pauses. She narrows her eyes, casting them over the faded red blotch on the kitchen wall, the crockery dents on the fridge, the miscellaneous food stains up the side of the door into the living room. Then she looks a little further, into the living room itself, at the biscuit tin on the mantelpiece.

'Are you serious?' she says.

Isaac looks bewildered. He turns, looks at the biscuit tin, feels a hot flush spreading across his cheeks.

'She likes it here,' he says.

This is why Isaac didn't want anyone coming round. He's being forced to think of things he doesn't want to think about. Like the drinking. Like the funeral. His mind sears with new, old images. One of Joy wearing black, unable to break down because she's too busy holding her big baby brother upright. One of Esther wearing black, smaller than he'd ever seen her, unable to complain about the journey down south, unable to say anything at all. And one of himself, still wearing black the week after the funeral. Drunk again, alone again. Tipping an urn into an empty tin of Walkers shortbread rather than allowing its contents to be laid to rest in Scotland while he festers down here, alone. Shame burns in the pit of Isaac's stomach.

'You're keeping her hostage,' Joy says.

'No, I'm not.'

Yes, he is. Esther has called about forty times, and every time he's been 'Too busy to talk'. Isaac looks through the living-room doorway, at the biscuit tin. He coughs, but only to mask the fact that he can't breathe. His eyelids flicker. He holds himself up against the nearest counter. There's a long pause, in which Joy looks her brother up and down again. He knows she'll have spoken to Esther, to Dr Abbass. He knows they probably all want the best for him. But what they want only makes him feel worse. While Isaac concentrates on not sliding to the floor, Joy closes the mug cupboard and waves a dramatic hand in front of her nose.

'You really need to have a wash,' she says. 'And a haircut, for God's sake.'

'I haven't been out of the house.'

Joy goes to say something else, but stops herself. She raises an eyebrow instead.

'Apart from therapy,' Isaac says.

Joy's eyebrow raises a little further.

'And the odd walk,' Isaac says, his voice rising with it.

'Come on, Isaac,' Joy says. 'We both know where you've been.'

Isaac's hot panic returns, along with the battery-acid sensation in his throat. He squirms like a cockroach under a thumb.

'I . . .' He's at a loss for words. 'I don't want to talk about that.' Isaac swallows. His eyes reflexively glance upstairs.

'She's worried about you,' Joy says.

'Dr Abbass?'

'No, not Dr Abbass.'

'Oh,' Isaac says.

'I don't blame her,' Joy continues. 'We're all worried about you.'

'I told you. I'm fine.'

Sensing she's fighting a losing battle, Joy scans the room.

'At least you've cleaned,' she says.

Joy's eyes settle on the magnet on the fridge, the one holding up the list. Isaac thinks he notices a quiver in her bottom lip. Joy sniffs it away, crouches and opens the cupboard under the sink. Isaac is still looking at the magnet. Joy used to bring back all manner of freebies from her legal conferences. Isaac would always take the pens, Mary the notebooks. He's pretty sure even the yellow one on her desk upstairs has the branding of some po-faced bankruptcy firm on the back. There was all manner of bric-a-brac: calendars, laser-pen keyrings, as well as those fridge magnets for the handy holding-up of lists. Joy used to scout the merch table when she was bored and begging for the day to end, sending pictures of potential steals to their WhatsApp group. Yes, he remembers now. The three of them had a WhatsApp group. They called themselves 'The Three Amigos'.

'Here they are,' says Joy, her voice muffled beneath the sink.

She stands and turns, now holding a roll of black bin bags. She taps the roll against the palm of her free hand and gives Isaac a look like she's about to rip off a plaster.

'So,' she says, ripping a bag off the roll. 'Are we doing this?'

'This?'

'You don't have to do it all today,' she says. 'But you know what Dr Abbass said. It's an important step in letting go.'

'She said that?'

'Yes,' Joy says. 'You told me. In your email. In capitals.'

Did he? 'Did I?'

Joy frowns. Isaac frowns back. Another blank. Isaac closes his eyes, rubs his temples, exhales slowly. Nothing. When he opens them again, Joy is gone. He can hear her in the hallway. Isaac chases after her, his eyes on the stairs. The hot panic is getting even hotter.

'Let's start with these,' Joy says, gesturing down at the ladies' shoes lined up by the door. A pair of running shoes rubs shoulders with some dirty wellies, themselves nuzzling up to some heeled ankle boots she barely wore because they made her so much taller than Isaac. Mary liked to reimagine herself, every so often, and her wardrobe was always the first thing demanding an overhaul. Isaac can't help but look back at the biscuit tin on the mantelpiece. The biggest reinvention of all.

'No, not those,' Isaac says.

He finds it hard to speak. He doesn't want to admit that getting rid of Mary's shoes would mean she'd have nothing to wear, if she were – *theoretically* – to ever wander back in through the front door.

Joy turns to the coat rack and grabs a handful of Mary's coat sleeves. One muted black, one leopard print, one Tactical waterproof. 'These?' she says, as if choosing something to try on.

'No, not those, either.' He wouldn't want Mary getting cold.

'OK,' Joy says, flashing him a weary smile. She's still holding the empty bin bag. 'We can start upstairs, if you like.'

Before Isaac can even comprehend the implications of Joy *starting upstairs*, she's already pushed past him again and, well, started upstairs. Isaac's hot panic is now so hot that he feels like he might evaporate before he can get to her. He climbs the stairs so fast that he ends up sprawled on all fours on the landing, eventually catching up with Joy by the time she's already in the bedroom. She's taking stock of the wardrobes and the drawers, deciding which to open first. The hairs on the back of Isaac's neck stand up as he pictures the worst: Joy flinging open the wardrobe doors, Egg unfurling in a blood-curdling scream, Joy echoing the scream. How would it end? Isaac suspects that Joy would not be as accommodating as he has been of the monster he found in the forest while contemplating flinging himself off a bridge. His mind conjures up an image of Joy beating the creature to a pulp with her fists, or the creature constricting its long arms around Joy like a deadly boa. Granted, neither seems likely, but Isaac has had enough bad luck to know that the worst possible scenario is the scenario that will probably happen. Whatever *will* happen, he knows that letting Joy see the egg is a bad idea. Joy has already opened one of the drawers and set to work. She picks up a pyjama T-shirt, briefly steadying her breath as if the sight of it might cause her to lose her well-kept composure. She wipes an eye, seeks Isaac's opinion. Isaac is looking at the wardrobe door. Joy holds up the T-shirt to get his attention.

'Keep or . . .' She breathes carefully again. 'Pass on?'

Isaac drags his eyes away from the wardrobe. *I Love My Bed*.

'What?'

'Keep or pass on?'

'Erm . . . keep.'

Joy puts it back in the drawer. She picks up another. *I Love New York*.

'Keep.'

I Love Us.

'Keep. Definitely keep.'

Joy shakes her head, puts the T-shirt back, closes the drawer.

'You can't just hold on to all of it,' she says. 'Something has to change.'

'I don't want anything to change.'

'I know you don't,' she says. Her voice sounds fragile. 'But look what it's doing to you.'

Isaac refuses to look down. At his untrimmed beard, at his unwashed clothes, at his undernourished body. 'What do you know?' he says instead, his voice laced with venom.

Joy speaks softly. 'I've been reading a lot of books about this stuff. They all say that this is an important part of the healing process.'

'I'm not in a book,' Isaac says. 'I'm not in a healing process.'

'That's the problem.'

Isaac has no response. And, having no response, he can't help but nervously eye the wardrobe.

'Good idea,' Joy says. 'We'll start with the wardrobe.'

Scalding panic. As Joy begins to move, Isaac hops from one foot to another like he's standing on burning coals. Then, as she crosses the room, he skids crab-like in front of her, slamming his back against the wardrobe door and spreading out his arms. He's sure he can feel the door trembling against his forearms.

'No,' he says. 'Not the wardrobe.'

Joy looks confused. She reaches out to touch Isaac's arm, but he shakes her off.

'It's OK, Isaac,' she says.

'Not the wardrobe,' he says again.

Isaac has another problem now. The door is *definitely* trembling. Whether it's the force with which he slammed himself against it, or the warmth in Joy's voice, Egg has decided to hatch. Isaac can hear the slither of his arms unravelling behind the door, a telltale purr from within the wardrobe which signals that Egg is awake and feeling frisky. Isaac had told him not to move until he'd given him the 'all-clear', but he only now realises that Egg has no idea what an 'all-clear' is. Perhaps he thinks this is the all-clear. What then? How long until he gets claustrophobic, starts wailing and flinging his flailing arms around? What *then*? Isaac hears a muffled '*Wob wab?*' from within. He tries to drown it out by talking.

'I think you should go,' he says, gritting his teeth.

'What?'

'This is too much. I think you should go.'

'I'm only trying to help,' Joy says, endeavouring to move Isaac out of the way.

'You're not helping.' He has a flashback to play-fighting as kids, Joy executing a flawless People's Elbow off the living-room sofa and on to Isaac while a horrified babysitter looked on. She was always stronger than he was.

'Isaac, I know it's hard,' she says, trying to manoeuvre herself under his outstretched left arm.

'Do you?' Egg is getting louder, so Isaac is raising his voice, too. 'Do you!?'

It works. Joy stops trying, steps backwards and bumps against the bed. She looks shocked.

'You're not a part of this,' Isaac says. 'None of you is a part of this.'

Even as he says it, he knows he's being unfair. More unwanted memories are tumbling behind his eyes, faster than he can fully process them. He remembers how Mary used to play on Joy's office netball team back in London, how they used to get roaring drunk together every Tuesday night after losing yet another game. He remembers how Joy and Mary used to go to the theatre together, that the Globe tickets Egg had scoffed from the post pile had been theirs for this summer, booked a whole lifetime ago. He remembers the Christmas morning when Joy had told them she was pregnant. It wasn't Isaac she had called. It was Mary. It wasn't Isaac she'd asked about being godparents. It was Mary. That's it: he knows Joy and Mary were best friends. He knows he doesn't have a monopoly on Mary Moray. But he's started, and he can't stop. It's that perverse little imp in his brain again, bashing on the organ, manipulating his vocal cords to say things they don't mean. The imp is selfish. It wants to grieve alone. And while Isaac might be shouting at Joy, it's the entire world at which he aims his rage.

'She was *my* wife! Mine. And I don't care how many books you've read. I don't need your fucking healing process!'

Joy goes to say something, but words fail her. She looks as if she's finally going to cry, but she just about holds it in. 'Isaac, I was only trying to—'

'Help?' he practically screams. 'I. Don't. Want. Your. Help.'

Silence. Joy says nothing. The creature in the wardrobe ceases making sounds. Isaac's sister sniffs, wipes her eyes, then heads for the bedroom door. Before she leaves, she turns back to him.

'You can't pretend the real world doesn't exist,' she says. 'It's not just yourself you're hurting by doing so.'

Then she's gone, disappearing into a puff of hard footsteps

on the stairs. Isaac closes his eyes and slumps against the wardrobe, shaking his head. He hears the front door slam, Joy's heels on the front path, disappearing down the pavement and into the distance. Eyes still closed, Isaac finds his way to the bed and sits down heavily. He puts his head in his hands and considers crying, but he's distracted by the creak of a door hinge. He looks up to see Egg, watching him from the open wardrobe.

'You heard all that?' Isaac says.

Egg heard, clearly. He's shaking his head, more like a full-body sway from side to side. He's crossing his arms, too, knotting them over each other, and over again, like a pair of Boschian serpents. Above his overly crossed arms, Egg's little face is tight. His ever-downturned mouth is even more pinched than normal, and his big eyes are squinting with concentration as if attempting to copy an expression which isn't quite his. It's an expression of disappointment.

'*Bloo blah*,' he says. It sounds like a judgement.

'I know,' Isaac says, shaking his own head. 'I was out of order. I'll call her and apologise.'

Egg now tilts forward and widens his eyes a little, as if saying, '*Go on . . .*'

'And I'm sorry for shutting you in the cupboard,' Isaac says. 'I was trying to protect you, anyway, so you should be saying thank you.'

'*Blam woo*,' Egg says, with a face which would look very much like he was raising his eyebrows, if he had eyebrows to raise.

'Great,' says Isaac. 'Now you've got an attitude.'

Egg seems pleased with himself. Isaac just feels guilty. He puts his head in his hands once again and moans, wondering what he's going to say to Joy, preparing to grovel. As he does so, he feels something. A small, three-fingered hand, ruffling his hair as he had done to Egg in the kitchen all those weeks before. Egg is comforting him. Or, no – the room is vacuumed away, as it was in the kitchen all those weeks before. The bed is sucked into the floor like jelly into a plughole, the wardrobes fly into the ether like butterflies, the walls spin off like sycamore seeds into non-existence. Though Isaac can still feel the mattress beneath him and Egg's hand on his head, he's once again floating in a black void, a haunting nothingness stretching as far as the eye can see. Isaac gasps. He isn't cold, but his breath makes a cloud in front of his face. He looks to his left, then to his right. More nothing. Only space. Then, just as he's about to start panicking, he sees something, far in the distance. A light, blinking. A beacon of some sort, floating towards him with a high-pitched hum like a beluga in the deep. Isaac attempts to swim towards it, but he floats still, unable to move. No matter. The beacon is coming close now, and Isaac can see that the blinking light is attached to the front of what looks like a pod. The little thing floats through the blankness, an even smaller shape just about visible through one side of its glass exterior. Up close, against the vastness of the void, it's tiny. It *beeps beeps beeps* as it floats past Isaac. He can't help notice that it's shaped a bit like a coffin.

Before Isaac can get a closer look, Egg lets go. The room comes back into being. And Isaac, once again, is slumped against the wardrobe in his earth-bound bedroom. He rubs his eyes. He looks at Egg. Isaac remembers him, back in the kitchen, answering the question of 'Where are you from?' by pulverising a grapefruit into the tabletop. Perhaps he was trying to tell him something, something Isaac was too wrapped up in his own problems to see. Isaac imagines Egg watching from the window of an escape pod as his home went the way of that grapefruit, that biscuit, that plate. He imagines a whole planet, destroyed. He imagines a vast mothership, filled with eggs just as lost as Egg, sailing through the cosmos in search of their missing son. And he imagines Egg himself, crash-landing in the forest. It's a heartbreaking image. He sees Egg, even more alone than himself. And he sees a purpose, one which might just help him find his own real world again. The ultimate project, right in front of his eyes.

'I'm going to help you find your way home, Egg,' Isaac says. 'I promise.'

He's speaking more to himself, which is good because Egg isn't listening. He's over by the drawers instead, picking out an old pair of Mary's bed socks. He turns them over in his tiny hands, then turns to Isaac, who is watching him. Egg presents the socks.

'*Beep oh bah wom?*' he asks. *Keep or pass on.*

Isaac almost smiles. But not quite.

'Pass on,' he says.

SEVEN

I saac Addy might be an alien. He certainly feels like one. Apart from Joy's flying visit and his sessions with Dr Abbass, he's barely interacted with anyone of his own kind in months. He looks like one, too. What did Isaac Addy look like last year, before he zapped all his human friends away? Not like this. *This*, whatever *this* is, is as alien as can be. His stalagmite hair and stalactite beard make him seem like he's from a world where the inhabitants are made of stone. His eyes used to sparkle, but now they shine only as much as two polished pebbles one would find on a beach. Isaac has hardened, calcified. He speaks to no one but his two-foot-tall inhuman housemate, a lack of human contact which has left him noticeably lacking in the acting-like-a-human department. Any humanity Egg hasn't learned from the TV, he's learning from the lonely human who found him in the woods. While Isaac is becoming less human with every conversation they have, Egg is becoming more so. Give it a couple of months and they might meet in the middle.

Now that Egg is getting more confident at speaking, Isaac is trying his best to glean why and how Egg came to be here. He's posited the escape-pod theory, but Egg's admirably short attention span has made it hard for Isaac to find out much. He's had to be creative. Hand movements work, as do tactile, colourful toys. Egg has learned to count, which proves helpful when trying to measure distances, time and height, though he is still confused that Isaac, at 'six feet', is far more than six times the length of a human foot. He and Isaac converse with much more than words, and Isaac has created his own basic understanding of Egg's journey so far. And 'so far' is right, as the only concrete fact seems to be that Egg is from far, far away. The rest has been interpreted by Isaac – a smashed plate, an obliterated grapefruit – all pointing to some cataclysmic event. What must it have been like, watching your whole world be smashed to smithereens like a biscuit against a kitchen tabletop? Isaac thinks he has an idea. To validate his theory, he's tried to catch more glimpses of Egg's past, sneaking up behind him and ruffling his furry head to bring about some new, more informative, vision. It doesn't work. Egg's magic touch seems to be something he can turn off and on. Still, if Egg crash-landed in the woods by the bridge about fifteen minutes from Isaac's house, it might mean that there are more of Egg's kind out there, somewhere. Isaac is going to help Egg find that great metal mothership from his vision. He's going to use the E.T.

approach, though this time he'll be playing Elliott. He'll be the hero on the bicycle. He'll help Egg phone home. But to do so, he needs the necessary components. That's why, after months of skirting around the outside world, Isaac Addy is going into town.

Egg seems to have noticed a difference in Isaac. He's watching him, again. Egg watches Isaac as Isaac whistles along to the sound of the saxophonist. He notices the skip in Isaac's step as Isaac ferries overflowing bin bags to the front door. And he stares as Isaac retrieves a set of keys from the console table beneath the TV in the living room, and uses them to let himself out of the back door and stride purposefully up towards the shed at the top of the garden. Isaac wouldn't have done this before, but in the days leading up to his big day out he's preparing as one would prepare for a marathon or a military exercise. That means fearlessly taking the bins out, to familiarise himself with short conversations with passers-by. It also means taking to Google Maps to plot the shortest route that takes in the charity shop, the hardware shop and his usual barber, without the possibility of bumping into any old acquaintances. And it means mowing the back lawn, getting used to being outside without panicking, and even letting Egg play in the churned-up grass – albeit late at night, when Isaac is sure his neighbours aren't watching. This is something else that Isaac-in-the-weeks-before probably wouldn't have encouraged, but Isaac isn't the same as he was in the weeks before. One might even be inclined to think that he's on the road back to being human, even to being happy. He isn't. But he'll get to that later.

The stage is set for Isaac and Egg's trip into town. Isaac has at least got rid of some of Mary's older gym tops, her disused swimming costumes and her half-broken sunglasses. They're in the bin bag by the door, along with the shrunken sheets he'd found still idling in the tub of the tumble dryer. He's also making more headway on the list. He's crossed off another item: ~~Call Mum~~. It wasn't a long chat, and he batted away her suggestion that she come round and they cook an old-fashioned family feast together, but at least he could reassure her that he was still alive, still capable of speaking and still keeping himself somewhat fed. He's even crossed off ~~Plant flowers~~, which wouldn't have been possible back when he avoided going outside (as in, into his garden) let alone outside-outside (as in, into town). The flowers were a gift from Joy. They're dahlias, which were Mary's favourite, and which Joy says will mean there'll always be a memory of Mary when he looks out of his kitchen window in summer. He sent Joy a picture of the freshly planted flowers, then he called her to apologise for being a dick. She forgave him. Then he told her about his grand plans to go into town for a haircut, leaving out the part about the space-age communication device he's hoping to build. Joy seemed happy for him. If she knew he was hiding something – about the egg, about how much he's really been leaving the house – she decided to hold her tongue.

Isaac and Egg stand by the front door, ready to leave.

Isaac has calculated that just after lunch on a Tuesday is the optimal time to avoid the attention a busy town centre would bring. And, with the same military precision as Isaac's planning, Egg has thrown himself head first into the technicalities of the transponder that he and Isaac are going to build. He sketched out plans, using vast sheets of Isaac's old drawing paper and a sausage finger smeared in charcoal from the grate. He oversaw Isaac's construction of a rudimentary aerial out of coat hangers, cocktail spoons and twine, now flimsily fixed to the roof via the upstairs bathroom window. And he started his own list, one which Isaac is suspicious only exists because Egg had been jealous of Isaac's. According to Egg, *this* list consists of all the items he'll need if he's going to try to communicate with his own species, to find a family that Isaac assumes is somewhere out there, waiting to be found. Egg dictated, plodding back and forth and stroking his chin-fur, while Isaac did the writing.

Batteries (AA)
Gaffer tape
Paperclips
Laser pen
Fertiliser (tomato)
Strong white bread flour
Garden gnome (any)

The translation took a while. Isaac queried a few of the items. He conjured up a Google image of a garden gnome to make

sure Egg was asking for the right thing. He showed Egg
a half-full bottle of fertiliser in the shed, but Egg seemed
adamant that only high-potash tomato feed would do the
trick. Not knowing the specifics of Egg technology and not
really wanting to find out, Isaac didn't ask any further questions. At least he already had the flour, safe from the food
fight in a forgotten corner of one of his kitchen cupboards.
Now the list is in Isaac's pocket, within a pair of jeans he's
wearing for the first time since . . . a long time. So long,
in fact, that Isaac practically had to snap them out of stiff-
ness as if he were activating a glow stick. Even then, they
didn't fit him, nor did any of his belts – he's had to fish out
one of Mary's, a garish yellow chequerboard number from
her short-lived *Clueless* phase. Somehow, he still looks more
dignified than Egg.

What? It's not like you can waltz into a suburban town
centre with a bug-eyed monster by your side and expect
people not to notice, so Isaac has had to take precautions to
ensure that Egg doesn't cause panic. Rooting through the
bin bags of soon-to-be-discarded clothes and the furthest
recesses of his bedroom wardrobes, here's what he's settled
on. Egg is strapped to Isaac's chest in a hastily fashioned
papoose, so as to make him look like a human baby. While
it would have been cruel to make him go full egg, Isaac has
stuffed Egg's arms into a tightly wrapped blanket to prevent
them flopping down on to the pavement and tripping Isaac
up. While doing so, he made sure to use one of Egg's stubby
hands to ruffle his own hair, just in case. No vision presented

itself. Now Egg is in his papoose, with his face just about visible above the blanket, Isaac has covered his large eyes in an even larger pair of plastic sunglasses Mary bought during her Audrey Hepburn era. This leaves only the tufting top of Egg's bright white head, which Isaac has covered up with a novelty sun hat which Mary once bought Isaac from a fishing shop on a trip to Mingulay. **Women Want Me, Fish Fear Me** it says in bold letters above the brim. With Egg strapped to his chest, Egg's list in his pocket and Mary's clothes in a bin bag clutched in one hand, Isaac takes a final look in the hallway mirror before he leaves. Beneath his sunglasses, Egg scowls.

'It's better than stuffing you in a rucksack,' Isaac says.

Afraid that Egg will find a way to free his arms and flail them in protest, Isaac wastes no time in flinging himself out of the front door, down the front path and on to the pavement outside. He regrets his decision before he reaches the street. Like a baby bird out of its nest, he feels overcome. Normally by this point, he's battened himself down in his car. Normally, he's definitely pointing that car in the opposite direction to the centre of town, driving straight past Dr Abbass's office and on, on, on to the only other person that Isaac goes to see, but never admits he's visited. Guilt crackles over Isaac's skin like an electric current, and he almost finds himself buckling against his car. It's cloudy, but the sun still seems impossibly bright. It's near-silent, but the street still seems impossibly loud. Drivers scream past like fighter jets and cherry blossom petals rain down like artillery fire. Isaac does his best to keep his head. He trips, stumbles, but regains his balance before he hits the ground. Eyes screwed up, he orients himself to face in the right direction. Then, one careful step after another, he begins to claw his way to town. He grimaces at a whistling postman and nods at a baguette-toting passer-by with a monumental ginger beard. He suspects this may be the saxophonist, but he's too disoriented to investigate further. Both men watch Isaac with raised eyebrows and slightly open mouths, but Isaac pays no attention. He concentrates on forging on. By the time he's reached the end of the road, his breathing has at least returned to non-panic-attack levels. While dizzy, he's no longer falling over, and he's now managing to stand without holding on to street signs or strangers' fences. He takes a deep breath in, straightens up and exhales. You've got this, he tells himself. 'You've got this,' Egg presumably echoes, but his mouth is covered by the blanket so his words come out as a barely audible 'MmgGfhmm'.

At the end of Isaac's quiet cul-de-sac, he turns left on to a similarly leafy but slightly steeper residential street. Right at the end, left again, then round the corner and he's in town. By this point, he's sweating. It's partly because of the weight of the bin bag full of gym shoes and leather jackets. It's partly the nerves that come with strapping a strange creature to your chest and smuggling it down a busy suburban high street. Mostly, though, it's town itself, a place the entire layout of which may as well be a map of Mary Moray. For Isaac, these streets are a criss-cross of places where he and she used to walk together, drink together, eat together, exist together. He's not even at the southernmost edge of the town centre and he's already walked past the estate agents who sold them their house, the newsagent who delivers their papers, their favourite butcher, their least-favourite baker. He can't escape her. She's everywhere. Look, his brain says. There she is, giggling at the window table of the overpriced Italian deli because she can't eat garlic prawns without the oil dribbling down her chin. And look, there she is again: loitering outside the off-licence because she's sent you in to buy beer. She's left her ID at home and she's optimistically worried that they'll mistake her for seventeen. Can you see her? She's browsing for books on the ten-pence-a-volume rack outside the old bookshop, despite the fact she's never once found a book worth buying, for all the times she's tried. She's waiting for a bus. She's flagging down a taxi. She's peering out of the top window of the wine bar. She's mouthing something out of the basement window of the nail salon. *I'll be five minutes*, she's saying. *Wait for me.* Isaac can feel himself getting overwhelmed again. He feels fragile, like a shell. He remembers worrying about a yolk spillage, that night he first found Egg. Swallowing thickly, wiping his brow with his free hand, Isaac makes a hard left into the charity shop. With a considerable amount of effort, he manages to hand over the bag full of Mary's clothes.

'Is that a wickle baby?'

The woman behind the counter leans in for a closer look at the child strapped to Isaac's front. Even with Egg's yellow skin and bug eyes concealed, there's something inherently creepy about the egg-shaped bundle strapped to him, wearing a grown man's hat and staring ever ahead through a stand-offish pair of a grown woman's sunglasses. The woman's face drops.

'He's sleeping,' Isaac says.

Isaac emerges from the shop. Free of the weight of Mary's belongings, he feels that perhaps he made a huge mistake. He almost turns back, but shuts his desperation away. He focuses on feeling lighter. He doesn't exactly float down the high street, but he doesn't stumble, either. He's unbothered by the light and the noise, and he's even mostly unbothered by the fact that Egg is getting restless and poking his yellow fingers out of his papoose in an attempt to try to remove his Audrey Hepburn sunglasses. Each time, Isaac pokes the roving hand back into its blanket, while patting Egg encouragingly on top of his fisherman's hat to reassure him that it won't be long until he's free. Isaac weaves around a pair of arguing octogenarians and presses the button at the pelican crossing. Distracted by Egg's roaming hands and unused to navigating traffic, he's almost flattened by a bus as he goes to cross the road without looking. He survives, loudly apologises, then crosses the road. He pushes into the hardware shop through its heavy door, navigating his way through a precarious display of plant pots and brooms which bear down on him from above and around the entrance.

'What you looking for, mate?'

Egg pipes up beneath his blanket, attempting to squeak

'*Batteries*', but it sounds more like '*Babwheeze*'. Isaac coughs to cover him up, then takes the screwed-up list from his pocket and unfurls it. Meanwhile, the man behind the counter flicks his eyes over the pretend child strapped to Isaac's chest. He coughs, looks away, feigns being busy.

'AA batteries,' says Isaac, reading from the list.

'Yep, got those.' He fetches some.

'Gaffer tape.'

'Yep, got that.' He fetches some.

'Paperclips.'

'Yep, here you go.' He fetches some.

Isaac squints at the list. In the pause, Egg squeaks again. '*Wayzer bem*,' he seems to be saying, beneath the blanket. The man looks back down at the baby, but Isaac coughs and regains his attention.

'Laser pen.'

'Laser pen?'

'Laser pen.'

'I'll have a look,' he says, frowning. After a while, he finds one at the bottom of a dusty old bargain bin. 'What next?'

'Fertiliser,' Isaac says. 'Tomato fertiliser.'

'Yep, we've got some outside.' He fetches some.

'And finally,' Isaac says. 'Garden gnome.'

'Garden gnome?'

'Garden gnome.'

'What kind?'

Isaac looks back down at the list. 'Any,' he says.

The man heads back outside and fetches a couple to choose from. Once he's back by the till, having filled a plastic bag with the items on Egg's list, the shop assistant tries to enquire about the hat-and-sunglasses-clad infant gurgling on Isaac's front.

'What's his name?' the man says, leaning over to inspect the baby. When he gets closer, he visibly shudders and quickly averts his eyes.

'Eg— Edgar,' Isaac says, pulling away with the plastic bag in hand. He notices the assistant's haunted face. 'He's sleeping.'

Further up the high street, past Mary's old dentist and Isaac's second-favourite pub, is Isaac's barber's. He has a sudden flashback to standing in this same spot, screaming in terror, wearing his dressing gown and not much else. His spine tingles, and he cringes at the memory. He walks straight past it, turns left into the alleyway, and hastily removes Egg from his papoose.

'Sorry about this,' Isaac says.

Back at the door of the barber's, Isaac mouths a silent prayer, holds his breath, and heads inside. His entrance is announced by a tinkling bell above the door.

'Isaac!' says Tommy. He looks surprised.

'Hello,' Isaac says, the warmth of Tommy's greeting making him feel uncomfortable. He deposits the heavy plastic bag by the door. The gnome inside hits the tiles with a *clunk*, and the egg inside with it squeaks like an agitated dog toy. Isaac masks the sound with a loud cough, as if to further announce his arrival.

'I am here for a haircut,' he says, alien that he is.

Tommy blinks down at the near-bursting plastic bag, then gestures to an empty chair. 'OK, take a seat,' he stutters.

Isaac falls heavily into the chair. There's a long pause, as Tommy surveys Isaac's unkempt appearance. He looks like he wants to say something, but he stops himself. He looks like he wants to say something else, but this time Isaac does the stopping for him.

'I'm fine,' says Isaac. 'How are you?'

Tommy hadn't asked. Having presumably read one of the local papers in a stack by the door, Tommy will already know that Isaac is far from fine. Isaac thinks of the 'Dog Suicide Bridge'. What headline might they have used to succinctly sum up his own suffering? Isaac shakes the thought away, shakes his knee against the barber's chair, shakes his head at the mere sight of Tommy's sad smile. He wishes he hadn't come here. Tommy fiddles with a pair of scissors, gives Isaac some earnest eye contact in the mirror.

'Look, mate . . .' he says. 'I've been meaning to reach out. Ever since I saw you a couple of months ago, out on the street. You were—'

'It's fine,' Isaac says. His chest tightens.

'I was so sorry to hear about—'

'It's fine,' Isaac says. His ears are ringing. 'I'm fine.'

'Are you?'

The question falls like a scissor blow on the back of Isaac's head. Tommy used to listen to him so intently and nod so sagely that it'd seem as if he'd forgotten he was cutting Isaac's hair at all. They were friends, probably. Isaac would talk to Tommy about anything. Yet he couldn't talk to Tommy about this. Isaac's whole body has tensed up. Even if he wanted to answer the question, he feels gagged. The things Tommy wants to hear about are locked in an attic to which Isaac has hidden the key. Isaac tells a tiny portion of the truth, once a week, to Dr Abbass. He lies to everyone else, himself included.

'I'm OK,' Isaac lies. 'I'm just tired. From work.'

In truth, Isaac hasn't worked in months. The spot in front of his door where the snowdrift of letters once was is now populated mostly by credit-card bills and threats to turn off his electricity. He doesn't feel much like drawing, and injuring his hand has given him the perfect excuse not to. He really *is* too tired, too busy with Egg. He's got one more place to go after the barber's – the pawn shop, with his watch and a handful of Mary's jewellery. The thought of having to do so is already pre-emptively triggering another mind blank.

Tommy tries a different tack. 'What happened to your hand?'

Isaac stretches the hand out in front of him. The fingers are still trembling slightly, the scars at the base of them still purplish-red. Judging by the zigzag pattern of scabs across his knuckles, he must have had stitches. Imagine that.

'Work injury,' Isaac says.

Tommy knows that Isaac is an illustrator, but doesn't

push the subject any further. He looks pained, as if he wants to help but knows he's fighting a losing battle. He drops his eyes, picks at a comb.

'Well, if you want to talk . . .' he says.

He leaves the sentence open, as if he knows it's hopeless. There's a pause. Isaac says nothing. His stony eyes stare into the middle distance. Tommy coughs, forces a smile.

'Let's put a bib on you.'

Without saying anything else, Tommy shrouds Isaac in a black cloth, which he fixes around Isaac's neck with papery white tape. Tommy still looks troubled, but regains his composure whenever he notices Isaac looking at him. He straightens up. He smiles. Then he grabs a tuft of Isaac's shaggy beard, a spiral of Isaac's unruly hair. Though he seems to want to say a thousand other things, he sticks to the basics.

'What we gonna do with this?' he says. 'The usual?'

Isaac considers 'the usual'. He stares at his thick beard and his wild hair and the spiderweb of worry lines on his face, worry lines which weren't there last time he sat in this chair. He stares at the plastic bag in his peripheral vision, from which an anthropomorphic egg is trying to wriggle free. That wasn't there, either. The usual, Isaac realises, is no longer an option.

'Just make me look human again,' he says.

With a freshly done fade and a face free of stubble, Isaac feels like he's shed his skin. He feels free, and no doubt Egg feels even freer. Here in the park with barely anyone around – it *is* the middle of a weekday – Isaac has allowed him out of the confines of both papoose and plastic bag, a treat which ensures Egg won't even ask about their pawn-shop detour. It's almost T-shirt weather, and Isaac and Egg celebrate the sunshine by sharing the kind of blissful afternoon most friends could only dream of. They get ice creams from the ice-cream van: a Flake 99 for Isaac and a Fab for Egg, Egg hiding behind a bush while Isaac hands over the cash. The creature experiences brain freeze for the first time, and the experience upends him and leaves him wriggling on his back. They go to the kids' park. It's fairly quiet, and the swings are just about secluded enough to hide them from the other, more authentic, families. Isaac quietly pushes Egg in the swing, which is all fun and games until his long arms get so tangled up that Isaac worries he'll have to alert the fire brigade.

Once Egg has been untangled, they wander home via the farm on the edge of the park. If town really were a map of Mary Moray, this would be right at its centre. It's the farm he and Mary used to go to, in order to make vague plans for their own. It's the farm on which Mary would spend whole days, chipping in, mucking out. Here, around the whinnying animals and the wide-eyed children, she felt more at home than in any ostentatious wine bar or over-priced Italian deli.

It's funny, isn't it, she'd said once, with a smile. *The thing that makes me most homesick is the overpowering odour of manure.*

Isaac buys some miscellaneous feed in a brown-paper bag, and – when the coast is clear – he frees Egg to allow him the opportunity to feed the animals. Egg is frightened by them at first, hiding behind Isaac's legs, but his long arms come in handy as he tentatively offers handfuls to the goats and the donkeys and the pigs. Eventually, he enjoys it. Here, among beasts, it strikes Isaac just how unlike an animal Egg actually is. He watches and he considers and he reflects, like a human. He can almost talk like one, although certain consonant-heavy words are scuppered by the fact he has no teeth. Like the word he tries to say when he turns to Isaac, standing by the fence of a muddy enclosure, staring at a smattering of aggressive-looking geese. The geese posture at Egg, and Egg gets great satisfaction out of blowing endless raspberries in their direction. Eventually, the geese become bored and waddle away.

'*Bibbub?*' Egg says, to Isaac. He always sounds like he has the world's worst cold, but Isaac is getting better at understanding him.

'No gibbons here,' Isaac says. 'Maybe at a zoo. Not here.'

Egg turns back to the fence and stares through the slats. The geese have all but disappeared. He shifts on his little yellow feet and smacks his little yellow lips.

'*Wawooo,*' he says, sadly.

Egg perks up on the way home, despite the fact he's been stuffed back into his papoose and once again hidden under Isaac's hat. At least this time he's not being forced to wear sunglasses, mainly because he flung them into the pig enclosure while Isaac wasn't looking. Isaac is similarly perky, perhaps owing to the spring sun setting on his freshly shaven face, or the haircut which has lifted a weight from his head. Even with the heft of the garden gnome and a full bottle of fertiliser in his plastic bag, Isaac walks with a spring in his step. Egg, meanwhile, *ooooooo*s almost every single thing they pass. He *ooooooo*s a street lamp stuck all over with stale chewing gum. He *ooooooo*s a milky-eyed pug so obese and so ancient that it has to be pushed in a buggy. And he *ooooooo*s Isaac's house, which he's never seen from the outside, admiring the unruly bushes in need of a prune and the towering, pastel-bricked facade which looks like it's being squeezed in an architectural line-up by the burly shoulders of the houses on either side. As Isaac steps on to the front path, he isn't admiring the facade. He's looking at the package on the doorstep.

'What's that?' he says, as much to himself as to Egg.

Taking this as an instruction, Egg pokes both hands out of the papoose and allows them to flop on to the ground below. They move like dropped rolls of toilet paper, skidding towards the door in a constant unrolling motion until they bounce against the parcel. At the door at the other end of the path, the yellow hands feel around until they grasp either side of the brown-paper package. Then they pick it up and retract, bringing the package to a stop in front of Egg's and Isaac's eyes.

'*Eh bah blime ooo odda goob gibe,*' Egg says. '*Wub woy.*'

Isaac realises that he's reading a label, which is attached to a green ribbon around the tall, flat parcel. Isaac grabs the label between thumb and forefinger, then reads it himself.

'To remind you of the good times,' he reads aloud. 'Love, Joy.'

He says nothing. He checks the coast is clear, then releases Egg from his papoose. He unlocks the front door and opens it, depositing the plastic bag on the floor by Mary's shoes. As Egg plods off into the kitchen, Isaac takes a seat at the bottom of the stairs. He reads the label again, undoes the ribbon and carefully unsheaths the package from its brown paper. Underneath is a black frame, about as tall as Egg and twice as wide. Inside the frame, beneath glass, is a black-and-white collage. It's the pictures of himself and Mary that Isaac sent to Joy, plus plenty more, pictures he's never seen before, pictures he didn't even know still existed. One from their first book launch, cradling *That's Not a Dog* like it's a baby. One from a Christmas pub crawl, the pair of them holding a fake baby, dressed up as Joseph and, well, Mary. One from Scotland more recently, a cloudy June day on the bridge, just after Mary had very nearly managed to push Isaac into the water below. It's a whole montage of Isaac and Mary, and it's devastating in how perfect it is. Isaac notices a peculiar, unfamiliar feeling rising in his chest, and for a moment he's worried that he's going to vomit over the frame. It's only when the first tear drops that he realises the feeling is something else entirely. He's crying. When was the last time he cried?

It must be weeks. He screws up his face, balls his fists over his eyes and bawls like a baby. Great, hacking sobs envelop his whole body, and tears stream down his cheeks with such velocity that he feels as if they might drown him. He cries and he cries and he cries, and he wonders if he'll ever stop feeling like this. Then he stands up, wipes his eyes and hangs the frame in place of the mirror on the hallway wall. He goes to get a tissue, and to check on Egg.

'I'm just going to call Joy,' Isaac says, after blowing his nose. He plonks the plastic bag down on the kitchen table, at which Egg is sitting patiently. 'You work your magic on this stuff, then we'll phone home.'

It sounds strange to say out loud. He feels nervous about the thought of Egg leaving. He shakes his head, takes out his phone and dials Joy instead. He thanks her. He cries some more. He tells her about his haircut, all the while keeping an eye on Egg, who is watching motionlessly from his seat at the kitchen table. Isaac nods at the bag. Egg does not move. When Isaac hangs up, he gestures at the bag again. Nothing.

'What are you doing?' he says to Egg.

Egg simply nods at the phone in Isaac's hand.

'I need this,' Isaac says. He pictures Egg taking the device apart, gaffer-taping it to a flour-and-fertiliser-filled gnome and studding it with paperclips. Then he sighs, and reluctantly hands the phone over. 'Please don't damage it beyond repair.'

Egg makes Isaac check that the aerial outside the upstairs bathroom window is properly fixed in place. It is. Egg makes

Isaac charge his phone to one hundred per cent battery, then remove the battery, blow on it, then put the battery back in. He does. Only then does Egg take the phone, giving Isaac a secretive look, turning it over in his chubby little hands. Egg clears his throat. He looks at the screen. Then he jabs in some jumbled numbers with his sausage fingers and puts it to his ear. Or, the space at the side of his head, where his ear would be. Does Egg have ears? Did he just dial a phone number? Isaac can't ask either question, because Egg is already speaking. A short conversation ensues, of which Isaac only captures Egg's half.

Bab!

Eb bee. Wob wab.

D'ah. D'ah d'ah d'ah.

Obie. Dee bah doo.

Wawooo.

Egg hangs up. He looks pleased. Isaac's mouth hangs open a little. He looks from Egg to the phone, from the phone to Egg.

'What was that?'

'*Ebb bobe bobe.*'

'Egg phone home?' Egg hasn't even seen the film. He

just knows the phrase from Isaac. Isaac points at the plastic bag on the table, still untouched. His voice is high-pitched. 'Why did you make me buy all that stuff if you could just use my phone?'

Egg looks at the bag. Then he looks back at Isaac, and actually smirks.

'*Bubby*,' he says, shrugging. *Funny*. As if to clarify this, he blows yet another raspberry.

Isaac stares for a while, unsure what to say. Isaac used to pull pranks, but it's been a long time since he was on the receiving end of one. The planning, the homemade aerial, the items which were the reason for the entire trip to town. Isaac realises now that they never needed any of it. Egg was having him on. Isaac looks back at the bag, at the phone, then at the raspberry-blowing egg. He notices a similar feeling in his chest again, a peculiar rising which makes him think he's about to burst into tears in front of Egg. But he isn't. His face tingles, his eyes smart, but his mouth contorts itself into an unnatural mirror of Egg's smirk. The smirk spreads into a smile, which spreads further into a grin, and suddenly Isaac is hooting deeply and resonantly, from his very core. He doubles over. He holds on to the back of one of the kitchen chairs. Isaac is crying again, but they're not tears of sadness. For the first time in months, Isaac is laughing. *Really* laughing. He laughs and he laughs and he laughs, and he feels like scooping up the egg and hugging him tight to thank him for giving him his first good day in God-knows-when. But he doesn't.

'That *is* funny,' he says instead, when he finally straightens up and wipes his eyes. Then he crosses to the fridge and pulls out two untouched, unopened beers which have been gathering dust since before Isaac last laughed. Isaac turns to Egg, who blinks expectantly. He gestures towards the back door.

'Open that,' he says. 'And take out those chairs. I think it's time for a toast.'

Egg starts thwapping towards the toaster, but Isaac stops him and explains the other meaning of the word. So, always learning, Egg bypasses the bean cupboard and instead heads straight for the right-hand drawer of the console table beneath the living-room TV, where he's learned Isaac keeps the keys. Isaac isn't even paying attention. He's checking his phone's call log to see who Egg dialled. The digits aren't any symbols he recognises. The area code is '+ō♭'. Isaac contemplates calling the number again, but doesn't want to get stuck in a conversation with Egg's mother. If her son is anything to go by, he assumes she's formidable.

'*Dose*,' says Egg. *Toast*. But not as he knows it. He's opened the back door, set out two chairs and even retrieved a bottle opener from the drawer next to the hob. He goes to hand it to Isaac, but hesitates.

'I know,' Isaac says. 'I'm not supposed to. But one night can't hurt.'

Egg shrugs and hands Isaac the opener. Isaac opens both bottles. He goes to hand one to Egg, but now he's the one hesitating.

'How old are you?' he asks.

Before he can get an answer, Egg has grabbed the bottle with a viper-like strike of one arm and headed outside. Isaac shrugs and follows him, taking a seat on the cushioned chair opposite the one already taken. It's dark. The sun has all but set, and what remains is a deep purple above the trees blending into a rich indigo overhead. Isaac and Egg sit at a trestle table on the patio, beers in hand, and survey their surroundings in silence: a freshly mown lawn, a shed, some unkempt trees and the vastness of the night sky above them. Isaac, as freshly shorn as the grass, looking like a human being again. And the egg, fur still unruly, looking about as alien as he always does when sitting comically undersized in an adult earthling's chair. Isaac stares at him. Egg's orb-like eyes reflect the stars as if they contain every single one. The skin of his face is as yellow as the sun, cratered all over like the surface of the moon. Even out here, in the darkness, his fur still seems to glow. Isaac half remembers reading an article in a men's magazine, a dubious list of things which purported to help with low moods. Sunlight was one of them. Golden retrievers another. Egg is somehow both. Isaac and Mary did always want a dog. Having a little ball of sunshine around on a gloomy day is never a bad thing. Isaac decides, with a faint smile, that Egg is a good egg. Then, with a lump in his throat, he realises just how much he doesn't want Egg to leave.

'Did you manage to make contact?' Isaac asks.

'D'ah.'

'And you're going?'

'*D'ah.*'

'When?'

'*Borrow.*'

'Tomorrow!?'

'*D'ah.*'

Isaac tries his best to hide his upset. 'Why so soon?' he says.

Egg merely shrugs.

Isaac breathes out slowly. He feels as if he might fall off his chair. He feels the old chasm opening in his chest. He stuffs the emotions back down, speaking with a voice which is suddenly a notch deeper.

'A toast, then,' he says.

'*Dose.*'

'To those we've lost.'

'*Dobie doss.*'

'And new friends we've found.'

'*Doo bendy bound.*'

They clink bottles. Or, Isaac clinks Egg's, and Egg watches suspiciously as he does so. He even recoils a little, as if worried Isaac will take the bottle away. Isaac smiles, takes a swig of his own beer. Then he sighs.

Don't go, he wants to say.

'How are you getting back?' he says.

'*Boobs.*'

Isaac looks at Egg, eyebrow raised. Egg blinks, then repeats himself. He lengthens the *o*, goes to considerable effort to pronounce the *w*. He's never looked more like a monkey.

'*Woooooooooooobs*,' he splutters.

'Woods,' Isaac says, nodding. 'You're getting picked up from the woods?'

'*D'ah.*'

'Got you.' Isaac drinks some more beer.

'*Biff*?'

Isaac chuckles, but there isn't much humour in it. 'Yes, of course I can give you a lift.'

Egg nods in appreciation, then takes a large sip of his own beer. He chokes, screws up his face and lets out a disgusted '*bleh*'.

Isaac smiles again. Sighs again. 'What am I going to do without you?'

Egg doesn't answer. Isaac takes another, longer sip of beer, this time mainly to quell the rising panic in his throat. That's it, then. Tomorrow, Egg is going to leave him. Tomorrow, Isaac is going to be all alone. What will he do? Isaac watches Egg take a sip of his own beer, feigning enjoyment this time. At least *he* won't be alone. Isaac can't help but envy him. What is he thinking? What's going on behind those cosmos-sized eyes? He imagines excitement. He imagines Egg thinking about his family, about finding a new home. He doesn't for a second imagine what Egg is actually thinking about, because locks and keys and secrets behind doors are, ironically, locked away deep inside Isaac's own head. Unbeknownst to Isaac, Egg had two questions he wanted to ask him. And though he's more or less gained the linguistic proficiency with which to ask them, Egg has now decided he may as well bypass the asking and figure out the answers for himself. Egg now knows that Isaac keeps his keys in the right-hand drawer of the console table beneath the living-room TV. And if that's where all the other keys are kept, there's a good chance that's where Egg will find the key that opens the door to the room at the top of the house.

Tomorrow, Egg is going to use that key. Tomorrow, Isaac's house of cards is going to come tumbling down.

EIGHT

I f this were one of Mary Moray's stories, illustrated by Isaac Addy, Egg would never open the door at the top of the house. Or perhaps he would, but it would be filled with farm animals, friendly gibbons, plates of beans on toast and all the other things that Egg has come to love during his time on earth. If this were one of Mary's stories, Egg wouldn't leave, and Mary wouldn't have left, either, and Isaac wouldn't need to keep things locked away because he'd be perfectly happy, ever after. Good things happen to other people, don't they? So why does it seem like only bad things happen to him? This isn't one of Mary's stories, and life isn't a children's book. Egg is going to open that door, and the flimsy reality that Isaac has spent the last few months constructing is going to be blown apart when he does. So much for a coping mechanism. So much for a happy ending.

The day begins like any good picture book, with the protagonist waking from a dream. In it, Isaac imagined he was in a spaceship with Egg by his side, hurtling towards the mothership while 'Raindrops Keep Fallin' on My Head' boomed out of the radio. Isaac knew he was in a dream, because even if spaceships had radios, he's sure they wouldn't have the signal for Smooth FM. He wakes. His heart sinks at the absence of Mary, but it doesn't sink quite as much as it did a few months ago. He imagines it's like learning to walk with a missing leg. Then his heart sinks again, remembering that today is supposed to be Egg's last day on earth. Isaac sits up in bed and tries to ascertain what time it is from the sun spilling in through the curtains. It's no use. It's rising earlier and earlier every day, now. Instead, he yawns and turns his attention to the door. Egg should be arriving any minute. From now. Any minute from now. Isaac frowns, leans on his elbow, tries to peek around the crack in the door. No sign of Egg. Granted, he's long since stopped screaming, but there'd normally at least be a *thwap thwap thwap* to signal that he's coming down the landing with breakfast. He racks his brain for something, and comes up with something bad. Yes, today is the day that Egg is supposed to be leaving. But Egg never gave him an exact time. Isaac gulps, jumps out of bed, dons his dressing gown and sprints down the stairs.

Egg isn't in the kitchen. Egg isn't in the living room, either. Egg isn't in the hallway, nor the downstairs bathroom, nor the cupboard under the stairs, where he sometimes likes to build forts out of the tins of beans. Looking out of the kitchen window, Isaac can't see Egg in the garden, and there's no way he's hiding in that well-mown grass, nor the locked shed beyond it. Where on earth could he be? Or, if not earth, where else? Isaac's heart is racing as he begins to wonder whether Egg has left, for good, without saying goodbye. But he couldn't get to the woods on his own. Could he? He can't drive. Can he? There's still so much that Isaac doesn't know about Egg. So much he never will.

Thunk.

Isaac smiles. He exhales. He knows exactly where Egg is.

Thunk.

Isaac finds Egg in Mary's office, once more pulling books out of the bookshelf and allowing them to tumble to the floor. This time, he's at least stopped at two.

'What are you doing?' Isaac says, arms crossed, from the doorway.

'*Wee bin.*'

'You're not reading. You're just throwing books on the floor.'

'*D'oh.*'

Egg slaps his forehead. Isaac reckons he's trying to be funny again. Crouching down to Egg's height, Isaac picks up the most recently toppled book, the one that's landed by his feet. He looks at the cover.

UNDONE
under
LONDON
Written by Mary Moray
Illustrated by Isaac Addy

It was Mary's least favourite of theirs. A story about a journey into a secret city beneath the city, where Battersea was a literal sea of bats, and so on. She didn't like the finished product, but not because she realised halfway through that Neil Gaiman had already written basically the same thing. She disliked it because of the patronising title slapped on it by her publishers – bigwigs who'd decided that 'Undon', the name of the city under London, would be 'confusing for younger readers'. They'd changed it to 'Undone' with an *e* and infuriated her in the process. *It ruins the whole syntax*, she'd roared. *Since when did we live in Lon-done?* The latter syllable pronounced like 'dome' in a faux-English accent. Isaac had laughed so much that he'd given himself hiccups.

'I'm guessing you want one final lesson?' Isaac says.

'*D'ah.*' Egg nods enthusiastically. He picks up the other book on the floor, turns it over, does his best to read the title aloud. '*Fwah fwah fwah fwah.*'

Isaac wipes Egg's spittle from his face. Then he takes the book and reads the title himself. He smiles. It was always a bit of a tongue-twister.

FRED FOUNDS
A FARM
Written by Mary Moray
Illustrated by Isaac Addy

While Isaac was more of a *That's Not a Dog* fan, *Fred Founds a Farm* was always Mary's favourite. A story about a cramped city-dweller turning the shed into an animal sanctuary. What could be more Mary than that? Isaac smiles, flicking the book open to its first page. Then he sits cross-legged on the floor and begins to read aloud.

One summer day
To his parents' alarm
Fred pinched some money
and founded a farm

Egg sits bunched up opposite him, not so much like a child at a library reading, more like a bean bag that the child might sit on. His pudgy yellow mouth is set in its usual perpetual grimace, but he blinks up at Isaac with mesmerised eyes. Isaac turns the page past his own illustration of a muddy-kneed boy, then continues reading.

He started with chickens
And one or two pigs
And a half-baked enclosure
of mud, leaves and twigs

Isaac looks up from the book, out of the window, and sighs. Then he looks down at Egg, who seems to be trying to form another sentence with his puckered little mouth.

'What?' Isaac says.

'Wobbid ah bow?'

'What's it about?' Isaac thinks on this for a moment. 'Building a home, I guess. Finding a family.'

'Ah,' says Egg. *'Wawooo.'*

Isaac continues staring at Egg. He half opens his mouth, half closes the book. A thought comes to him.

'Does *Wawooo* mean family?' he says. 'Does *Wawooo* mean home?'

'D'ah.'

'Which one?'

'Bobe.'

'Both?'

'D'ah.'

Isaac stares at Egg for a minute. Egg stares back, galaxies swirling in his eyes. It's as if he's looking into Isaac's soul. It's unnerving, but somehow soothing. Isaac feels calmed, momentarily forgetting that Egg will be gone by the end of

the day. He remembers. He trembles. He keeps on reading.
Egg sits in silence as Isaac reads him the rest of the book.
He drags it out as long as possible, and feels a catch in his
throat when he reaches the last page.

And his mum said:
'For now, Fred,
let's get you to bed'
For the farm in Fred's shed
had been all in Fred's head

Egg has no such emotional response. He's already barged past
Isaac, on to the landing, and begun to march down the stairs.
He's clearly ready for his breakfast, if the fact he's yelling
'*Beebs! Beebs! Beebs!*' is anything to go by. Isaac shakes his
head, clambers to his feet with knees that click, then puts the
book back in its rightful place on Mary's bookshelf. Before
he leaves the office, he can't help but field a glance at Mary's
yellow notebook. It still lies untouched, at the edge of the
desk where she'd left it. Her final big idea. The book she'd
never write. He considers opening it, but he already knows
what's inside. The contents of the notebook try to burrow up
to the surface of his brain, but Isaac is a master suppressor by
now. It's like whack-a-mole. He beats the intrusive thought
back down, then leaves the office. He follows Egg downstairs.

Breakfast is – as one would expect – beans on toast, eaten on the sofa. And though Isaac hasn't yet brought himself around to fully opening the blinds at the living-room window, they're at least at a half-slant, meaning some rays of sunshine can sneak in. Despite the weather, Isaac has already decided on the last film he wants to show Egg before Egg has to leave. He doesn't call it that, though, because acknowledging Egg's departure will make him panic. He merely turns on the TV and loads up the film in silence. A Christmas film, really, but he's sure Egg will make an exception since he's not sticking around for Christmas. Isaac's lip trembles. He turns up the volume. *It's a Wonderful Life*. His favourite. A flurry of snow welcomes them to Bedford Falls, a chorus of voices prays for the soul of their suicidal friend, and suddenly a man stands on a bridge in the middle of nowhere, one dark night in the middle of winter.

'*Eh woo!*' shouts Egg, jumping up and down on his sofa, pointing so hard that his yellow hand slaps the screen like a thrown fish.

'It's not me.'

'*D'ah!*' Egg says. '*Eh woo.*'

'You're only saying that because it makes you look good,' Isaac says. 'You think you're my guardian angel.'

'*D'ah,*' repeats Egg, with a self-satisfied nod.

'Lucky me,' scoffs Isaac. Despite his tone, he knows he actually means it.

Later, after it's happened, Isaac will try to understand it all from Egg's perspective. There must have been a reason for Egg to do what he did. There must have been something Isaac did wrong, for Egg to go behind his back and betray him like that. So, yes, he'll try to see things from Egg's point of view. He'll put himself in Egg's shoes. Or, Egg's shell. Here's what he'll see.

While Isaac watches the film, Egg pretends to watch the film, too. It's only when Isaac pauses to go and boil the kettle that Egg betrays what he's really been watching: the right-hand drawer at the top of the console table beneath the TV. Egg's a little embarrassed about this. You see, he meant to investigate the room at the top of the house last night, while Isaac was sleeping. But – despite himself – Egg fell asleep, too. What? It was a busy day. He liked the farm animals. The excitement got to him. So now, while Isaac fills the kettle from the tap, Egg decides to grasp another chance. He peers at the door into the kitchen to check that Isaac isn't watching. While Isaac searches for teabags, Egg slithers his arm over to the console table and up its shiny wooden side. And while Isaac realises that he's forgotten if Egg settled on seven or eight sugars for his perfect cup, Egg slides his hand over the handle of the drawer.

'How many sugars?' Isaac says, from the doorway.

Egg's arm pings backwards with elastic speed, knocking him over on to the pile of cushions at the sofa's edge. Luckily,

Isaac has not seen why, and assumes that Egg is just being Egg.

'*Dibe*,' squeaks Egg from under the cushions.

'Nine sugars. Got it.'

Having learned his lesson, Egg doesn't try again while Isaac is nearby. He sips his tea calmly, eats his teabag pensively and wonders when he might next get a chance to strike. His chance doesn't come during the film, not even towards the end when Isaac is tearing up and hiding his face behind a blanket as George's guardian angel informs him that 'No man is a failure who has friends'.

'That's my favourite line, in any film, ever,' says Isaac, his voice high-pitched and wobbly.

Egg nods, stealing a glance towards the drawer while Isaac wipes his eyes on the blanket. Isaac has already returned his gaze to the screen by the time Egg considers taking action. He doesn't get another chance until the film is over, nor does he get one during snack-time – an old tin of tuna, halved – nor during the time spent watching *The Breakfast Club* afterwards. Isaac has a surprisingly enduring bladder, Egg realises, so his toilet breaks are few and far between. Egg bites his tiny lip. Egg taps his tiny feet on the sofa cushions. If Egg had a tiny watch on his tiny wrist, he'd be checking that watch impatiently. Time is running out, and he knows he needs to get to the bottom of what's in the top room if he's ever going to feel comfortable leaving Isaac on his own. Wouldn't you? The man's a mess. He doesn't seem like he'll cope well on his own, despite all the faux optimism and the 'not looking back'. He's keeping especially busy today, presumably because he's upset about Egg leaving. Egg has noticed that, too. Even when their film ends, and Egg hopes that Isaac will announce that he's off for his afternoon nap, the man still wants to spend time with Egg. He's made a plan to ceremoniously finish crossing off the list. Isaac leads the way, and Egg rolls his eyes behind him when Isaac isn't watching. Still, he plods obligingly into the kitchen after Isaac.

Isaac takes the list down from the fridge. He hands Egg the Sharpie, then scoops him up with one arm. In this moment, Egg could easily enter Isaac's mind, and Isaac could enter Egg's. But Egg doesn't want that. When it happens, Egg sees only darkness. And though Egg wants to know what Isaac has been hiding in the room at the top of the house, the thought scares him. Egg would rather open that door himself than be sucked back into the black abyss behind Isaac's eyes.

'OK,' says Isaac. 'Let's do this.'

Egg is hovering at Isaac's height, now, a permanent marker in one stubby little fist. His free hand is still on the kitchen floor, and he briefly tries to send it back into the living room to retrieve the key from the drawer. It's not quite *that* long, though, so Egg grits his gums and obliges when Isaac hands him the list and tells him he's in charge of crossing-out. Isaac reads aloud, cradling Egg in the nook of his right arm. Egg uses his wobbly penmanship to strike off each item, glancing every so often back into the living room.

'We mowed the lawn, didn't we?' says Isaac.

'D'ah,' says Egg, fondly remembering the flavour of fresh-cut grass. He crosses out ~~Mow lawn~~.

'We sorted Mary's clothes, too.'

Egg nods. He crosses out ~~Sort Mary's clothes~~.

'And we donated the clothes,' Isaac says. 'So that can go.'

Egg crosses out ~~Donate clothes~~.

'Did we get a haircut?'

Egg feels the tufty hair on top of his head, notices that he hasn't, then slaps himself between the eyes. 'D'oh!'

'Not you, idiot,' says Isaac. 'Me. I did.'

Egg thinks, nods, crosses out ~~Get haircut~~.

'Clean Mary's office,' Isaac says, reading the next one aloud. 'Well, it's still a mess. Notebooks everywhere. And now books all over the floor.'

Egg chuckles mischievously.

'Yes, well done,' Isaac says. 'Cross it out. I think we can afford to leave it as is, for now.'

Egg crosses out ~~Clean Mary's office~~.

'There we go,' says Isaac, with a deep exhale and a satis-fied nod.

Egg worries about Isaac. Egg wonders what Isaac will do next. Egg knows that Isaac thinks he hasn't been a good brother, a good son, a good son-in-law. That if *no man is a failure who has friends*, Isaac is a bigger failure than he ever thought possible. Egg knows that though Isaac's been saying he'll **Call Esther** the decision seems at odds with the fact that Isaac still sometimes sleeps with the biscuit tin in his bed. Egg knows that though Isaac's been saying he'll *Start drawing again* his hand still shakes where the stitches were laid. He's been sneaking out more and more in the last few weeks, and the credit-card bills haven't stopped piling up by the front door. Egg knows that Isaac is far from fixed, that Isaac would rather he stayed. 'Why so soon?' Isaac had asked him. The answer lay in something Egg had heard the other day, in a conversation between Isaac and his sister on the other side of the wardrobe door. *You can't pretend the real world doesn't exist, Isaac.* Egg is from another place. His kind have always come and gone as they please. But only now has Egg realised that Isaac's path to being human again lies in other human beings, in time spent with his own people. He's doing more harm by staying than going. While Isaac's favourite quote is from *It's a Wonderful Life*, there's a line in *Mary Poppins* which has stuck with Egg ever since he and Isaac watched it, in the first weeks of his time on the sofa with his only human friend. *I shall stay until the wind changes.* And so shall Egg. But there's one thing he wants to do first.

'All done,' says Isaac.

'*D'oh*,' says Egg resolutely, flaring his nostrils. He taps his pen against the bottom of the list, at an item which remains conspicuously uncrossed.

Sort top room

Egg looks up at Isaac. As Isaac's eyes flicker over the sentence, his entire disposition changes. It's as if the mask showing his fair-weather face had been held in place with a single stitch, and that stitch has just been unpicked. His smile drops. His face sags. Worry lines creep around his mouth and eyes and cheeks like cracks in china, while a grey cloud passes over his eyes. Then the stitch is fixed as quickly as it was unpicked. His features are winched back up. As Isaac's face comes back together again, he tears the list out of Egg's hand.

'All done!' Isaac says again, his voice terrifyingly chirpy.

With one arm, he deposits Egg a little too roughly back on the floor. With the other, he screws up the list and throws it into the kitchen bin. Before Egg can protest, Isaac has already returned to the living room and turned his attention back to the TV. But halfway through *Fight Club* he seems to have a crisis of conscience, as he switches off the TV and faces Egg with a solemn, sombre expression. Egg thinks he's about to tell him where he disappears to, and what he's been hiding. But he isn't.

'Do you know what time it is?'

Egg doesn't. He hasn't told Isaac the time he plans to leave. Egg pushes out his bottom lip and shakes his head.

'I thought we'd have a final toast,' Isaac says. 'To say goodbye.'

Egg's eyes light up. He's developed a taste for beer since Isaac let him have one last night, so the thought makes his mouth water. He smacks his lips.

'Beans on toast, that is,' Isaac says. 'Our tradition.'

Egg stops smacking his lips. He masks his disappointment.

He can't deny that the thought is a sweet one, though, so he nods and follows Isaac back into the kitchen once again. Isaac cooks and chatters nonchalantly to Egg as he does so, about whether Egg wants to take some beans with him for the journey, about whether he'll be warm enough without a blanket. Egg has the impression that Isaac is hiding something – not just the usual things that he hides, but something else. Anxiety. Sadness. Though he's clearly scared of saying goodbye, his stiff upper lip grows stiffer with every minute closer to Egg's departure. Before Egg can offer to stay a little longer, Isaac has plonked two plates of beans on toast down on the table and started to eat his own. Egg takes a bite, then looks out of the kitchen window. The sun is setting on their time together, and the sky is turning a peculiar shade of yellowish-white, devoid of the warmth you'd expect in any normal sunset. The moon is already visible above the unkempt trees at the end of the garden. Beyond it, the first stars of the evening. And, somewhere beyond that, family. Home. Egg turns to Isaac, and realises that Isaac has been watching him. Isaac's toast is held static beside his mouth, beans in freefall down towards his plate. For the briefest of moments, Isaac looks desperately sad. Or, no, trapped. He seems to want to say something, but is unable, as if he's holding himself at gunpoint. His eyes plead with Egg. *I need to tell you something*, they seem to say. *I need to tell the truth.* Then Isaac's phone starts vibrating on the wooden tabletop, his mask is restored, and the opportunity is gone.

Isaac looks at the phone. Egg furrows his yellow brow,

and Isaac's eye twitches in response. It's that woman's name again.

'I need to take this,' he says.

He's about to leave the room, but Egg protests with two waving hands. This is his moment, although he won't let Isaac know that. It's now or never. Egg hops off his chair, grabs the plates and – with arms high above his head – deposits them into the sink. Then he waddles off through the door into the living room. Aware that Isaac is watching him, waiting for him to leave before he starts speaking, Egg makes a show of closing the door behind him. Isaac starts talking. Because they're now separated by several inches of wood, and because the saxophonist has just started tuning up again, Egg can once more only hear a smattering of the words Isaac is saying to whoever is on the other end of the phone.

better   no,

        emergency?

    is   OK?

                                complicated?

                sick   waiting

        listen!

The conversation is terse, and Isaac's voice is getting more and more strained behind the door. Egg has stopped listening. He's focusing all of his attention on the right-hand drawer of the console table beneath the TV, which calls to him from the other side of the room. Egg sneaks over the rug, skirts around the coffee table and, with one glance back at the closed kitchen door, pulls his dragging arms up towards the drawer. He opens it. A cloud passes over in the sky outside, sucking away all the light that had still been streaming through the cracks in the venetian blinds. A pause behind the door, presumably as Isaac listens to an answer he does not want to hear. Even the saxophonist is taking a pause. The room, no, the whole house, seems to be holding its breath. Then Egg's hand rises from the drawer clutching a set of keys. The cloud passes. The saxophonist continues to play. And Isaac continues to raise his voice in the kitchen.

'I don't understand!' he's shouting, now. 'You said things were looking better. You said things were going to be alright.'

In the hallway, Egg can hear Isaac more clearly. He sounds angry. He hears Isaac's chair scrape backwards from the table. He hears the more subtle scrape of Isaac's slippers as he paces back and forth on the kitchen tiles. Egg is petrified that Isaac is going to fling open the kitchen door in a rage and catch him here, yellow-handed, holding a set of keys he isn't supposed to be holding. So Egg hops up on to the bottom step and hides himself behind the banister. If he were a human, his heart would be racing. At least, like a human's, his mouth is dry. Though he's almost weightless, the bottom step still creaks uncomfortably beneath him, and he's sure he feels the banister tremble, as if in fear. The clouds outside are gathering swiftly overhead. Or perhaps the sun is just setting behind one of the houses opposite. Either way, the hallway is dim, verging on dark. The only light making it through the frosted window of the front door is unhappy, agitated. The whole sky seems to be worrying, and Egg could swear the walls of the house are worrying along with it. Above him, ahead of him, every stair creaks a warning. *Don't come up here*, they seem to say. *Don't do what you are about to do.* But Isaac is shouting even more loudly in the kitchen, and there's a desperation in his voice which makes Egg afraid. Putting two floors between himself and his host seems like the best option. So, swallowing thickly and clutching the set of keys in a tight, stubby fist, Egg climbs the stairs – something he's learned to do by throwing his arms ahead of him like grappling hooks, then winching himself up and up and up via the banister.

By the time he's reached the top of the stairs, Egg can barely make out what Isaac is saying. The sax seems to be getting louder and louder, squealing as if the saxophonist has got caught in a squall and is playing as a last-ditch attempt to get help before he sinks into the ocean depths. The whole house feels as if it's on a rough ocean, too. The stairs sway beneath Egg's puffy toes, and he feels the need to grip the banister tightly just to safely reach the first-floor landing. Up here, it's even darker than downstairs, although the last cold, yellow rays of sunlight are still trying to claw their way through the window of Mary's study opposite. The mood of the house is descending with the darkness, and Egg is sure he can hear a battering wind. Strange, because earlier it was perfectly still, but then the wind doesn't seem to be coming from outside. Egg looks into the study, at the books still strewn on the floor, and considers turning back. Then he takes a deep breath, pivots, and turns to face the second set of stairs. Although this can't consist of ten or more steps, the locked door at the top of them is shrouded almost entirely in shadow. While the walls around it creak and the carpet under Egg's feet bristles, this door is entirely silent, sucking away sound like the emptiness in the middle of a maelstrom. And though this silence is somehow scarier than anything else in this suddenly haunted house, the keyhole under the brass doorknob seems to exert a magnetic pull on the keys in Egg's hand. Egg can't help himself. He climbs the first step, then the second, then the third. Downstairs, Isaac has stopped shouting.

With some effort, Egg reaches the top of the stairs. He reaches the door. In the darkness, he holds on to the cold wall with a firm palm, as if he's worried the whole house is about to come apart at the seams. At least the walls have stopped moaning, and the carpet isn't quivering any more. In fact, the only thing trembling is Egg's hand, which shakes and shakes as it unfolds and reveals the set of keys it had been clasping so tightly. While Isaac's been running off to God-knows-where for days on end, Egg has been famil-iarising himself with the films Isaac never lets him watch when they're together. The sad films. The scary films. And, thanks to the scary films, Egg knows exactly what unhinged human beings keep behind locked doors. In *The Sixth Sense*, it's a malevolent ghost in the attic. In *Psycho*, it's the hotelier's decomposing mother in the basement. Egg is prepared for the worst. The wind is prepared, too: it's stopped howling. So is the saxophonist: he's stopped playing. The only sound in the darkness at the top of Isaac's house is the tinkling of the keys on the keyring as they make an uneasy journey out of Egg's palm and up towards the keyhole on the tall, silent door. The sound of a key entering a keyhole, a door failing to open. The nervous fumbling of more keys, then, finally, the right one turning in the lock. The unnerving groan of a brass doorknob being twisted, and the horrible squeal of a stiff door slowly opening.

When the door has opened fully, Egg stares into the room at the top of the house and tries to make sense of what he sees. Meanwhile, at the bottom of the stairs, Isaac Addy starts to climb.

If an alien came down to earth, there are a thousand everyday things it wouldn't recognise. To a human being, knowing what a spoon is, or an iron or a pack of cards, might be second nature. Yet to an alien who has never seen a spoon, or an iron or a pack of cards, understanding the purpose of these objects would entail an enormous cognitive leap. What is the meaning of a spoon? What could one possibly achieve with an iron? What use, besides decoration, is a 'pack of cards'? Just look at Egg: even now, after so long here, he still sees things every day that he doesn't quite understand. Yesterday, Egg saw a moped for the first time. The day before that, it was a yoga mat. Chalk those up with pineapples, shoehorns and the concept of 'rosé wine' on the list of things he has discovered in the last week alone. There is still so much about this world that Egg does not know, which is why it's understandable that there are certain things in the room at the top of the house that Egg can't even begin to understand. The newspaper on the floor, for example, or the flaking pots of long-unused paint. These things Egg doesn't understand. But the thing opposite, the main thing, the boxy wooden thing, the thing which is the centrepiece of the room? Egg has seen enough of them in kids' films and cartoons to understand what one is for.

The sun has set entirely behind Isaac's house, but the streetlights on the right and the moonlight on the left provide a ghostly sort of illumination in which Egg can see everything clearly. The room is a converted loft. Newly converted, if the fresh paint and the unused furniture is anything to go by. The ceiling slopes on one side, and each slanted wall has a circular window, one looking out on to the street and the other on to Isaac's garden. Inside the room, Egg surveys a wall which seems like a window of its own. He's not seen many paintings, and definitely none this big. He doesn't understand why the newspaper is there, laid down to protect the cream carpet. He doesn't understand the meaning of the paint, several pots of it, that has been used to create *this*. This, Egg doesn't know, is a mural. It covers the flat wall beyond the sole piece of furniture. And though it's dark in the room and the mural is half finished, it still manages to take Egg's breath away. It's a marvellous masterclass of colour and perspective, starting at the bottom with brown mud and green grass, spreading up into fields of corn and wheat which seem to extend into a seemingly endless distance. Egg knows the things in the foreground from his time spent with Isaac. He recognises the tractor from *Footloose*. He recognises the huge red barn from their adventure on the way back from town. And he recognises the animals from *Fred Founds a Farm*, though most of them are only some way to being complete. A pig is a head and half a body. A cow stands complete but for its spots. Two chickens run headless across the bottom of the wall, while a distant horse is all legs and little else. Isaac never finished the mural. For some reason, he decided to drop his paintbrush and lock the painting away for good. Perhaps that reason is something to do with the empty cot in the middle of the room.

'What are you doing up here?'

The voice is heavy, hoarse. It causes Egg to jump out of his fur. Closing his eyes and holding on to the doorframe for support, Egg turns slowly to meet his maker. He opens his eyes. He looks up. Even a few steps down from him, Isaac looms large. And, in the windowless, lightless stairway, he looms terrifying. There's nothing where his eyes were before: just black holes. His face is devoid of expression, devoid of anything, a featureless granite slab which hangs in the air above Egg, threatening all kinds of retribution. Standing over Egg, in the darkness, Isaac is merely an outline of a human being. A shadow of his former self. Egg shudders. Even in the darkness, he can see that Isaac isn't smiling.

'You have no right to be up here.'

What *is* he doing up here? Egg realises immediately that he doesn't have an answer. And, trapped in the doorway between Isaac and the barren room, he doesn't have an escape route, either. Egg looks back at the cot, at the mural, then up at Isaac. Isaac looks up at the cot, at the mural, then down at Egg. There's a long silence in which Egg scrambles to find the words to say, but he already knows it's too late. He knows where Isaac's been disappearing to. He knows what Isaac's been hiding. And, as Isaac's deafening silence crashes down on top of him, he knows too late that he was never supposed to know.

'Get out,' Isaac says, his voice trembling, its volume rising. One shaking hand points back into the shadows, down the stairs, towards the front door. 'Get out of my house.'

Egg is frozen to the spot. So, suddenly, Isaac ascends the last two steps and grabs hold of him roughly, his hand closing around the top of one skinny white arm. Isaac is yelling, now.

'Get out of—'

But Egg panics. Out of options, he allows that magic touch to work, one last time. Isaac has barely planted his feet on the top step when he feels it wrenched away beneath him. He is once more in Egg's head. Or, perhaps, Egg is in Isaac's. Wherever it is, that same black expanse opens up. Though one hand still grips Egg's arm and the other still grips the door at the top of the stairs, Isaac's stomach is barrel-rolling into the upper atmosphere until his eyes are no longer in his own house, or even on his planet. He floats and shudders and tries to catch his breath. He's angry, but in the darkness there's nowhere to direct his anger. He tries to focus. He tries to settle his breath. He tries to see something, anything. At first, there's nothing. Then there's that same pinprick in the distance, glowing like a distant star but floating closer and closer. Isaac expects the escape pod to appear, as it did before. But it's not the escape pod. It's a ball. No, a bundle. A bundle of rags, wrapped tightly into an egg shape. It's the bundle which, last time, was inside the pod. Isaac assumes it is Egg. But then the bundle moves closer, and he realises that it isn't. For unlike the escape pod, or even the mothership, the bundle is not some strange and floating other in the great expanse of space. It is a bundle of blankets, carried by a pair of human arms, attached to a human body, with a human head and a human face and a human smile which beams down at the blankets, then beams up at Isaac. The human holding the bundle is smiling. What's more, the human holding the bundle is him.

Isaac gasps. Isaac lets go of Egg's arm. And as Egg flees through the open door and down the stairs, Isaac chokes. He's only half aware of crashing back down to earth, then crashing down on to the carpet of the room at the top of the house. He retches. He wheezes. He rolls on the floor, clutching his chest. He clutches his stomach, then his head, then his eyes. He's contending with the head-splitting feeling of a mind filling up with things it had been trying to forget, his self-told lies collapsing around him like a cardboard shelter in a hailstorm. As Isaac kneels on the floor of the nursery and shields his vision from his own half-finished mural and his own hand-built cot, his comprehension of recent events shifts like a *Magic Eye* picture. He sees the looming metal structure in the abyss, daunting and imposing and fifty feet tall. It's not a mothership. It's a hospital. He sees the lonely glass box, glowing like a beacon in the void. It's not an escape pod. It's a tiny bed, housed on all sides by glass. And he sees the bundle of blankets, first in his own arms, then trapped inside that self-same glass box. It's not Egg. It's not even *an* egg. It's his son.

NINE

Isaac Addy might be a ghost. He's been fading away for months now, present, but never really there. As he holds his right hand up, up, up in front of the sky, he's surprised he can't see right through it. He focuses on the hand. He focuses on the sky. Not the real sky, but the sky he once painted on the wall of a nursery in which no one has ever slept. He focuses on the cot. He's been avoiding this room. Can you blame him? In the spectral months he's spent floating around his house, Isaac's never felt strong enough to face what lay behind this door. He's been afraid. He's still afraid. He can't remember a time when he wasn't.

Before Isaac was a ghost, he was a father. And well before Isaac was a father, he was already afraid. It's not that he didn't want kids. On the contrary. He drew pictures for a living. His wife was a children's author. Kids were the obvious end-goal. It's just that kids always felt like something that happened to other people, to older people. Fathers knew how to get their act together. Isaac still couldn't eat without getting food down himself. He always reckoned he'd have a little more time, time to figure it all out and become a grown-up before he had to help a child grow up itself. Yet by the time he was staring down the barrel of his late twenties, Isaac realised that he'd sleepwalked into being old enough to have kids. He was still a man-child, not capable of having his own child. Right? Wrong. Before he could hold up his hands and say, 'I'm not ready,' a positive test result after book three's launch party made it pretty clear that the world had other ideas. Failure had always crouched on the fringes of Isaac's life, that ever-present fear of letting others down. Fatherhood had the potential to be Isaac's biggest failure of all. Perhaps that's why he found himself more afraid than he'd ever been before.

Everything's going to be OK, Isaac.

He remembers that day on the bridge, in the snow, when Mary was barely three months' pregnant and Isaac could already barely make ends meet. The commissions had dried up. He was stuck in a spiral of self-doubt. The baby was on its way, and his paltry contribution to their household income would never be enough with another mouth to feed.

'You wouldn't need to tell me everything's going to be OK if everything's going to be OK.'

It's in your head. We'll manage with money, like we always do. So what's wrong?

'I feel like I'm going to fuck it all up.'

Then we'll fuck it all up together.

The briefest of arguments, but one which stays with him still. He said things he shouldn't have. Even then, he knew he wouldn't be better off alone. Mary's cold breath floated over the water in a plume of smoke which still haunts him.

Why can't you act like an adult, for once?

She'd stormed off, her feet crunching over the snow. The drive back down south had been even frostier. Even later on, when he'd cooled down, he'd never apologised. He assumed she knew that he'd said what he'd said in the heat of the moment. Besides, they'd made up by the next morning. And she'd proven him right, after all. The work had come back, the money hadn't run out. Everything had seemed like it really would be OK. Isaac stares at the cot. He stares at the mural. He kneels on the carpet of the nursery at the top of the house, and he allows himself to remember the rest of it. Months of nail-biting. Weeks of worry. Then, eventually, no time left to be afraid. *It's happening*, Mary had said, prodding him awake one humid August evening. After a perilous and panicked drive over the old bridge on the outskirts of town, Isaac skidded into the car park of the hospital and found himself holding her hand through twelve agonising hours of labour. There was a lot of screaming. Some of it was Mary. Much of it went by in a blur: nails digging into his palms, cold towels, bloodied blankets. Then, Mary was fast asleep. The midwives were smiling. It was all over. And, looking down at the bundle in his arms, Isaac wasn't afraid any more.

He gets to his feet. He has to focus all of his energy on not collapsing, on putting one foot in front of the other. He turns from the mural, finds the door, descends the stairs shakily and in near-total darkness. He can't remember how long ago it is that he heard the door slam. He can't remember why it did. He can only remember everything else, everything he's been forcing himself to forget. He feels his way down the first-floor landing, finds himself in Mary's office. He rubs his temples, blinks through the shadows. He's looking for something. A notebook. Yes, that's it. A yellow notebook. He finds it on her desk, almost incandescent in the dark. Just seeing it sends spasms through his amygdala. He sees things in flashes, things he hasn't seen for months, presented to him like family photographs in an old-fashioned slideshow. A crushed-croissant-and-mashed-carrot food fight in the kitchen, his infant son in a high chair. Taking the wee man to the farm on the outskirts of town, letting him feed the pigs and intimidate the geese. Baby's first Christmas, baby's parents passing out pre-midnight on New Year's Eve. A few days later, he and Mary spending that last night together with a bottle of red and a beef bourguignon. The yellow notebook. They'd talked about the yellow notebook, about the book, Mary's next one. She'd been writing again. He was so proud. He remembers telling her, he was so proud. Did he? His memory is foggy. The next morning was foggy, too. He remembers the wee man fidgeting in his car seat. He remembers Mary reminding him to take down the Christmas tree, to bin the Christmas cards. He remembers kissing her goodbye, quickly, through the open car window.

'I'll see you in a few days.'

Not if I see you first.

The trembling fingertips of Isaac's weak right hand come to a rest on the cover of the notebook. He breathes, unsteadily, out. He tries to take hold of it, but his hand won't follow his head's instructions. He feels like he's falling, as if he *will* fall, and he grabs the desk with his other hand to stop himself from doing so. He takes hold of the notebook in his left hand and, with his right, moves the computer mouse across the desk with unsteady fingers. The blackness is cleft in two by a blinding light, the beam of a computer screen coming to life. Isaac stops shaking. He looks at the screen. He sees a bridge. Mary's bridge. He thinks of that white winter, Mary in the snow telling him everything's going to be OK. He thinks of those purple summers, Mary stretching out her toes to touch the water. But that perverse little imp in Isaac's head, the one he thought he'd shaken by now, won't let him think of such things. *Think of the other bridge*, it says, shaking its cage. *That bridge was much more important to Mary.*

He sees it now, with a startling clarity as bright as the blinding light on that screen. He sees the bridge near their house. He sees his wife and his son upon it. And he sees what happened. He allows himself to remember. She'd been away for the weekend. Back home. The wee man was approaching six months old, and she wanted him to see Scotland for the first time. A delayed Hogmanay, she'd called it. Isaac would have gone with them, but he'd had his first big commission since the birth, and his sleepless self had been putting it off since way before Christmas. Besides, he'd been looking forward to the rest. How selfish he seemed, now. But Mary had told him to stay. *It's just a weekend*, she'd said. How did Isaac even spend that weekend? Seventy-two hours yawned ahead of him but, looking back, he could barely remember doing a single thing. He must have drawn a lot, obviously. But he must have eaten, too. He must have slept. He thinks he watched *It's a Wonderful Life* on the Friday night, *E.T.* on the Saturday. He'd done a little of the mural in the nursery, the one he'd spent months saying he'd finish. It proved a damn sight more enjoyable than wrestling the dying Christmas tree out of the front door, or the 'easy-build' cot which had helped him set a personal record for swearing under his breath. The wee man had been sleeping in their bedroom. Isaac was never one to stick to deadlines. He remembers talking to Mary before she set off back down south that Sunday, the wee man giggling on the other end of the phone.

'The house feels empty without you.'

I think that's more him than me.

'How so? You're the one who cries all night.'

Pot, kettle. I know you're crying yourself to sleep without us.

He remembers telling her what he was making for dinner. Lamb kofta kebabs. He remembers telling her to text him when she was about to leave. He remembers their exchange.

About to set off. Maps says should take 8 hrs
but probs a bit longer if you factor in nappy
changes. See you soon x

> You have to change
> your nappy en route?

Shut up

> Lol. Drive safe.
> Send me your location xx

Alright, stalker x

The last thing she'd ever say to him. He's reread the message a million times since. Isaac is sure a Mary who knew her fate wouldn't have ended it all with *Alright, stalker*. If she had known, if either of them had, Isaac would have composed a thousand-word sonnet in response. Or perhaps he'd have chosen three words, all careful, all capitals. DON'T DRIVE HOME or GET A TRAIN or WATCH FOR ICE. In reality, he didn't even reply.

Mary sent her location. A bubble appeared, promising to show her whereabouts for the next twelve hours. When Isaac rereads his texts to Mary, her last location is still there. He's considered deleting it, but he's worried that would somehow be worse. There it sits inside its box, rectangular and grey and final. Like a tombstone.

Live location ended

A picture of Mary in that bubble. And that bubble, floating forever over the last place she'd ever be. He doesn't remember what he was doing when Mary set off, but he remembers taking the initiative to put their bedsheets in the tumble dryer when he checked and saw that she'd just passed Glasgow. He was making breakfast – eggs, perhaps, or beans on toast – when he saw that Mary had stopped off somewhere around Carlisle. He checked her location again, guiltily, when he realised he'd shrunk the bedsheets. Expensive, linen. She wouldn't be happy. Still, his excitement outweighed his nerves. They barely ever spent time apart. Add the wee man into the equation, and he basically spent those last couple of hours with one eye trained on that chat, that map, that ever-moving bubble. Isaac checked Mary's location, then removed the mince from the fridge. Isaac checked Mary's location, then chopped up some coriander. And when he checked Mary's location and found her not too far away, Isaac smiled, put his 'Italian Cooking Songs' playlist on, and got down to chopping onions. *O bella ciao, bella ciao, bella ciao, ciao, ciao.* It was only when he'd washed his hands, wiped them on his apron and gone back to check again that he realised that Mary had stopped moving. Strange, seeing as there was nowhere to stop off around there, and no reason to stop off so close to home. Then again, the signal around those parts was rubbish, being several miles from the nearest clump of houses on either side. Perhaps Isaac frowned, but he didn't give it much thought. He shrugged it off and returned to cooking. It was only when he checked five minutes later and Mary still hadn't moved that something began to tingle in his stomach. Five minutes after that, no movement, that battery-acid taste in his throat. Five minutes later. No movement. Isaac's heart was beating a little fast, but he convinced himself he was being ridiculous. The connection would have timed out, or her phone would have run out of battery after playing music for the long journey. Isaac set to putting the kebabs together, thinking that doing so would help budge the heavy knot of panic coiling in his gut. Five more minutes, and his phone began to ring. Mary must have broken down, he thought, and even that thought gave him some relief. He washed his hands. He dried them on his apron again. He half smiled as he thought about how to answer the phone, but his face dropped when he saw the screen.

'Are you sitting down?'

If this were a children's story, Mary's bubble would have floated home to their castle and everything would have been happily-ever-after. Instead, Mary's bubble burst fifteen minutes away from where he's standing right now. Fifteen minutes later, and they'd both have been back in his arms. How cruel is that? Isaac has since wondered if he's cursed, if she was cursed, if all three of them were. He thinks of the black spot from *Treasure Island*, the inky curse which condemned pirates to their deaths. That's what the police had called it, after all. A black spot. A stretch of road where accidents often happen. Perhaps this time it was black ice, or a crossing deer, or a fault in the car that even they couldn't see. Whatever it was, it sent Mary into a tailspin which ended against the heavy stone parapet of the old bridge fifteen minutes from their house. Every time Isaac thinks of them there, deathly still in a crumpled car at the end of a dark and silent bridge, his stomach falls out and his legs turn to jelly. Based on that bubble, she was there for at least twenty minutes before the police and paramedics arrived. A cursory search on her shattered phone had them calling 'Mum', who passed on the message to 'Isaac' because he wasn't saved as 'Husband'. He answered the call.

'Are you sitting down?'

That's all Mary's mother had to say. And while Isaac's own mother has always said that only fools deal in what-ifs, what if he'd never picked up the phone? What if the police and the paramedics had never found her? What if the evening had been a little warmer, or the night had been a little lighter, or their house had been on the other side of that bridge? What if Isaac had been in the car with her? What if he hadn't been so eager in agreeing to a weekend off? Perhaps it wouldn't have happened. Perhaps Mary would still be here. Perhaps his son would be here, too. But there's no use dealing in what-ifs. Isaac didn't go. Mary didn't come back. And their son didn't come home. He was found unconscious in a baby seat in the back of a smoking car, and now he lies, still unconscious, on a ventilator in a hospital on the other side of that bridge. Which brings Isaac to a whole other set of what-ifs. Such as, what if the doctor on the phone was right? What if there are complications with the surgery? What if his son never wakes up?

Isaac haunts Mary's old office. The light on the computer screen dwindles, dies. He looks down at the yellow notebook he now holds in both hands. His breath rattles in the empty house. He imagines it forming a cloud of its own. He looks up at the window, blinds still open, the lamp-lit street eerily silent and empty. Somewhere beyond it, the bridge. Somewhere beyond that, the hospital. He left a part of himself there. It's as if he were a panel of glass, and that night, the hospital, was a hammer. It smashed him into pieces, and he hasn't managed to put himself back together since.

Isaac's been having mind blanks. But now, with everything out in the open, he can think more clearly than he has in months. Isaac remembers. He remembers it all. He remembers arriving at the reception desk, dumbstruck, screaming her name. He remembers the painfully bright lights, the morbid beeping of the machines, the nurses with grave faces and clipboards like tombstones. He remembers surgeons who wouldn't answer his questions. *What's happening, doctor?* He remembers feeling as if he were watching himself on TV. He sees it now in the frayed-edge frame of a Charlie Chaplin farce, or a slapstick cartoon with a perpetually unlucky lead. *What's up, doc?* A low trumpet wobbles on the soundtrack. The audience laugh. You can't see your wife right now. But you can see your son.

Isaac remembers seeing that tiny hospital bed for the first time, its raised see-through sides like a claustrophobic glass box, the fragile-looking figure inside hooked up to all manner of tubes and wires. He remembers thinking the bed looked like an escape pod. He also remembers thinking it looked like an open casket. After all, his son wasn't moving. And while Isaac wanted to punch his way through the Perspex and cradle the child in his arms, those arms may as well have been made of tissue paper. He remembers a nurse's arm around him, instead, remembers crying into her scrubs. He remembers saying, 'I'm sorry, I'm sorry, I'm sorry,' but he doesn't remember who he was supposed to be saying it to. He remembers being told about Mary. He remembers being taken to see her body. He remembers thinking, this isn't my Mary. Not because of the skin, even paler than normal, or the unfeeling look on her face. No, no. My Mary only ever slept on her front.

What happened next? His memory gets foggier. He vaguely remembers the following weeks, not sleeping, curled up in an uncomfortable wooden chair by the hospital bed, searching for any sign of life in his son's face. He remembers fainting on the floor of the funeral parlour when he caught sight of a child-sized coffin. He remembers turning up drunk in front of the doctors, embarrassing himself, despite having promised Joy that he'd at least stay sober enough to drive. He remembers drinking again, this time for courage, the week after the funeral. Pint after pint in the nearest pub to the crematorium, still wearing his funeral suit from the week before. He hadn't yet managed to take it off. He remembers collecting the ashes, decanting them into an empty Walkers shortbread tin, finding himself aghast and alone in the small hours of the morning, on the bridge where she died. The months since then blur together. There are the bits he's allowed himself to experience: the therapy, the list which was supposed to make him better. Then there are the bits he's forced himself to forget. The guilt-stricken panic attacks. The tearful phone calls with his son's consultant, Dr Park. The days on end spent sleeping in the paediatric intensive care unit, nurses bringing him blankets on the nights he couldn't bring himself to go home. While fear used to define Isaac Addy, guilt has overridden everything about him since the accident. Every time he's left the house to go to see his son, guilt has seeped from every pore of his being. He blames guilt for his broken brain, and guilt blames him for everything else.

Though Isaac and Mary used to fill their favourite weekends watching feelgood films, she'd always loved *Titanic*. She was a sucker for a weepy romance. Isaac never watched *Titanic* with Egg, because he felt it would hit too close to home. He remembers the thought, in the days after Mary died, while he was watching their son cling on to life on a hospital bed a third the size of Rose's floating door. He wished he had been in the car with them, like a captain going down with his ship. Instead, he feels like a man who'd forced his way on to the lifeboat, stealing the place of the women and children left behind. Isaac Addy should have been on the boat. Instead, he watched from safety as his wife and child drowned. Isaac Addy should have been in the car. Instead, he stayed at home, and now he's drowning in his own guilt. Isaac Addy is a man who wears many masks, but he never thought he'd have to wear this one. Widower. And if he has to wear the mask of a single father, he's sure he can only fail at that, too. Here Isaac stands, in his dead wife's office, staring out of the window at the lamp-lit street which is eerily silent and empty. The hospital beyond it. The bridge, between here and there. Isaac looks up further, at the moon, and the stars, and his brain starts to come back down to earth. He looks at the notebook again. He looks at the books on the floor. Then he mutters something under his breath, something quiet.

'Egg,' he says.

Egg comes back to him, and with Egg comes another wave of guilt. Already he's seeing things from Egg's point of view. And already he's seeing that, in the story of Isaac and the egg, he's the bad guy. Why wouldn't Egg be curious? Why wouldn't Egg want to know what was in the room at the top of the house? After all, Isaac's been lying to Egg, hiding things from him, all this time. Egg simply saw through his lies, and Isaac repaid him by banishing him from his house. Isaac looks out of the window and sees nobody on the street.

His car is still there. Besides, Egg can't drive. How far could an egg get, on foot, on a night like this? How far *will* he get? Isaac's heart starts to beat again. The muscles in his neck are tense. He shakes his head and leaves the office, barely aware of the fact that he's taken the yellow notebook with him. Outside the office, he heads down the stairs. The cloud of smoke hits him before he reaches the bottom. Did he leave the oven on? No, he hasn't used the oven. Besides, there's no smell accompanying the smoke. Egg is long gone. And the front door is closed, so the smoke isn't coming from outside. Isaac stands on the bottom step, holding the banister with one hand and shielding his eyes with the other. He squints through the fog, searching for its source. When he realises it's coming from the living room, his eyes widen.

'Mary,' he says.

The scene in the living room is post-apocalyptic. Particles hang in the air like ash from a nuclear reactor; the floor is coated in a fine layer of what looks like moon dust. The mantelpiece wasn't exactly a solid resting place at the best of times, and the slammed front door seems to have finally dislodged the Walkers shortbread tin and sent it clattering on to the carpet. The lid has been blown off by the impact, and a mushroom cloud of Mary has filled the air. Isaac, coughing and choking and banging his shin on the coffee table, skids over to her. He drops the notebook on the table, places the tin upright on the carpet, then sets to work in a frenzy, trying to scoop up as much of Mary as he can. It's a fool's errand. Growling and spitting and swearing under his breath, he shakes the cushions and blankets out over the tin. He scrapes powder off the surface of the table, as one might scrape countertop crumbs into a bin. He even tries to squeeze Mary out of the carpet. It's no use. On his knees, panting and panicking, Isaac stares towards the ceiling and starts to cry. The tears carve tracks through the ash on his cheeks. There's more ash on his T-shirt, on his forearms, caking the outside of his dressing gown. He sniffs, wipes his chalky nose with two chalky fingers, looks down at the ruined carpet and his own ruined clothes. He looks at the remainders of the ashes in the biscuit tin, picks it up. He kneels, weeping at the altar of their mantelpiece with a biscuit tin full of Mary in his arms, like a reversed pietà on the living-room floor. She would find this funny, he thinks. Mary would be laughing at the absurdity of all this. Kneeling in front of the fireplace once more, with the tin clasped tightly to his chest and with Mary's ashes all over him, Isaac feels as if she's embracing him. He allows his mind to trick him once again, to convince him that she's really here, that she can hear what he has to say. He imagines she can answer.

'I don't know what to do,' Isaac tells Mary, through tears. 'I thought I was getting better, but I'm not. And now I'm all alone.'

Stop crying, you big wuss, Mary says. *Go and find him. It's about time he was home.*

Isaac sniffs. He wipes his eyes. He looks down into the tin of ash, its surface puckered by the odd full-stop tear drop like craters in the surface of the moon. Isaac looks up at the moonlight streaming in through the venetian blinds. It illuminates the TV screen, which, covered in ash, bears the crime-scene fingerprints of one of Egg's chubby little hands. Despite everything, Isaac manages to smile.

'You're right,' Isaac says to the tin in his hands. He looks at the clock on the mantelpiece. 'You're right. I made a promise. I'm going to get him back where he belongs.'

He contemplates asking for Mary's permission to let her go. Then he contemplates taking Mary with him, his partner in crime, along for the ride. He can imagine her response to that, too.

I won't be much use, will I? You've trapped me in a bloody biscuit tin.

Isaac smiles a snotty smile. He laughs to himself. Then he climbs creakily to his feet, wipes his eyes and his nose once again. He picks up what's left of Mary and puts her lid back on. He presses it to his forehead. The metal is cool against his skin.

'Thank you,' he says. 'I love you.'

She doesn't need to say it. Isaac knows she loved him, too. He kisses the tin, puts it back in place on the mantelpiece. He shakes off the dressing gown, takes the car keys from the console table under the TV. He starts to head for the door, but he falters. Something pulls him back. Not Mary, now quiet on the mantelpiece, but something else. Something on the coffee table. Something yellow, something white. Isaac sighs, picks up the notebook. He dusts the ash off the cover, turns it over in his hands. He knows what he's holding. But he also knows that, before he goes back into those woods, back to that hospital, he needs to read it. He needs to confront what's inside. Isaac knows. He knows that reality is fragile. He knows that it only takes a gentle tap to break its shell. And yet – and yet – he knows what he needs to do. Isaac swallows thickly, then opens the notebook. He begins to read. He allows himself to remember one last thing.

Its fur is <u>white</u>

Its eyes are <u>black</u>

Its face is <u>yellow</u>

Its name is <u>Egg</u>

'What's that?'

Isaac had noticed the notebook as soon as he entered the kitchen. It wasn't exactly hard to miss, bright yellow and box-fresh. The room was hot with the pot of stew cooking on the hob, and condensation had formed on the windows. Mary, her hair tied up and her glasses perched on her nose, looked distracted. She was writing something in the notebook. She either hadn't heard Isaac's question, or was pretending she hadn't heard it. Either way, she asked a question of her own.

Is the wee man asleep?

Another one of her Scottish-isms, but one which refused to budge. She used to say *What in the name of the wee man?*, as her mother did, when something confused her. Now 'the wee man' was what they called their son. Not on his birth certificate. He had a given name, obviously, but for now neither of them used it. 'Wee man' seemed more apt for a half-formed little thing which couldn't even crawl yet.

'Out like a light,' said Isaac, heading straight for the wine rack and grabbing a bottle of burgundy. 'For now.'

He crossed to the cupboard and fetched two glasses. He opened the bottle, gave it a cautionary sniff, and began to pour. Mary closed her notebook, sat back in her chair and watched him.

You're a natural, she said.

'Sommelier?'

No. Dad.

'Don't call me "dad". Creep.'

She rolled her eyes. *See? Dad joke, right there.*

'A natural dad.' Isaac stopped pouring, rolled the words around his mouth, as if tasting the wine. Then he smirked. 'Nope. Not quite. Nice try, though.'

You are, Mary said, her voice high-pitched on the second word, her eyebrows raised. *Seriously. I never get him to sleep that quickly.*

Isaac shook his head. He continued to pour the wine. 'Maybe he just finds me boring,' he said. 'Although I was reading him one of *your* books.'

Mary snorted. Isaac was still smiling at his small success, although part of him was focused on the inevitable crying fit which would come in about half an hour, signalled by the squawking of the baby monitor on the counter by the door. Another part of him thought of the botched bathtimes which always ended with soap getting in both his and his son's eyes, while another was needled by the nappy changes he was still regularly making a mess of. He was taking it one day at a time. In his lower moments, during the tantrums which came with his own sluggishness and selfish self-doubt, Isaac was convinced he was little more than an infant himself. He felt sorry for Mary, having to look after two children at once. Look at her now, tired and beautiful, sitting at the kitchen table with her fogged-up glasses on her face and her yellow notebook hidden beneath her hands. She makes it all look so easy. Isaac wanted to scoop her up and kiss her like he used to, but he was even more tired than she was. He'd been on baby duty ahead of the big weekend. He'd drop Mary if he tried to carry her, and neither of them needed that.

'What time are you off in the morning?' he asked, instead.

Bright and early, Mary said. *Eight-ish, I reckon. Long drive ahead.*

Isaac crossed the room and handed her a glass. They clinked a cheers, and Mary took a sip. She sighed a contented sigh.

'Are you sure you don't want me to drive?' Isaac said, probably not as forcefully as he should have. 'It's a long way.

We could split it.'

Don't be silly, Mary said. *It's my family. And you've got to make us some money.*

She signalled 'money' like a cartoon gangster, rubbing her thumbs against her index fingers. Isaac laughed.

Besides, you need your beauty sleep, she said.

Isaac leaned over and kissed her. 'I'm going to miss you,' he said. 'Both.'

It's three bloody days, Mary said. *Besides, you'll be too caught up in your own world to miss anyone. Or you'll be horizontal and snoring.*

Isaac smirked. 'Touché,' he said. He sipped his wine. 'You can sleep for a whole week when you're back. That's a promise.'

There was a crackle on the baby monitor. Both of them winced. They heard the sound of the wee man murmuring, turning, but – mercifully – not crying.

Don't make promises you can't keep, Mary said, raising her glass.

They both smiled. For a moment, neither of them said anything. Silence, even silence punctuated by the bubbling of the bourguignon on the stove and the white noise of the baby monitor on the counter, was a rare commodity nowadays. Isaac felt like a valve had been released between his shoulder blades, the stress seeping out of him and fogging up the kitchen windows. He closed his eyes and exhaled. Then, putting a hand on Mary's shoulder, he gestured towards the notebook once more.

'New project?' he said, pointing at it with the hand that held his glass of wine. 'You evaded my question. Don't think I didn't notice.'

No, Mary said, a touch too defensively. She once again covered the yellow cover with her hands. *It's just . . . nothing.*

'It doesn't look like nothing,' said Isaac, detaching himself from her shoulder and trying to get a look. Mary sighed, but didn't put up too much of a fight when Isaac took hold of the notebook.

OK, it's not nothing, she said. *But it's far from anything yet.*

Isaac flicked it open. Immediately, he smiled. 'You're writing again?'

I'm trying. She was uncharacteristically coy. *I can make us money, too, you know.*

'Wow,' said Isaac. 'I'm so proud of you. How long's it been?'

A minute, Mary said, grinning. She gestured upstairs. *Been a bit busy.*

They both laughed. Then Isaac settled on a page. He stared at the simple sketch for a while, smiled again, held it in front of Mary. He pointed at the picture.

'Who's this guy?'

Even Mary's better drawings looked like stick men scribbled down during an earthquake. That didn't stop her trying, especially not when she had an idea she wanted to get down on paper. These sketches would usually serve as a basis for Isaac to go off and create something better. Or a little more refined, at least. That's how their books always began. She was the brains. He was the steady hand with the crayons. Now Isaac stood pointing at her newest invention, a protagonist with big black eyes and an oval-shaped body and arms which were little more than glorified squiggles. It looked like Mr. Tickle might look, if he'd accidentally been put through the washing machine.

You need the whole story, Mary said, blushing. The open book. *Otherwise it won't make sense.*

Isaac pulled up a chair next to her. 'I'm all ears,' he said.

So she told him. The whole story. It's a tale which might sound familiar: Isaac's been telling it to himself for many months. The story of a boy finding an alien egg in a forest, and doing everything in his power to help the alien get home. Reality is fragile, remember? All it takes is a gentle tap to break its shell. And because Isaac's own shell is broken beyond repair, everything he's been experiencing can be put down to the gooey stuff leaking through the cracks. Now Isaac finds himself speeding in his car towards the place where his wife died, towards the bridge where he found himself all that time ago. In the forest beyond that bridge, an egg which Isaac may or may not have made up is embarking on a journey which may or may not lead him home. In a hospital beyond that forest, Isaac's son is undergoing surgery from which he may or may not wake up. Isaac will get there. He needs time. For now, real or not, all he knows is that he promised Egg he'd help him get back to his family. All he knows is that he's not prepared to break another promise.

'You didn't answer my question,' Isaac said, back then, after Mary had finished telling her story.

What question?

'Who is he?' Isaac tapped the sketch of the egg. 'What's his name?'

Mary looked at the egg. *It says right here*, she said, turning back a page.

'Egg? That's his name?'

Sure is. Call an egg an egg, and all that.

'You're ridiculous.' Isaac said, shaking his head. 'And the boy? The one who finds him?'

I don't know yet, Mary said. Then she smiled. *What would you call him, Isaac?*

TEN

As Isaac speeds down an empty road towards an old bridge on the outskirts of town, he's adamant he's in his right mind. After all, he's thinking practically. He knows that his son's surgery is taking place right now. He knows they won't let him in. He knows all the doctors by name, and they don't need that pressure if something goes wrong. Isaac knows he'll hear some news in about an hour – Dr Park said she'd call him straight away – and Isaac fears the news will not be good. But at least it gives him an hour of blissful ignorance, just enough time to find Egg and apologise and see him on his way. If he's still on earth, that is. Oh, and if he actually exists. Isaac's self-prescribed practicality has limits, because he's not quite sure if his new best friend is the product of a particularly nasty psychotic episode. At least he's asking the question. He's asking other questions, too.

Is Egg real?
If not, what else isn't?
If not, where am I even going?
If not, what else have I made up?
No – was it Mary who invented Egg?
I saw it. In her notebook. Did I? Didn't I?
Did she know Egg? Did he visit Mary, too?
How could she keep that a secret from me?
How could Egg not tell me about it, either?
What else might Mary have made up?
But Egg looked so real. Didn't he?
Did he? Didn't he? Is he real?
Is he real? Is he real?
Isn't he real?

Isaac has drifted, and the car has drifted with him. He can feel his mind unravelling, like Egg's arms from his body. It's only rapidly approaching headlights and the roar of a beeping horn that bring him back to reality. He sees the flat, black road, the glaring beams, the shocked-looking bark of the looming trees on either side. He gasps like a drowning man. Stupid, he thinks. Stupid, stupid, stupid. Then he swings the car back on to his side of the road, and his stomach lurches with it. Not because of the threat of imminent death, but because his brain is threatening something worse. He's fixated on something. He's in a deathly spiral. He's starting to convince himself he made Mary up, too. Could he have? Surely not. He remembers it all so clearly. The cold hands. The warm laugh. The flecks of emerald green in her eyes. Yet every day since Mary died, everything he thinks he remembers drifts a little further into the realms of fiction. Every single day, he's making up a Mary who's a little different to the Mary he actually had. What will his Mary look like in a year? In two? In ten? Will this Mary, Isaac's Mary, even come close to the Mary who existed? Worse, will his son even know the difference? Oh God, his son. He doesn't even know if his son will survive to hear about his mother. Dr Park was upbeat on the phone, but last time she mentioned this procedure she'd talked about 'success rates', about survival. Isaac wonders, with a lump in his throat, if he might have made his son up, too. Is anything in Isaac's life real any more? Is he truly alone? He thumps his palms against the steering wheel, strains against his seatbelt like a Rottweiler on a leash. He screams at the top of his lungs. Oh God, Oh God, Oh God.

Isaac has reached his destination. He passes it, actually, realising at the last minute that he's sailed straight over the bridge and consequently slamming his foot down hard on the brakes. The car skids to an abrupt stop in the dry dirt, inches from a dense bank of trees. No black ice tonight. The evening is surprisingly warm, verging on humid, as if a thunderstorm is brewing. Isaac can't tell. It's dark down here on the road that slices through the forest. The only light comes from Isaac's headlights, which reveal nothing but a few yards of road, the shadows of the first flank of trees, and the vague suggestion of a forest beyond. He departs the car and stumbles back over the road towards the bridge, leaving the door open. The *ding ding ding* plays a duet with the muffled sound of the river in the distance. Isaac reaches the bridge, taking care not to step on the plastic bouquet wrappers. The flowers they hold have long since rotted away.

Isaac touches the flinty edge of the parapet. The stone is thick and ancient, but here on this side of the bridge it's also broken and battered. He traces the imprint of a car bonnet, imagines it lingering like the outline of a clumsy cartoon character in a wall. He pulls away a loose chunk of stone and holds it between his fingers. Then he places his flat palm on the parapet itself once again, bows his head, closes his eyes. Over the *ding ding ding* of his car idling nearby, he's sure he hears the faintest rustle in the leaves on the branches behind him. He hasn't felt this close to Mary in months.

'I'm going to save him,' he says to the bridge, to Mary. Isaac isn't even sure which 'him' he's referring to.

Opening his eyes, Isaac takes his hand off the parapet and wipes the chalky residue on his tracksuit bottoms. It leaves no stain on top of the white ash, Mary's ash, which coats the fronts of his trousers and the entirety of his already-dirty T-shirt. Perhaps that's why she feels so close. If she *were* here, she'd make fun of the way he looks. Sure, he's still in his crusty old slippers, but at least he left the dressing gown at home. Yesterday's haircut is now unwashed and uncombed. Stubble is starting to break through the skin. His cheeks itch as if they're covered in ants. He feels like . . . he looks like . . . he feels like he looks like he's lost his mind. It figures. He's lost everything else. Isaac peers to one side of the nearest tree to him, into the dark and silent woods beyond, into the place where he found that last, lost thing all those weeks ago. He contemplates heading into the woods, but a voice of sense carried on the wind stops him. Egg isn't real, remember? The wind has a point. When he tries to imagine what Egg's fur felt like between his fingers, he can't. Only now does Isaac realise he's been expecting the 'mothership in the woods' denouement because that's what happens in *E.T.* He thinks of thanking the wind and heading home. Or, no, to the hospital. Then he hears another sound. Not the wind, not the river, not the *ding ding ding* of his idling car. A scream. Surely not? He remembers the clearing where he found Egg in the first place, and the scream which preceded his discovery. He imagines the mothership swooping down into that same clearing, flattening trees as it beams Egg up into its belly. For some reason, he pictures a thousand Eggs, streaming out of the forest like Ewoks, babbling and waddling, his own worthless self drowning in a vast sea of them. Isaac shakes his head, refocuses on the scream, then takes one step over the rotten flowers, towards the trees at the end of the bridge. He soon finds himself on the muddy bank of the woods, once more about to descend the slope into the undergrowth and the shadows beyond. Before he can take another step, he hears the scream again.

It's not coming from the forest. It's coming from the bridge. Isaac turns, blinks, tries to see into the distance. Although his eyes are beginning to adjust, he still can't make out much of the road or the bridge beyond where the beam of his car headlights end. But he knows where the scream came from, and he knows what the scream sounded like. It's a blood-curdling, skin-crawling, stomach-churning scream. It's a scream that isn't human, isn't animal and isn't anything in between. It's a scream Isaac knows well. A hopeless scream. A helpless scream. A scream which used to mean '*Hello*'. Isaac is already following it. He steps back off the precipice and forges forwards into the darkness – not down into the forest, but up and back on to the road. Away from the glare of the headlights, he can see much more clearly. He passes the beginnings of the thick parapets, the mulched flowers and the imprint of the car on one side of the bridge. Isaac grips the parapet again, the rough stone back beneath his fingers. He feels his way forwards, not blinded by the darkness, but thrown off balance by the absence of noise from below. It's not a roar. It never was. The river washes lazily over the weir beneath him; the trees, which previously loomed over the bridge, now seem frail and far away. Halfway across, Isaac allows himself to look down. Last time, he'd thought about throwing himself over the edge, into the abyss. Now he sees that void for what it really is – a relatively short drop into a shallow river. Isaac would have been lucky to break his legs.

Isaac rubs his temples, runs his hands through his unkempt hair. Nothing at all is as it seemed. Even the memories he hasn't lost are playing tricks on him. He groans, and the unthreatening river groans back, white foam churning over small rocks and scattered twigs. Dead dogs and pine martens. He'd remembered that wrong, too. The 'Dog Suicide Bridge', another story he'd told himself. Another Mary Moray tale he'd borrowed. It was an article she'd showed him in her parents' local paper, about a nearby bridge they'd never even visited. Haunted, apparently. Dogs had a strange tendency to jump off. Not Mary's bridge, of course, and definitely not this one. You'd never get pine martens this far south, and a dog diving from this height would only be in for a short shock and a pleasant swim. Why had he thought of it, then? Why the intrusion, Mary? Isaac closes his eyes, breathes out steadily, and wonders if there will ever be anything inside his head which isn't hers. He thinks of Egg again, either entirely invented or entirely alone out here, just as confused as he is. Isaac opens his eyes.

He looks towards one bank of the river, then the other, the side on which he found the egg in the first place. His eyes trace the edge of the trees down to their twisted roots, the steep slope of toppled branches and tossed litter that signals the beginning of the river. He's looking for anything white, anything yellow, but all he sees is black water boiling over as though from a pot on a stove. It churns up plastic bottles and scraps of metal and long-abandoned items of clothing, origin unknown. He squints down towards the weir, at the foaming scum and the detritus within it. He sees something else. Something which makes his eyes widen, and his breath stop short.

There's something in the water. Not just anything: something white, something yellow, something still. Isaac lets go of the parapet as if he's touched an electric fence. He steps backwards, into the road, his hands still raised in front of him. He begins to shake, a full-body shiver which starts in his fingers and ends with his knees practically knocking together. Then, whispering, 'No, no, no,' under his breath and willing a God he barely believes in to give him just one break, he steps forward and peers back over the parapet again. God isn't listening. Egg is down there. Egg is, by the looks of it, unresponsive. Isaac lets out a wail, an inhuman cry of agony. Then, before the tears even begin, he's climbing over the parapet. One leg, then another. He couldn't tell you why. Perhaps he's climbing over because he's planning to swim to Egg's rescue. Perhaps he's climbing over because, just like all those months ago, he hopes the fall will prove more fatal than it looks. He's seen Egg face down in the weir, and wants to join him. This time, the imp in his head isn't trying to warn him off. It's too busy singing 'Humpty Dumpty'. *Isaac Addy sat on a wall. Isaac Addy had a great fall.*

Up here, sitting on the parapet, the breeze is stronger. It's colder, too, coming off the river. Isaac lets it wash over him. He stares straight ahead, breathing slowly, unblinking despite the breeze. The sound of the river doesn't bother him any more. He wills himself to look down at the weir. His body listens. With a gentle bend of his neck, he looks. Down past his own tracksuit bottoms, past the parapet he sits on, past the empty space over the black water. His eyes settle on the white foam, the bubbling current. Perhaps the wind in his face has given him more clarity, for he now sees the unmoving egg for what it really is. Yellow circle, white plastic. It's a shopping bag.

'Shit!' shouts Isaac.

What on earth is he doing up here? He should be at the hospital. He shrieks again, grips so tightly on to the stone beneath him that his palms start bleeding and his knuckles turn white. He realises, too late, that breaking his legs wouldn't be so lucky, after all. Isaac slips, just an inch, but enough to send a few chunks of rock hurtling into the river. He's petrified, unable to even think of swinging his feet back over to the safety of the pavement behind. He attempts a look backwards, but he's worried any movement at all might compromise his already-precarious position. He feels like Mary on the mantelpiece, and is worried he, too, will explode if he falls and hits the shallow riverbed. He feels like crying, but even his tears are frozen in his tear ducts. He doesn't know how he's going to get out of this one alive. He doesn't want to do this to his son, on the off-chance that his son is getting out of this one alive, too. He doesn't know how he could have been so blind. He doesn't . . . know what that sound is. Suddenly, Isaac stops panicking. His grip relaxes ever so slightly. Still sitting upon the edge of the bridge, he cocks his head to one side and wrinkles his brow. What is that? It's a low rumble, louder than the river, yet so low that it hits him at a frequency far beneath that of the water on the weir. It's a bass-y sound which fills his whole body, perhaps because it's causing the very parapet beneath him to vibrate. He removes his hands from the parapet. He looks at the spot where his hands were, at the tiny shards of stone jumping and dancing like water droplets on the surface of a drum. Then he looks up, first at the river, then at the dark panorama of the forest beyond. Where is the sound coming from? It's getting louder now, rising in frequency, all-encompassing in its volume. It seems to be coming from everywhere at once. Isaac feels as if he's in an advert for surround sound. He squints once again into the trees, and this time he sees something. Lights. Dim, in the distance, but moving rapidly closer. He knows what's about to happen before it even happens.

The mothership appears all at once. Within seconds the sound from beneath the river is drowning out the river itself, and Isaac is shrivelling under the roar and the wind of the black metal beast swooping down over him. The spotlights rise from behind the trees, then they're upon him. Isaac is frozen under them, under all the noise. He feels as if he's being sucked into a tornado of light and sound. The lights are blinding, that much is clear, but by shielding his eyes he can just about make out that there are several of them, some blinking red, others white. The white ones beam down upon him, and he wonders if they're about to beam him up. He has to look away, they're that bright. As he does so, as the ship hovers above him, he has a moment to catch his breath and focus on the sound. Not a continuous, reverberating hum, as he'd thought it was before. Now it's above him, the sound is disjointed. It's more of a *thub thub thub thub*, each *thub* beating against him with a new blast of air. He's just on the cusp of realising what's actually up there when the sound of a voice on a tannoy confirms his suspicions.

'Don't jump!' it says. The voice is crackling and distorted, but it sounds too much like his own to be an alien. 'You have so much to live for!'

The rotors of the helicopter keep beating wind into Isaac's face. He's so blinded by the spotlight that he can't see if it's the pilot operating the tannoy, or someone else. How did they know where he was? And since when did they send in helicopters, out here? They're just as likely to blow you forwards as they are to force you backwards. Besides, *how* would a helicopter be hovering here, above a squat bridge on a narrow river, between two dense banks of trees? All of these thoughts occur to Isaac in a nanosecond. And it's as if the crew of the helicopter know exactly what he's thinking, for almost as soon as the voice on the tannoy has spoken, the helicopter spins mightily on its axis and proceeds to disappear. The spotlight turns and vanishes into the trees. The great noise ceases to be great. And the wind dies down, albeit with one final gust which has Isaac's arms windmilling. He loses his balance. His centre of gravity shifts forward. He finds himself falling, unable to hold on to the parapet, staring down into that black abyss once again. The water rushes up to meet him. He closes his eyes and waits for the worst.

It doesn't come. Isaac opens his eyes again. His mouth opens, too, a little bit of nervous dribble seeping out and spiralling into the river, just feet away from his face. He can see his tired-looking reflection in the rolling water. He stares at it with incredulity, blinks back with comical confusion. He stretches out his hands, sees them reflected in the river, too. He's hovering. He's floating in mid-air, above the water. He thinks, for a second, that he's acquired superpowers. Then he notes the tightness around his chest, and thinks he must have forgotten that he's wearing a parachute, a bungee cord. He can see it, in his reflection, wrapped tightly around his T-shirt. So he feels for a safety vest, and finds a form of it in two sets of rough, pudgy fingers gripping tightly on to his torso, and two soft, furry arms enveloping him on either side. As if being winched up by a pulley on a ship, Isaac feels himself being pulled back up towards the bridge, despite gravity trying its best to drag him back down. Gravity loses.

Isaac is dragged roughly over the parapet and deposited head over heels on to the hard pavement whence he came. Lying on his back and regaining his senses, Isaac blinks up at his saviour. With two enormous, black eyes that still contain multitudes, Egg blinks back.

'I thought I made you up,' he says. The helicopter already seems somehow more absurd than Egg himself.

Egg considers this, pushing out his lower lip. Up close, his face is a screwed-up yellow squish of pockmarks and wrinkles. No worry lines, though. Just Yoda-like creases of deep thought. After a while, Egg simply shrugs.

'*Wab wob,*' he says.

Isaac still doesn't know what this means. It doesn't matter. He takes Egg's little yellow hand, which is outstretched and surprisingly strong, and allows himself to be pulled up into a seated position.

'I don't know what I was thinking,' he manages to say.

As he lies there catching his breath, it strikes Isaac how quiet things have become. There's no roar of rushing water, no breeze in the leaves on the trees on either side. Just him and Egg, sitting on a bridge, sharing a moment. Egg's toes have retreated into his body, but his arms are out in full force. They pool at either side of his body, heaped up on the pavement like piles of old-man hair on a barbershop floor. Even in the darkness, his fur is astonishingly bright. *Especially* in the darkness. It never gets dirty, that fur. And, even if only softly, it really does glow.

'I shouldn't have told you to leave,' Isaac says. 'I was

upset. But I think I see things more clearly now.'

Egg laughs. It's the first time he's done it, and it's a distinctly simian sound, a near-silent *hoo hoo hoo* which comes right from his belly. Although, really, he's all belly. When he's stopped laughing, Egg's arm rises like a puppet's, and he places one three-fingered hand on Isaac's shoulder.

'*Bo bab ibba waywer hoo hab bwebs,*' he says.

It takes Isaac a moment to understand. *No man is a failure who has friends.* It only tangentially applies to the present moment, but Isaac still appreciates the sentiment. He places his own hand on Egg's shoulder. Or, flat on Egg's side, at the point where either his shoulder or his ear should be. Then, unable to help himself, he climbs to his knees, grabs Egg and gives him the tightest hug he can. His hand doesn't hurt any more. It doesn't even shake. Isaac thinks again of a fluffy hot-water bottle, as if hugging Egg might cause him to burst between his arms. Egg doesn't. In fact, though Egg seems startled at first, and despite his barely audible '*bleh*', he obliges. With arms which slither round and round and round Isaac like the tentacles of an octopus, Egg hugs him back. Isaac didn't know how much he needed the hug, and he didn't know how much he needed it to be just that: a hug. No vortex this time, no abyss. Egg's fur smells a little like warm oats, and it's as soft as a comfort blanket against Isaac's face. Isaac's chest is full, and he holds his breath to stop from sobbing.

'Thank you, Egg,' he says, instead.

The hug continues for a moment. Then, when it's just about to start getting awkward, Egg retracts his arms. He takes a couple of duck-like steps back from Isaac and fixes him with those bulbous eyes.

'*Owwible,*' he says.

With that, he spins and starts walking back down the bridge. In the newfound silence, Isaac can hear his feet as they *thwap thwap thwap* on the tarmac. He thinks of Mary's feet, crunching over the snow. Isaac climbs to a standing position, preparing to give chase. This time, he won't fail to apologise.

'I know I was horrible!' Isaac shouts after Egg. 'I'm sorry.'

Egg stops. To an outsider, they'd look like drunken lovers having a tiff. Or two actors, playing out a dramatic final scene on an ancient bridge over a churning river. Isaac thinks of Reeves and Swayze in *Point Break*. While Isaac looks nothing like Keanu Reeves, he supposes that Egg does have Patrick Swayze's hair. Further down the bridge, Egg turns again. Now he's facing Isaac, framed by a backdrop of bridge and forest and idling car. How tiny he seems against it all.

'*D'oh,*' Egg squeaks, in a voice a little larger than himself. '*Oww-sih-bull.*'

He lisps out the word with some difficulty, but Isaac gets his point. Egg has already turned around again. He continues his little march, not towards the forest and the mothership, but towards Isaac's car.

'Hospital,' Isaac says, rolling the word over in his mouth. 'But what about getting you home?'

'*Wawooo!*' Egg shouts, without even turning.

Wawooo. Home. Family. Isaac thinks he's starting to speak Egg's language. And even if '*Wawooo*' doesn't exactly mean 'Home is where the heart is', it's probably as close as humans have got. With a smile, Isaac starts running after Egg. At the end of the bridge, Egg is already letting himself into the driver's seat. A stern look from Isaac, newly arrived and breathless, encourages him to budge over. Before he gets into the car, Isaac takes one last look at the bridge, the broken parapet, the remainders of the flowers at its base. Then he climbs in, closes the door on the *ding ding ding* and the din of the rushing river, and turns to his passenger. Egg has put his seatbelt on, and is staring up at Isaac with a sense of purpose. Isaac nods and Egg nods back, as if he already knows what Isaac is going to say. Isaac turns to face the road. He grips the steering wheel. He revs the engine.

'Let's go and save my son.'

All good stories end with a car chase. Isaac and Egg's is no different. And while Isaac feels like Egg should be in his bike basket, with the pair of them pedalling through the sky towards salvation, a car is better suited for their current mission. Here they are, speeding down a dual carriageway, towards a hospital and a kid who's undergoing surgery which may or may not save his life. 'Raindrops Keep Fallin' on My Head' booms out of the radio, Isaac swerving in and out of traffic as if they're outlaws being tailed by hired guns.

Egg, as if he's in a spy movie car chase, bleats directions like he's plugged into a headset and a GPS monitor. In reality, his directions are nonsense. But Isaac likes the fact that he's along for the ride. They make a good team. And if there was ever a time that Isaac would need a sidekick, it's right now.

'*Weft!*' shouts Egg.

There's no left turning, just straight road, so Isaac continues driving. The rumble strips go *thunk thunk thunk* beneath the wheels of the tiny Ford Fiesta, and the streetlights over-head zip by in luminous lines like stars in hyperspace. It's a classic race against time. Isaac imagines they're in a two-man spaceship, flying away from bandits in an asteroid field or a particularly hungry black hole. No, flying *towards* something. A new home for Egg, a new beginning for Isaac. And, just like that, the mothership appears over the ridge of the road. It's a metal structure, about fifty feet tall, looming in the blackness under a canopy of stars. Generous observers would describe it as 'postmodern', as they often do with anything hewn fifty years ago from boxy concrete and angular steel. The Barbican, the whole of Milton Keynes, this particular hospital in the north-west of nowhere, all like spaceships from old episodes of *Doctor Who*. You can see why Isaac got confused. Lights blink across the hospital roof, spotlights flaring and fanning out over the car park. Above the entrance is a glass pyramid. The reception, not the cockpit. Above and behind that is the great body of the beast itself, an enormous cube of glass and iron which twinkles all over with lights. Behind one of those windows, Isaac knows he will find his son. What then? What if he's too early? He can't burst in and distract the doctors. What if he's too late? Surely he'd know. He'd have felt it, like he did with her. And even if he's wrong, he can't allow himself to think like that. This is one intergalactic mission which cannot afford to fail.

'Keep your wits about you, captain!' Isaac yells, gripping the wheel, embracing the persona of a Starfleet commander. Spittle flies from his mouth. 'No time for losing your head tonight!'

'*White!*' yells Egg.

Isaac takes the left turning, careening around the round-about like a ball on a roulette wheel and soon finding his car skidding into an empty space in the hospital car park. No time to pay for parking. It's fairly empty, which is fortunate, because Isaac leaves the car parked across two spaces with the driver's side door hanging open. He turns to Egg. Egg turns to him. There's so much unsaid, so much *to be* said, but both know that now is a time for action. Egg winches up one arm and grips Isaac's forearm with a firm hand. He might be small, but he's mighty. Isaac looks down at the little egg, its yellow face resolute, its white fur phosphorescent under the night sky. Egg says nothing, but the stars in his eyes say exactly what Isaac needs to hear. *Go*, they say. Isaac turns and starts running. And, as he starts running, it's as if his very being splits in two. Perhaps they did pass through a black hole. Perhaps he's been cleft apart in a time-warp. Or perhaps he's just having déjà vu. He remembers everything from that night: the painfully bright lights, the morbid bleeping of the machines, the busy doctors, and the nurses who stopped him from hitting the floor. He's not sure he's ready to face it all again.

Isaac bursts into reception. The waiting area is silent save for the hum of the air-conditioning and the distant voices of practitioners, and his entrance makes quite the impression. Several sets of eyes look up from the benches. He scans the faces, considers shouting something dramatic, but refrains. He strides with purpose towards the white-topped desk, places two firm hands on the countertop. In a steady voice, he speaks.

'My son,' he says. 'I'm here to see my son.'

Isaac is led down a slightly too-bright corridor by a nurse who already knows him by his first name. And, if he thinks about it hard enough, he knows hers, too. At the end of the corridor, they reach a lift.

'You know the way from here,' she says.

Isaac can't bring himself to press the button. He feels as if it's all a trick, as if stepping through the doors will send him tumbling down the lift shaft. But he doesn't need to press it. The doors open, anyway. It's not his fate awaiting him inside: just an old man who hasn't done up his dressing gown. Isaac lets him shuffle past, then steps inside the lift. He waits. He's alone inside, save for his reflection, repeated ad infinitum on all four sides. Above the door, a counter counts up towards the fifth floor. Isaac watches it, one foot tapping incessantly on the metal beneath his feet. He breathes out heavily. He clenches his fists, the fingers of his right hand tingling only a little this time. He stares at the side of the box, not into his own reflection, but into the door. Through the door. Up towards the fifth floor, towards his destination. The counter reads '3'. Now it reads '4'. The lift trembles slightly. Don't stop now. Isaac steadies himself on the metal railing to his side. Then the number reads '5', and the doors begin to judder open.

Isaac closes his eyes. He takes a deep breath in, exhales slowly. He opens his eyes again, steps out of the lift. Even though the corridor he steps into isn't any brighter than the box from which he emerged, the pupils of his eyes feel as if they need to adjust. And they do. Now he sees everything. He sees the waxed linoleum floor and the buzzing strip lights overhead, and he knows that he's arrived in the PICU. He sees the curved built-in reception desk to his right, the blue plastic clipboard and the ballpoint pen on a metal chain, and he knows that 'Sir, visitors have to check in before entering the ward'. He sees the doctors and nurses lining the corridor, and he knows all of their faces as if they're old friends. They watch him with sympathetic eyes. He looks back at them with desperate eyes of his own, eyes which plead for help.

'Don't turn the ventilator off!' he yells. 'Please don't give up yet,' he begs.

No one's told him they're turning the ventilator off. No one's given him any indication that they're giving up. He's not even sure if the surgery went ahead, as planned. But Dr Park sounded apprehensive on the phone. Didn't she? Isaac looks towards the fourth door along on the left-hand side of the corridor. The door is open. The light inside is on. He doesn't know if this is a good or a bad thing. Outside, through the window at the other end of the corridor, the night is still and dark. The ward is silent, save for the squeak of medical shoes on the rubbery floor and the distant bleeps of heart-rate monitors behind other, closed, doors. Is he too early? Is he too late? He doesn't know to whom he should address these questions. Perhaps the woman with the green dress and the black handbag, standing at the desk, turning round to face him. He sees her tired eyes, her lively lime earrings, her seven-months-pregnant stomach. He knows that he's looking at his sister.

'Joy?' he says. 'What are you doing here?'

'Isaac,' she replies. 'Where have you been? I've been calling you.'

Isaac frowns at her. In recent months, he's become accustomed to frowning at everything. As if hoping to prove her wrong, he fishes his mobile phone out of his pocket with two unsteady fingers. There it is. Twenty-eight missed calls, eighteen texts, thirteen Facebook messages and nine voicemails. Isaac shakes his head, returns the phone to his pocket, looks at Joy with the same pleading eyes. He's expecting bad news, but he can't bring himself to hear it. He doesn't want to know.

'Tell me,' is all he can manage to say.

But Joy doesn't tell him. Instead, she does something very strange. It starts with a faltering twitch in her cheeks, as if her mouth is filled with mouthwash and she's about to spit it into Isaac's face. Then one side of the trembling lip draws back.

Then the other. Is she going to snarl, like a rabid animal? No, her mouth isn't foaming. It's stretching, each corner extending upwards, lips parting to reveal her teeth. Perhaps it's because he isn't used to it, but Isaac instinctively draws back and bites his lip when Joy starts doing the very strange thing that she's doing. Her eyes fill with tears, although the shape of them is all wrong. Her eyebrows, which should be drawn together, are lifted high. Despite everything, these are happy tears. And she's smiling. No, not smiling. Grinning. Beaming. Joy is overjoyed.

'It worked,' she says, barely able to get the words out. 'He's awake.'

Who's awake? Oh. *He's* awake. Wait. He's awake? He's awake!? Isaac's eyes widen. One eyelid starts to flicker. He grabs Joy by the elbows, half because he can't use words to respond and half because he thinks he's going to keel over and hit the linoleum floor. The sound has been punched out of his eardrums, as if he's been sucked into a vacuum. He hears nothing but his own heartbeat. Unable to focus on Joy, he draws his eyes away from her face and looks over her shoulder, down the corridor, towards the fourth door on the left. Somewhere in between stands Dr Park. She'd been worried about him, Joy had said. Now she's smiling, too. Isaac lets go of Joy. He takes a tentative step around her, then another. He walks like a toddler finding its feet for the first time. He walks like a man just landed on the moon, achingly slow, stepping into parts unknown. Someone's clapping. Someone else is shaking his hand. He feels like he's underwater, and he thinks of *Titanic* again. That last scene, in the afterlife, a whole supporting cast applauding him down the hall. Or, no. It's a mothership, isn't it? Isaac wades down the corridor as if the airlock has been compromised, as if the vacuum that's opened up has sucked gravity out of the window with it. Up is down, down is up, and the only way he'll reach room four is by clinging on to the doors and walls which lead him there. No, perhaps there's *too much* gravity. His legs are heavy. His feet are sticking to the floor. No matter how close he gets to room four, the further away it is. Or at least it feels that way. But he's in a hospital, not a mothership, so he actually reaches the room in no time at all.

Isaac feels as if he might pass out. He holds on. Both mentally, to the room, and physically, to the door. Turning into the doorway, blackness fringing his vision, he realises what this reminds him of. The feeling of being sucked out of his own body and deposited somewhere in space, of seeing something as if it's very far away. The void and the blinking lights. The clear-sided hospital bed looks so tiny against the vastness of the space around it. Just the sight of it wrenches at something in Isaac's chest. He pushes the feeling away, taking a step into the room instead. He looks through the Perspex window of the bed. And, up close, he realises it's nothing like he remembered at all. The tubes are gone, most of the wires stripped back, and where there was previously something deathly still, there is now a living, breathing human baby. It's got fuzzy hair which sticks out in all directions, a squashed-up little face which looks as if it's made of bubblegum. Its eyes are open, and within those huge, bug-like orbs Isaac feels as if there exists an entire universe. The baby is awake. The baby recognises him. The baby is his son.

Just like that, the blackness disappears. The fog is lifted. Isaac is brought back down to earth. What's left is a bare room in a hospital ward with a tiny hospital bed at its centre, a baby in the bed, a father staring down at the baby. The baby looks up at him, makes a sound like a burp, gurgles with recognition. He's grown, despite being kept in a box. He looks so full of life. One of the nurses – Isaac doesn't notice which one – unclips a couple of wires. She gives him the go-ahead, tells him to be gentle. And Isaac, with arms which are strangely steady considering the circumstances, reaches down and picks up his son for the first time in months. He cradles him in his arms, and it's like a key has been turned in a lock. Everything makes sense again. Isaac sighs and stands there for what must be minutes, eyes closed, the wee man warm and wriggling against his chest. He feels a feeling he hasn't felt in a long time. He thinks the feeling is fulfilment. He thinks the feeling is what his friend would call *wawooo*.

Egg. Isaac opens his eyes. He looks at his son. Then he looks at the door. The baby in his arms is now fast asleep, so Isaac steps gently and carefully across the room, rocking him all the while to avoid waking him. Isaac's vision is sharp, his mind focused. He cycles back to when he last saw Egg. The reception desk? The car park? The car? He can't remember.

Isaac reaches the doorway, pushes the door open with one foot, then peeks out. He looks down the corridor for any sign of his companion, but there are too many people. Everyone in the corridor is either beaming or crying or clapping, but Isaac doesn't notice them. He peers over their shoulders, between their legs. He sees Joy, smiling at the other end of the corridor, and he smiles tearfully back. Then he notices something behind her, out of the corner of his eye, and he looks at the space behind her right leg.

The lift doors are open. From inside pours a steaming mist of what Isaac swears could be dry ice. It might be the whine of the hospital equipment, but Isaac is sure he can hear a rising overture of synths and electric guitars. It could be the clinical strip lighting overhead, but the whole corridor seems bathed in neon. Isaac blinks, and all the people disappear. Within that otherworldly light, within those four mirrored walls, stands one figure and one figure alone. It's about two feet tall, sprouting bright white fur in all directions. Its belly sags while its arms – way too long for its body – pile up in heaps at either side of its stubby yellow toes. Its hands are yellow, too, as is its face, which sits about two-thirds of the way up its torso with two pinprick nostrils and a downturned mouth. Its eyes, enormous eyes which gleam like polished marbles, stare back at Isaac from the empty lift. The music swells, the mist spreads. That little mouth turns up just a little bit. And Isaac, rocking his sleeping son in his arms, feels tears brimming in his own eyes once again.

'Thank you,' says Isaac.

'*Wawooo*,' says the egg.

Then the lift doors close, and he's gone.

THINGS TO DO

- ~~Clean kitchen~~
- ~~Clear fridge~~
- ~~Sort post~~
- ~~Sort Mary's computer~~
- ~~Clean house~~
- ~~Mow lawn~~
- ~~Call Mum~~
- ~~Plant flowers~~
- ~~Sort Mary's clothes~~
- ~~Donate clothes~~
- ~~Get haircut~~
- ~~Clean Mary's office~~
- ~~Sort top room~~

SOMETIME LATER

Isaac Addy stands on a bridge, sure that he's exactly where he's supposed to be. He places one hand on the warm, flat stone of the parapet. He breathes in a view that seems to go on for forever. It's vast and unbroken, purple heather spreading across the hills like an alien landscape. The wind skims the top of the water, rustles the leaves on the tree at the end of the bridge. A sleeping Border Collie stirs beneath it. Next to him, Esther Moray holds her grandson. He babbles and wriggles in her arms, her husband and sons watching them with doting eyes. Isaac smiles at his second family. He smiles at the wee man, too. Like the kid, Isaac has put on some weight around his face. *Baby weight*, Mary would say, pinching one of his cheeks between her fingers. Isaac turns his smile to the Walkers shortbread tin in his arms.

'We got here,' he says. 'Welcome home.'

Home. It's where the heart is, as an old friend used

to say. Or perhaps it's where you hang your hat. It struck Isaac recently that he never did get an exact translation of *wawooo*. But here, with his second family, he feels like he's got the gist. *Everything's going to be OK*, Mary told him, the last time they stood together on this bridge. And while Isaac might never be completely fixed, he's definitely on his way to getting better. He hasn't seen Egg again. He never expected to. He imagines him light years away, somewhere with a thousand eggs just like him. As he should be. Isaac isn't an alien, after all. He isn't a robot, either. He's a human being, surrounded by other human beings who care. His family. Her family. Their friends. Demanding clients, caring neighbours, a sometimes too-chatty barber, a top-notch therapist who won't let him give up. And a son, with a smile stolen straight from his mother.

The dog barks. One of the twins blows his nose. Isaac stares out at the river, at the rolling purple hills, at the late-summer sky. Mary's favourite view. There's a stillness in the air. And, while he might be making things up again, he's sure there's a slight vibration of the metal tin in his hand. Mary would never have wanted to be buried, with a grave and a gravestone and a coffin six feet below it. So morbid. So final. *So clichéd*, he can hear her saying. *Toss me to the ocean winds, or burn me on a pyre like the Vikings of old.* Scattering her here is the next best thing.

'Are you sure about this?' says Esther.

Isaac tears his eyes away from the view. He's already made up his mind. Besides, he hasn't told Esther that there's still a fair amount of Mary trodden into his living-room carpet. Another portion of her ended up in the Hoover bag, and it's this that Isaac used to fertilise the dahlias in the bed just beyond his back-garden patio. Hence why he encourages the wee man to refer to those flowers as 'Mum'.

'It's what she would have wanted,' Isaac says.

Esther sets her attention on calming the crying baby in her arms. Duncan, Dennis and her husband are all crying now, too, while Clyde the Collie has fallen asleep again. That just leaves Isaac, standing at the edge of the bridge, opening the lid of the biscuit tin in his hands. It comes off with a *pop*, and the surface of the dust inside dances in the wind as the vacuum is broken. He looks once again at the fields and the hills and the stick-and-poke white dots of sheep in the distance, and allows himself – just for a moment – to picture it. The farm. Isaac would shear the sheep, sure, but Mary would collect the eggs from the hens and top up the troughs with chicken feed. They'd be happy like that, just the two of them. Then, eventually, more of them. The wee man, his younger siblings. Five cows, forty chickens and a Border Collie or two. They always liked to dream big. Isaac still does.

If Mary had lived, the first thing Isaac would have told her was that home meant nothing, and everything, to him. That home was wherever she was. And perhaps home could be here. Well, not *here*, but somewhere like here, without an overpriced Italian deli or a direct line to London. If Mary had lived, Isaac wouldn't have been joking. And he wouldn't have been talking about the far future, as he had every time before. He'd have found a farm that night. He'd have moved to the middle of nowhere, the very next morning. If Mary had lived, he wouldn't have delayed growing up. He'd have run headlong into it, whooping and cheering and diving into the rest of their life together like a skinny-dipper into the sea. This is it, Mary, he'd have said. This is the first day of the rest of our lives. And what lives they would have led. If Mary had lived, the royalties from their book about an egg-shaped alien lost in the woods would have been more than enough for a mortgage, perhaps a tractor, a combine harvester, a few cows, a handful of sheep, a sprinkling of chickens. Isaac isn't sure what type of farm it would be, and he's still fuzzy on the specifics of how farms actually work. If Mary had lived, she'd have helped him work out the rest.

When pets pass on, you tell your kids that they end up on a farm. Perhaps, for now, that's what Isaac will tell the wee man about his mother. He likes the idea: Mary, somewhere else entirely, waiting for them on the farm. I'll meet you there, he thinks. And he does, from time to time. Isaac meets Mary in the middle of the night, in dreams which come with no rhyme or reason. The only thing regular about these dreams is that he never sees her in a crowd. He always sees her here, in her happy place, on this very bridge over this very river. Mary, the only imaginary friend he'll ever need. Mary, the only one he wants to see when he closes his eyes. In these dreams, sitting side by side on the parapet with their legs dangling over the water, it's like no time has passed at all. They laugh about all the things they did together, and they moan about all the things they never got to do. Most often, they talk about their son, about how fast he's growing and how proud of him Mary is. Sometimes, they just sit in silence, holding hands and watching the view. And every so often, when reality is proving especially hard for Isaac, he cries into her shoulder, and she wraps her arm around him. He tells her how much he misses her, how he can't cope without her. She just smiles and laughs and punches him in the arm.

Miss me? she says. *I'm with you right now, you eejit.*

Back in the real world, the breeze off the river ruffles Isaac's hair. The pattern on the surface of the water shifts ever so slightly, as if inviting him to climb over and stretch out his toes towards the water. A bird dances like a kite on a string overhead, and a conker falls from the tree at the end of the bridge. It lands with a soft thud on the grass, next to the sleeping dog.

'Happy birthday, Mary,' Isaac says.

Then he reaches into the tin, pulls out a handful of ash, and lets go.

ACKNOWLEDGEMENTS

This book wouldn't have existed without a lot of people. I'll start with two. Thank you to my agent, Millie Hoskins, for taking a punt on my strange first novel all that time ago, for your guidance and incisive edits since, and for helping me find the right home for *Isaac and the Egg* back when it was nothing more than a badly-formatted Google Doc. And thank you to Frankie Edwards, my editor, for providing that home. From our first ever chat I knew that we were on the same page, and that the egg was in safe hands with you. Working together on making this story the best it could be has been an absolute delight.

For being such champions of this book, thank you to Fergus Edmondson, Alara Delfosse, Bea Grabowska, Hannah Cawse and Jessie Goetzinger-Hall at Headline, and to Amy Mitchell, Jennifer Thomas, Lucy Joyce, Alex Stephens and Jane Willis at United Agents. Thank you also to Patrick Insole, Headline's art director supreme, for creating a visual world for Isaac, Mary and Egg that I could only have dreamed of. This book looks so good thanks to him.

As for first readers, I could only ever start with my mum, Ann – it's not an overstatement to say I wouldn't be a writer if it weren't for you. Thank you for giving me my love of reading, and for paying the price by being forced to read every single thing I've written in the twenty-something years since. Thanks also to my dad, Mike, for your endless support and for reading this book so eagerly despite there not being a grizzled Scandinavian detective in sight.

For giving me advice as a wide-eyed aspiring author, thank you to Katie Brown. Thanks to Flo Lindeman, Becky Jones and the entire Griffith family – Lindy, Jeremy and Matt – for your early reading, invaluable advice and diligent spotting of typos, and to my brother, Alex, who normally only reads footballers' autobiographies but cried in the bath when he read this. Thank you also to Matt's cat, Mish, who stayed with us for most of the writing process, and without whose mannerisms Egg couldn't have come to life. You are sorely missed.

Am I forgetting anyone? This book wouldn't – couldn't – have existed without you, Nina. Not only because some (perhaps too much) of Isaac and Mary is us, but because you helped me start it, endured me continuing it, made sure I finished it and, let's be honest, added in all the funny bits yourself. Egg screaming every time he enters a room? Genius. You deserve your own space on the cover, but in lieu of that I'll just say thank you, and I can't wait for our farm, here.

READING GROUP QUESTIONS

- What were you expecting Isaac to find in the woods?

- The egg appears in Isaac's life during one of the darkest moments imaginable. How does humour and absurdity relate to Isaac's grief? How do you picture the egg?

- How far do you think that traditional masculinity and gender roles play a part in Isaac's difficulties with processing his grief?

- Would you consider Isaac a reliable narrator? How might our view of characters like Mary, who we only see framed through his memories, be influenced by this?

- *Isaac and the Egg* draws on the literary tradition of the stranger who arrives at a time of need but can never stay for long. Did the novel remind you of any other stories?

- *Reality is fragile. All it takes is a gentle tap to break its shell.* Isaac seeks solace in all kinds of storytelling, including books, TV and film. How do stories help us understand the world around us? And what might happen when the lines between fiction and reality become blurred?

- Were you surprised by what Egg finds in the room at the top of the house? Why?

- By the end of the novel, Isaac and the egg have found a common language. What do you think *Wawooo* means?

- Parts of this book are laid out on the page in unconventional and perhaps surprising ways – how did the text design shape your reading experience and understanding of the novel?

- Do you believe the egg is real? Does it matter?

SMALL HOURS

the new novel by Bobby Palmer

will publish in spring 2024

and is available to pre-order